NEVER LET GO

NEVER LET GO

Gloria Cook

This first world edition published 2012
in Great Britain and in the USA by
SEVERN HOUSE PUBLISHERS LTD of
9–15 High Street, Sutton, Surrey, England, SM1 1DF.

British Library Cataloguing in Publication Data

Cook, Gloria.
  Never let go.
  1. Cornwall (England : County)–Fiction.
  I. Title
  823.9'2-dc23

ISBN-13: 978-0-7278-8157-1 (cased)

All Severn House titles are printed on acid-free paper.

Severn House Publishers support the Forest Stewardship Council [FSC], the
leading international forest certification organisation. All our titles that are printed
on Greenpeace-approved FSC-certified paper carry the FSC logo.

MIX
Paper from
responsible sources
FSC
www.fsc.org   FSC® C018575

Typeset by Palimpsest Book Production
Falkirk, Stirlingshire, Scotland.
Printed and bound in Great Britain by
MPG Books Ltd., Bodmin, Cornwall.

To Roger
Thank you for the good times

One

The house should be empty. Dorrie Resterick had just waved hello to the four members of staff taking their afternoon break on the bench by the garden pond. Dorrie's niece, Verity, and Jack Newton, the owner of Meadows House, were currently on their six-week safari honeymoon.

So the old house should be empty.

But someone was upstairs, someone who had just slammed a door so heavily it juddered on its hinges and that someone was now running along the landing and heading for the stairs. The stairs were right in front of Dorrie.

She hightailed out of the hall and hid behind a tall cabinet in the vestibule, nervous and spring-taut, ready to tear outside and call for the burly Kelland to face the intruder, the apparently angry intruder, the living and breathing intruder. Dorrie did not believe in ghosts – she *did not want* to believe in ghosts, here or anywhere else, but the two housemaids, sisters Cathy and Tilly Vercoe, had both nervously related feeling the horrible sensation of someone watching them, and hearing strange noises, dragging noises like furniture being shifted about, and ungodly sighs, and, scariest of all, footsteps creeping up behind them, but when they spun round fearfully to see who was there . . . no one was. Dorrie hoped there were no such things as earthbound spirits, some lost residue of existence that could haunt the living. But there were so many eerie tales cast in the world concerning man, woman, child and beast; so many happenings of the unexplained and the impossible. And Cathy and Tilly Vercoe were not fanciful girls. Both had been badly scared by the unwelcome occurrences they swore started the very day Verity had moved some of her things into the house, a month before the wedding.

'It's the master's first wife,' Coral Kelland, the cook-housekeeper, had avowed, while stirring the wedding cake mixture with extra-ordinary passion. 'She died at her own hand and now Mr Jack is getting married again she don't like it one bit and has started haunting the house. The more I think about it the more I'm convinced she was an evil sprite. It's a pity Mr Jack ever laid eyes on her. She ensnared him into a comfortless marriage. What say you, Mrs Resterick?'

Dorrie had been helping with the baking, measuring out the ingredients. Despite the tight post-war food rationing, through careful squirreling away and generous donations from kindly Nanviscoe housewives there would be a real fruitcake – not iced, of course – to be shared out at the wedding breakfast, which would be held in a marquee in the grounds of the newly built village hall. Jack had donated the land and had had a lot to do with the welcome appearance of the hall. 'Lucinda Newton was certainly a deeply disturbed young woman, but to suggest she's suddenly haunting the house, well, I hardly think so. She came from an unloving background and was locked away, with only a nanny to care for her. She was bound to be troubled.'

'You would put it like that, Mrs Resterick. You're too nice; you see something good or excusable in everyone, you always have. I tried, like Kelland and Cathy, the only maid here during that creature's short reign as mistress, to make allowances for her because Mr Jack doted on the waif-like girl and saw himself as her protector. To say she was strange is an understatement. She dressed like a child, played with dozens and dozens of dolls – creepy things hers were – and got Mr Jack to deck her bedroom out like something between a nursery and the stage of a pantomime. She had no notion how to run a house, not that we minded the extra work, we'd all do anything for Mr Jack. Had a rotten young life here he did, thanks to the constant cruelty of his father. Randall Newton was a devil, and no mistake. Many a time I bathed poor Mr Jack's bruised strammed legs, and for dear tragic Mr Tobias, God rest his soul wherever he died, and for dear Miss Stella too. That monster even whipped that dear little girl. It's no wonder Mr Tobias is said to have drank himself to death, and that dear Miss Stella run away from finishing school. She obviously couldn't face coming back here. Randall Newton was no father at all. He was a monster. Monster, I say, and that's what Lucinda Newton was, too, a little monster.'

Mrs Kelland's lumpy, bumpy figure shook and wobbled as she wielded the big wooden spoon, a chunk of her grey hair falling out of her hairnet and bobbing against her ear. She wore a leafy print apron over a skirt and blouse. Wanting their new life together to be informal, Jack and Verity had decided to do away with uniforms, only white aprons for the Vercoe girls, declaring, 'There are no servants here, just staff, including loyal and trusted friends.' Dorrie was concerned the couple, so much in love, might have their happiness marred by these tales of disturbing, threatening haunting.

'Oh, I couldn't think of her like that, Mrs Kelland,' Dorrie protested, reaching for the spices, 'but just another tragic soul. After all we don't know what made Lucinda what she was, or what drove her to kill herself.' Dorrie, however, was unsuccessful at forestalling a shudder. Verity had helped Jack dismantle the disquieting effects in Lucinda's room. Verity had confided to Dorrie in a distressed, choked voice, 'You don't know the half of how dreadful those contents were, Aunt Dor. Lucinda had hacked some of her dolls to pieces and daubed them with red paint. She must have been quite mad. Jack was beside himself with horror.' Dorrie knew that a bonfire had seen the destruction of a lot of Lucinda's nasty belongings. In truth Dorrie had to admit, privately, that Lucinda had been insane and dangerous at the end.

'Thing is,' Mrs Kelland went on, beating eggs with a heavy hand, shoulders tensed. 'She was a suicide and was refused burial in consecrated ground, so she's stuck out here in the grounds of the house, down underneath Mr Jack's secret boyhood hiding place. No longer a secret when Kelland helped Mr Jack to bury her. When my husband goes to do the upkeep of her grave, he says it gives him the creeps.'

Dorrie wished Mrs Kelland would stop her scaremongering. She was spreading a sense of doom even in this recently modern-ized kitchen, which like much of the plain, colonial styled house had been brought up to date according to Verity's wishes. Jack loved to indulge her. Why couldn't the cook-housekeeper concentrate contentedly on the new enamelled Aga range, backed up with an electric cooker and a coke boiler to heat the water, a refrigerator and ventilated cupboards to use at her ease? The kitchen layout had been thoughtfully changed for the minimal of walking between preparation, cooking and washing-up. An old larder cupboard had been updated into a lavatory, with a modern low-level cistern and linoleum on the stone floor. A convenience to be envied by staff in a great many big houses.

'Kelland helped Mr Jack dig the grave and lower down her coffin. Weightless, Kelland said it was, as if there was no one inside, not even a young slightly built woman. Afterwards, in its own little box went her poor little dog that pined itself to death for her. I thought it was a very rum thing to have someone who can't rest in peace, as it were, still here, but of course, what else could Mr Jack do with her? Now it seems she resents a new mistress taking her place – not that she was a proper wife to Mr Jack. I said to Kelland only last evening, there'll be no peace here until that creature is dug up and laid to rest in a proper grave after a proper Christian ceremony.'

Dorrie had been about to reply but Mrs Kelland held up a sugary hand. 'I know you think I'm being uncharitable, but Cathy and Tilly aren't the only ones to have suffered strange goings-on. Kelland thought he saw Mrs Lucinda flitting through the trees, saw what looked like a white dress; she always wore white. He said his hair – what's left of it – stood up on end, but he followed those flashes of white to the stream. He didn't actually see her there but *felt* she was there somewhere. He heard a splash and then another, but there was nothing that he could see to have fallen into the water and made those noises. Mrs Lucinda used to sit by the stream dipping her bare feet in the running water. He was spooked and said he hastened away feeling as if something was about to jump on his back. My husband isn't prone to night-mares – well, not so often now the terrible memories of the trenches in the Great War are receding – but that night he woke up crying out and swore something was touching his feet. We spent the rest of the night with the bedside lamp on. Goodness, I'm getting the shivers. Would you put the kettle on, Mrs Resterick?'

Coral Kelland's tale had been unnerving, and Dorrie – who agreed that Lucinda Newton should have been allowed a decent burial in consecrated ground – had subsequently suffered a restless night herself, dreaming of a hideous spirit draped in white running and laughing manically through the woods behind Meadows House. Verity had confided to Dorrie on the night before her wedding that she didn't like having her predecessor's remains lying in the grounds. 'I know it's silly and selfish of me, Aunt Dor, but I want Jack to have moved on completely from her. It feels like she's still close to him – too close.'

The intruder was now at the top of the stairs. Dorrie gasped on her next breath and felt her blood jump in her veins and goose bumps prickle her flesh. *Was it Lucinda's ghost?* She peeped round the cabinet and caught a movement in the corner of her eye, a glimpse of something in the long bronze-framed mirror, and nearly shrieked in fright. Idiot! It was her own reflection, small and dainty in light spring clothes, including her favourite long cardigan and her beloved floppy crochet hat on her ginger, silver-flecked curls. Dorrie clapped a hand to her hammering heart. The sudden movement elbowed a cherub statuette in a niche in the wall, marble scraping on stone.

The game was up. Dorrie would have been heard. The footsteps coming down the stairs stopped. The owner of those feet called out, 'Hello? Who's there?'

The voice was a woman's, but to Dorrie's utter relief it was nothing like Lucinda Newton's had been – low and whispery, a girl's perpetual tones, either crooning or giggly with some secret excitement. This voice was strong and curious. The intruder was not a ghost then, but Dorrie felt no less nervous. She could no longer hide away. The stranger's voice had carried authority in it. Dorrie stepped out to where she could be seen.

At the same instant Dorrie and the stranger both affirmed, 'I know you!'

Two

Dorrie returned home to Sunny Corner, roughly a mile away from Meadows House. She gazed steadily at Stella Newton. 'It was quite a surprise, a pleasant surprise to realise it was you, Stella, after all this time. Your resemblance to Jack was a clear giveaway.'

The last time Dorrie had seen Stella was as an awkward, nervy sixteen-year-old. Although she had matured into a well-dressed woman of easy styling, with her mid-dark head held high, slim and tall, she was clasping and unclasping her hands on her lap. She was wearing a wedding ring, unconsciously displaying it, Dorrie felt, to denote that she was happily married. Dorrie was pleased about that. Like her older brother Jack and younger brother Tobias, after a difficult, soul-crushing childhood at the will of their heartless father, Stella deserved to know joy. She wore no hat and Dorrie was sure she rarely did, preferring informality after such a rigid, minute-by-minute ordered early life.

'Thanks for not giving me away, Mrs Resterick, and for agreeing to allow me to slip away from my old home unnoticed and then to call on you here. I've never forgotten Sunny Corner with its legendary beautiful gardens and mock pagoda, all tucked away just after the crossroads. Your parents always made Jack, Tobias and me very welcome when we were able to slip away from our gaoler of a nanny for a while. I remember the awful time you and your husband were visiting here and you so tragically lost your little girl . . .

'I would have loved to reveal myself to the Kellands, but of course it wouldn't be right until I've spoken to Jack. I was overjoyed when I learned, quite by chance actually, that he was searching for me. It was a surprise to learn from you that Jack is on his honeymoon, and married to your niece. I remember Verity a little. I was envious of her confidence and tomboy ways.' Stella was wringing her hands now. 'Do you think Jack will be happy to see me when he gets back from Africa?'

'He'll be absolutely delighted, Stella.' Dorrie smiled warmly. 'I've got his hotel number if you would like to telephone him.'

'Really? Oh, I will. It was silly of me to have doubted and worried, but, well, after everything, I never take anything for granted. It will be wonderful to hear his voice again. I always felt bad about not keeping in touch with him, but I was so afraid, you see, that my father would track me down and drag me back and lock me up for good. He was always threatening to. He would have punished Jack too for keeping my whereabouts secret from him. I can't tell you how much we loathed him, Mrs Resterick. I wouldn't have come down now, from Guildford that is, if I hadn't also learned that my father was dead. I was looking at the "seeking employment" columns in *The Lady* for an experienced nursemaid for my children – Jack must have remembered that I liked to read our mother's copy of *The Lady* – and then I browsed the personal columns and my heart stopped. It could only be from Jack. "*Jay for Ste. Good news. All clear, for good. Please get in touch.*" Jay and Ste was what Jack and I had called each other in our games. "All clear" were the words we used when our father was not in the house or had just gone off on his travels. I concluded that my father must be dead. The months he stayed away were the only times Jack and I, and Tobias, and poor mother were happy. We secretly did have happy times away from the snooping presence of the hateful Nanny Gill.

'I didn't mean to go inside the house today; I certainly didn't want to, not after all the dreadful times I'd been locked in the toy cupboard in my room, but seeing how different it looked from the outside, all the lovely new curtains and all the windows open to allow air in the house, something made me want to see if I could cope inside the place. I climbed up the cedar tree near my old bedroom window and slipped inside. I felt shaky at retracing my old escape route. My room had been changed, new voile drapes, white paint, and gentle furnishings, but I immediately felt the old vile panic crawling all over me. I remembered every beating my father and that malicious nanny gave me, every insult, every unfair accusation, every threat and punishment. I remembered every time Jack was punished, every extra castigation he received because in his anxiety he couldn't jump quickly enough to obey them; how poor little Tobias was stripped naked and left to sleep on a cold hard floor without a single cover after wetting the bed, and how hopeless we all felt because inevitably the bedwetting problem only got worse. I heard again my mother's despairing voice saying she'd run away with us all but she feared my father would track us down and make our lives even more unbearable than before.'

Stella shook all over with misery then thumped her fist down on her other palm, making Dorrie blink, startled. 'Then suddenly I was furious, unafraid of my father and wanting to tear him apart piece by piece. Wrenching open the door I slammed it shut and stalked for the stairs, forgetting about Jack and the servants for the moment, until I saw you. I felt rather lost then.'

'So I saw, Stella. I felt silly to have hidden away from what I thought was an intruder or a ghost,' Dorrie admitted.

'A ghost?' Stella made a puzzled face.

'Oh, that's some daft notion of Mrs Kelland's. Stella, may I ask if today was the first time you'd been back inside the house?'

'Yes, I swear. I'd only just arrived, after parking my car in the lane and stealing through the woods. Why? Has something happened?'

'No, not really.' Dorrie felt it was not her place to tell Stella that her brother had been married before and that his peculiar first wife was reputed to be menacingly haunting Meadows House. 'May I ask if you know anything about your other brother, Tobias?'

'No, did he run away too?' Stella stooped with disappointment. 'I was hoping to see Tobias again as much as Jack. My father was savage with Tobias because sometimes he would dare to answer him back. I could see Tobias was having the soul knocked out of him.' She was pulsing with indignant outrage, verging on distress, and Dorrie reached for her hand. Stella gripped on tight. 'It's no wonder he started to steal drink from the age of twelve to cope with things. Our mother was dead by then. The doctor said her heart just gave up on her. It's no wonder she died so young. That monster wore her out with his demands and cruelty. Oh God, I should have stayed for Tobias's sake. It must have got so much worse for him and Jack after I'd run away.'

'You mustn't blame yourself, Stella. Your father went off to Columbia soon after you left the finishing school, and Jack only recently got word he'd died of a snake bite. It was common knowledge, though, that Tobias drank heavily. One night, when he was about nineteen, he went out and never returned. No one has seen him since. Jack involved the police. They made sweeping inquiries, but I'm afraid they eventually came to the conclusion that Tobias had probably died somewhere in a state of inebriation. I'm very sorry.'

Stella cried wretched tears for a while then dried her eyes with her handkerchief. 'Poor Tobias. If he really is dead I hope he's now at peace.' Her voice was watery with emotion.

Dorrie understood. This had been a lot for Stella to take in.

'I'm going to tell you something, Mrs Resterick. It's something Jack knew about and so did Tobias. It was shouted at my poor mother and me in hate and accusation, often enough, that I'm not Randall Newton's daughter. I'm pleased it's the truth. Randall returned home from an eight-month trek to find my mother five months' pregnant. She refused to tell him who was the father. He used every way imaginable to punish her, including rape. Tobias was conceived by rape. Mother knew Randall wouldn't stop until he'd ruined me so she planned an escape route for me. She sold her jewellery and set up a savings account for me. For two years after Mother died I endured the old man's malice and hatred, then I absconded from the finishing school when I was sixteen and could access the money. Thanks to Mother's love and foresight and her pleas to me to make something good come out of my life I've done just that, because there is one thing I am sure of – my mother and real father, whoever he was, were in love.'

Heaving a mighty sigh of pride, Stella sat back on the sofa in Dorrie's comfortable sitting room. She picked up her handbag and took out cigarettes and a lighter. 'Do you mind? Would you like one?'

'Not at all, and no thank you, I haven't smoked for years,' Dorrie said, nodding at the cut-glass ashtray on the tea table. 'I'm so glad to hear all is well with you now. Jack is happy too. So you're married, Stella?'

'I am indeed,' Stella replied, leaning forward with energy and control and dipping again into her soft leather handbag. 'I'm now Mrs Oscar Grey and we have five children, all adopted. I've got some snaps. Are you and Mr Resterick down here on holiday?

I've never forgotten how kind you both were to my brothers and me, and Mr Greg was such fun.'

'I lost Piers during the Dunkirk evacuation. He'd sailed across the Channel in his own boat . . . He's buried beside our daughter in the village churchyard. It's just Greg and me here now; he should be home presently after his daily walk. And there's our dear Corky. We'd hate to be without him.' Dorrie patted the long, thick-bodied, squat-legged black mongrel lounging beside her armchair. 'He's not an old dog although he's just about deaf and blind and is lame in one hind leg, but he can scent something fresh or interesting from hundreds of yards away. He was a stray, obviously not wanted, and I found him near Piers' grave and fell in love with him. He's such wonderful company.'

'I know what you mean. We've three dogs, heaps of rabbits and other pets. I'm sorry to hear about Mr Resterick. Has Nanviscoe changed much? I would have loved to attend the village school but my father wouldn't hear of it. We weren't allowed to mix with anyone. Although Oscar and I school our children ourselves owing to their various needs we make sure they mix with lots of other children. They're all rather special, you see, like Corky, unwanted or handicapped. Oscar is wheelchair bound; his legs were paralysed from shrapnel in the spine.'

Dorrie was a smiler by nature and she beamed at every black and white photograph as she went through them. One boy had callipers on his legs, and one little girl a bad squint. All seemed happily occupied with toys, with pets or in dressing-up outfits. Oscar Grey looked about a decade older than Stella, in his forties. 'You all seem one big happy family.'

'A happy menagerie,' Stella laughed loudly.

In one rapid jump to his feet Corky was heading out of the room.

'Dor! Dor! Come quickly!'

The sudden anguished shouts from outside made Stella leap back in her seat, clearly alarmed.

'It's Greg.' Dorrie shot to her feet. 'Something's wrong.'

Three

'I don't see why I must stay in bed and have Nurse Rumford call on me every day. It's only a sprained ankle, for goodness sake,' Greg Barnicoat snorted, shoving back his bedcovers, his irritability making him sweat and turn red in the face. 'I fell in the hedge outside my own house and made a damned fool of myself, ripping my trousers and bloodying my head, and then I had the indignity of being hauled into the house by you and Stella Grey. She must have thought I was a doddering old codger only fit for the knacker's yard.'

'She thought nothing of the kind. In fact she remarked that you'd hardly changed at all, and that she always thought you had a touch of Errol Flynn about you.' Dorrie's patience outmatched her older brother's grumpiness. She was invariably a picture of tolerance. 'Sit up straight so I can put your breakfast tray across.'

'Did she really?' Greg smoothed at the ends of his spruce Clark Gable moustache and pushed out a swelling manly chest.

'Who?'

'Don't be silly, old girl.' Greg gratefully received the tray, for his stomach was grumbling with emptiness. His big-boned structure needed a lot of filling up. He usually did the cooking, something he excelled at, as it was not a fondness of Dorrie's, and in the five days since his accident he had niggled about every meal, drawing nothing more from Dorrie than an unwearied sigh, and her particular look that said, 'Well if you want to be childish . . .'

'Stella certainly did say that, but by rights you should look more like Boris Karloff as a monster. The lump on your head is still the size of an egg and your eyes are bruised like a boxer's. You should have gone to the hospital, as the doctor wanted you to. You had concussion and you could easily have taken a turn for the worse. So, of course Nurse Rumford has been keeping an eye on you.'

'Maybe.' Greg tucked into his dish of porridge with gusto,

chewing lumps of toast at the same time. He would have preferred a cooked breakfast, but at the present time eggs, courtesy of the hens he and Dorrie kept, and bacon from their own pigs were for main meals only. 'But I'll tell Nurse Rumford she no longer needs to call on me after today. She's got enough on her hands with so many young women in the village expecting, including that poor shamed deserted girl, Jenna, and her mum Jean expecting yet again too. Mind you, Dor, you can always lend a hand, you're an expert at midwifery after delivering the Templeton baby last year.'

'Don't be daft,' Dorrie said airily, picking up books, newspapers, notepaper, pens and pencils and other items that had fallen off the bed. Greg might be laid up but he somehow managed to make his room look a shambles. 'The women aren't due to give birth all at the same time. I've got some news concerning the village.'

'Oh?' Greg paused before demolishing his last spoonful. 'Someone planning an event at the hall?' He was proud of the fact that he had played a large part in getting the new village hall built and opened at the end of the previous year.

'Sawle has been sold. Stella's bought it to be near to Jack, isn't it wonderful? Her family will make a welcome addition to Nanviscoe.' Sawle was a modern house, an impressive piece of innovation, situated on the way to Meadows House.

Dorrie wandered off the issue a little. 'I wonder when old Petherton will be sold. Someone mentioned it would be a good thing if it was demolished and four bungalows built on the site. Can't see that ever being the case; Esther Mitchelmore would never sell the place she had put all her love and energy into for a building contractor to profit by.'

Dorrie's small, fine frame buzzed with her own speculation. Petherton was a rundown old manor house in the midst of Nanviscoe village. Esther Mitchelmore would have approved of Sawle being sold to Stella, a former local. Petherton and Sawle had been owned by two sisters, who last year had gone abroad to live after Esther Mitchelmore had been diagnosed with cancer. Dorrie believed it was a lie about the cancer but she had good reason not to declare this publicly.

'Trouble and strife,' Greg announced dramatically, lifting the tray into Dorrie's waiting hands.

'Why so?' She was amused at the twinkle running behind his eyes; eyes that showed his innate sense of fun and boyishness, eyes that were part of his overall attractiveness. She was proud her brother actually did have masculine film-star looks. He drew female attention but failed to notice even the most blatant attempt to gain his romantic interest. She knew exactly what Greg would say next, he was much given to repeated sayings. 'And problems for life,' she whispered under her breath.

'And problems for life,' Greg spilled forth as if in front of an avid audience. 'Well, every time we have newcomers they invariably bring all manner of troubles and problems with them, and poor you, old thing, always seemed to be plunged right into the middle of them. You've got too much of a trustworthy face, Dor. Keep your head down this time. Just look forward to our darling Verity coming home after her honeymoon and the secret welcome-home party we're planning.'

'I am, and Jack's reunion with Stella. He was over the moon at her contacting him. But Stella's hardly a newcomer and she has a happy life. She won't be bringing any trouble with her. Sometimes you say such silly things, Greg. She's moving down quickly from Guildford and will have brought her family to Sawle in time for the party.'

'Well, there should be no problems with a simple party, and one thing's for sure: I will be fit and well by then to go to Meadows House and I'll drive out any ghosts lingering there.'

Four

Stella and Oscar Grey and their five children, and two others, were all that remained in the empty Moderne-styled, half-rendered, half red-brick house in a quiet avenue in Guildford, Surrey. The furniture and series of labelled boxes, crates, trunks and cases, all carefully packed, were now being driven away in two large removal vans. After so much wholehearted activity the gathering were left bathed in the dust motes clearly visible in the sunlight streaming through the curtain-stripped windows.

The gathering had formed in a circle holding hands, something they did on important occasions to reinforce their family and friend and staff closeness, all there except for the new nursemaid who had declined to join the move down to Cornwall. Stella, the invisible cord that held the group together, with her habitual pencil and notepad hanging from a chain around her neck, was beside Oscar in his wheelchair. The checked blanket covering Oscar's ruined legs was in stark contrast to the force and vigour retained in his stocky build. Crinkly laughter lines traced off from his friendly eyes and he wore his hair Brylcreemed in place. Sitting on his lap, her oft-times perch, was the youngest child, tiny thirty-month-old, elf-like Libby, fated to never grow beyond her twenty pounds of weight, her rare condition a form of dwarfism. Wrapped in her baby-sized arms was her soft toy cat, made from a paisley-print cotton headscarf.

'Right then, our gang,' Oscar said in his hushed Manchester accent. 'We're up bright and early and already well into this new day of adventure. Our new house in Nanviscoe, all the way down in Cornwall, where Mummy and I showed you on the map, is much like this one, and we'll be able to spread out and have our rooms in roughly the same order. Mummy and Daddy will sleep downstairs as before, and Stanley will be temporarily in the sitting room until his own little room is completed. Cornwall has lovely lanes, woods and meadows much the same as we have here for you to play in, and some wonderful beaches all in quite easy reach, so there's plenty of scope for fun and learning.'

Oscar threw Stella a wide-eyed look, while kissing the back of her hand locked with his. She grinned back and shook her head in equal wonder, for this was the first time complete silence had reigned among their children – even Stanley, their nine-year-old constant fidget. His thin knobbly legs encased in harsh metal callipers, he was renowned for interrupting everyone's speech – chiding and encouragement couldn't prevent his cheeky rudeness – but right now he was completely still, his wavy lips slightly open in awe. Stella and Oscar loved him for his casual acceptance of his disability as a result of polio, his ever-friendly spirit, and quick clever mind. He was their cheeky moppet with a tumble of brown curls trailing across the top of his head and over his sturdy brow. He was born, it seemed, with a mischievous grin, was a perfect mimic, feigned innocence to a perfect pitch, and was already a seasoned rogue when he had been brought to the orphanage Stella had worked in. Stanley was silent for once, but only for a minute.

'Can we go to a beach soon as we get there?' The boy thrust up his stubborn chin then pitched off. 'Never been to a beach before. Gonna c'lect shells, seaweed and live crabs. There's a pond there, like here, you said, Mummy. Can I keep crabs in it? And can we bring back 'nough sand to play in? And can we have Cornish cream every day, like that d'licious stuff you brought home after going to Uncle Jack's? Can't wait to meet Uncle Jack. He got horses on his farm? Can we ride 'em? Can I have a horse, a black one so I can play Sir Lancelot, Dick Turpin and be a pirate?'

'Pirates don't have horses, bonehead,' chipped in six-year-old Pattie, her blonde prettiness marred by a severe squint. 'They have big wooden ships with sails and flags, and go "har-har, me hearties". Daddy said so.'

Pattie came from the same orphanage as Stanley and Libby. All three of them had no one else in the world except for their new family, formed after Oscar's recuperation period. Stella and Oscar had married before the airfield bombing that had crippled him. He was part of a Spitfire's ground crew. His crew mate and others had been killed.

'But I'm going to be a pirate who goes on desert islands and gets on his big black horse to search for buried treasure.' Stanley had an answer for everything.

'You can be Captain Blackbird and we'll be your swary mates,' Timmy, next to his eight-year-old twin Daisy, added to the theme. Their hair ginger and straight, their faces amassed with freckles, they hated being left out of anything and were always eager players, but their oval faces reflected wariness and they were apt to look over their thin bony shoulders, afraid their 'first' mother – a fist-ready drunk, regularly with a new man in tow, invariably a nasty man they must call 'uncle' – showed up and stole them away. Until Mummy and Daddy took them in – *rescued* them – they had never known what a full tummy, clean hair and bodies, and a full set of clothes felt like. Their miserable existence had been lice, bugs, filth and disgusting smells, sometimes imprisonment in a locked wardrobe for over twenty-four hours. They refused to be parted for long periods and shared a room, agreeing they would rather die than be forced back into their old life. Mummy and Daddy had promised that nothing bad would ever happen to them again, and now they were going all the way down to Cornwall, right at the bottom of the country, even further away from their former deprived existence.

'I think you mean *swarthy* mates,' Stella laughed. 'And Captain Black*beard*.'

'No, no,' Stanley bowled in. 'I'll be Captain Blackbird, not going to have a parrot but a talking crow.'

'And me the pirate cook,' Pattie added happily. Cooking was her favourite pastime and she spent heaps of time in the kitchen with Philly, who was in charge of the food and the laundry. Philippa Lindley was a much-older friend and former workmate of Stella's.

Now that the new nursemaid had left, the staff consisted of the children's middle-aged, firm but jolly and slightly eccentric nanny, Miss Noelle Lucas. She was a dramatic storyteller who used actions and characters aplenty to feed the children's imaginations. Philly and Nanny Lucas were as much loved by the children as Stella and Oscar were.

'And Libs can watch all the fun,' Philly finished off, her tones broad and low and husky from her many decades as a smoker.

Libby would never walk or be out of nappies, or talk apart from a number of sounds indicating her needs and moods. She chuckled a lot and was sometimes called 'the baby'. Philly played with all the children as often as she could. She had not known a happy secure childhood herself. Her start in life was as an illegitimate workhouse baby. She always wore a large pair of tied-on pannier pockets over her apron from which she invariably produced just the thing required at the moment – scissors, hankies, pencils, scraps of paper, string, nail file, cigarettes and matches. The pockets made her look as if she had enormous hips spreading out from her gangly form and she waddled rather than walked. Philly had been pushed out of the workhouse into service at the age of thirteen. She had met Stella during one of Stella's many jobs, working in a biscuit factory, in Salford.

The pair had clicked as friends and had soon shared a flat, confiding all to each other. Philly laughed off her lowly beginning and unattractiveness. 'Don't know who my parents were and I don't care to. Probably died of the pox or something equally as bad anyway. Don't know if I'm Jewish – I could be Jewish with this nose, but then again it could be a Roman nose.' Philly had grainy skin and man-sized hands and feet. Her breathing was noisy but it was a comfort to know she was there. Stella had told Philly that Randall Newton wasn't her real father and that she, Stella, was desperate to learn who was. And how she had carefully invested her mother's bequest for the future, and although initially scared at her escape into the world alone, she had been determined to support herself and discover other areas of life. Her confidence had grown. Wending her way about the country, Stella had worked as a waitress, a cinema usherette, a nightclub singer to show off her excellent crooning voice – but only for two weeks, hating the come-ons she'd got from certain male customers – and then on to the biscuit factory.

Still sharing digs with Philly, she had moved on to something she thought might be her calling, working in an orphanage. Although treated as an unappreciated dogsbody, mopping and scrubbing the dormitories, changing fouled bed linen, emptying chamber pots and sterilizing urine puddles, changing nappies, combing out hair nits and slogging in the kitchens, Stella had loved the time she had spent bathing the children, helping them to dress, reading stories to them and giving much needed cuddles. Soon Philly had taken a job as a cook in the orphanage and enjoyed being near the children too.

When the orphanage was evacuated during the war to a crumbling old parsonage away from the town, the conditions became even more trying. With other evacuated kids squeezed in beside them, the staff was much reduced as women went off to join the Land Army or ATS. Nothing on earth would make Stella and Philly leave the children. To Stella the children were her life's purpose, but that didn't stop love invading her heart when the rugged, quietly serious Oscar Grey turned up one day wanting to see his evacuated sister, pretty and lovable Olivia. Oscar had a heart-melting smile. He was a natural with the kids and loved to entertain them. One afternoon he helped Stella perform a puppet show at the orphanage, the last happy occasion for gorgeous little Olivia who died suddenly a week later from bronchial pneumonia.

'It's like she was blown away like a piece of thistledown,' Oscar had grieved, and Stella had taken him into her arms. 'I don't want to leave this place where Olivia last was and I don't want to leave you,' he had told her.

'I never want to let you go,' Stella replied, turning her consoling into passionate loving.

The pair married on Oscar's next leave. Weeks later a tiny piece of exploding plane pierced a lower region of Oscar's spine, putting him out of the war. After his long recuperation he had joined the orphanage as handy man, perfectly able from his wheelchair to bully the antiquated boiler into service, and to do carpentry at a bench. From a scholarship grammar-school background, he had taken over the office work when the manager had turned her back on the set-up and found a more lucrative post as a secretary in a munitions factory. By the end of the war Stella, Oscar and Philly were unofficially running the orphanage. Wanting to settle down to family life and a new beginning, the three adults moved to Guildford, adopting three of the special needs children to take with them.

The twins had been dumped several weeks earlier at the orphanage by 'an uncle', a rough, smelly individual with black teeth, of indeterminate age. 'Haven't seen their old woman for days. She stormed off, pissed to high heaven, drugged up too; mithering old bitch. Would've killed these nippers if I hadn't stopped her, they got belt welts all over their backs and legs. Reckon the bitch's dying of the clap. Don't let her ever have 'em back, for God's sake.'

Stella and Oscar had taken the man's plea to heart, taking the frightened little pair with them as foster children. As a safeguard in the event their mother was alive and searched for them, they had changed the twins' names and gave them Oscar's surname, the whole family, including the welcome addition of Noelle Lucas as nanny, embracing the subterfuge. Bruce and Marion Tilsley had become Timothy and Daisy Grey, and new papers had been obtained for them. The arrangement was not legal, but the twins' peace and protection was paramount to all. It had been a terrible, heartbreaking wrench to leave the other children who had been returned to the former orphanage.

Finding the best purpose for her mother's money, Stella had bought the house she and her family were now about to leave. Oscar was the strength behind the arrangement and Stella the cord that bound them all together.

'Right, gang,' Stella said, sad to be leaving the first Olivia House while greatly excited to be moving on to the next Olivia House and to at last be reunited with Jack. 'Everyone take a trip to the lav whether you feel you want to go or not, then grab your coats; it's quite chilly. Then we'll get the kids packed into the car; a picnic is already on board.' Petrol rationing was tighter than for food but Stella had begged for, inveigled and paid over the odds for the quantity of fuel that would take her on another long trip so soon. 'And Philly and Nanny will travel down by train. Philly has the taxi fare to our new house, and we'll all meet up there. The removal vans too, although we'll probably not all arrive at the same time. The dear lady I've told you about, Mrs Resterick, has the keys for whoever gets there first. Mrs Resterick is looking for a new nursemaid for us to join our gang. Until we get everything settled in it will be like camping out, all great fun. We'll soon be seeing your Uncle Jack and new Aunty Verity so we'll be an even bigger happy family.'

'Let's hope that's not brave last words,' Philly mumbled to herself. In her experience there was often a ruddy great obstacle to be overcome just round every bloomin' corner.

Five

'Have you heard, Mrs R?' Finn Templeton winked at Dorrie. 'That the Meadows House ghost has been walking again?' An amused scoff tempered his handsome young face as he playfully grabbed Tilly Vercoe, his girlfriend and the younger housemaid at the big house. 'Don't worry, darling, I'll protect you.'

'It's not funny, Finn,' Tilly admonished him, and to prove her words she shuddered inside his arm, her dainty oval face darkened with a chill, her bow lips trembling and neat chin wobbling. She looked younger than her seventeen years and even more so in her present frightened state.

Dorrie thought it a shame this sweet-natured, romantic dreamer should be scared out of her wits in the house she loved working in. Dorrie was at Merrivale, the restored cottage home of Finn and his mother Fiona. Dorrie was there to see her goddaughter. Baby Eloise was extra special to Dorrie, as she had delivered her nearly a year ago when Finn had panicked over his mother's premature labour. Fiona had been utterly depressed at the time and had rejected the baby, and Dorrie had been hers and Finn's mainstay. Made impoverished over Finn's disgraced council official father's imprisonment for fraud, Finn had been forced to forsake his university plans. However, thanks to Merrivale's owner, Guy Carthewy, Fiona's only reliable friend, who also happened to be in love with Fiona, Finn, after initially refusing Guy's ready help, had accepted Guy's offer to fund his ongoing education. Finn had chosen a small private art academy in Bodmin and he returned home at weekends to watch over his mother and baby sister, and to see Tilly. They were his priorities.

Holding pretty dark-haired Eloise up round her chubby waist while the baby bounced gleefully on her legs, Dorrie, never one to be dramatic, asked simply, 'Has something happened, Tilly dear?'

'It was dreadful, Mrs Resterick,' Tilly whispered, as if fearful that if she spoke normally the ghost would reach out and get her in this very spot, on the Templetons' boxy settee. She clung to Finn. 'Cathy left her room in the middle of the night for the bathroom, but somehow she found her way downstairs and, she said, she got that awful feeling someone was watching her. Then the ghost loomed up in front of her and when she screamed, the ghost, a girl in a long white dress just like the former mistress used to wear, screamed back at her. Cathy said she turned and fled and when she glanced back she saw the ghost's face, twisted up in horror and madness. Cathy came tearing straight in to me. Course she'd woke up the Kellands, and she explained everything to us. That was two nights ago and Cathy is too afraid to stay in her own room and sleeps in with me. I know my own sister and Cathy was terrified out of her wits and her teeth were chattering. Mr Kelland reckons she was dreaming. Mrs Kelland said that Cathy had surely seen Mrs Lucinda Newton, stirred up from her grave and really mad and insanely jealous that Mr Jack has got married again. Us women are all as nervous as kittens and none of us like going about the house by ourselves. Mr and Mrs Newton are back home from their honeymoon tomorrow – I must get back to my duties soon, only got an hour and a half off – and we don't know whether we should mention the haunting or not. It's not our imagination, Mrs Resterick, honestly. I swear there's something really strange and wicked going on in that house.'

Finn looked troubled over Tilly's fright and hugged her tight against him. Tilly had been his girlfriend for some months, and although Finn was experienced with women, he treated Tilly with pure romantic respect, on purpose. He had had an intense infatuation with a gorgeous young married woman, which had eventually been noticed by her angry husband. Belle Lawry had felt insulted and rejected Finn ruthlessly, shaming him in public, and in those humiliating moments Finn's feelings had changed to deep bitterness. He loathed Belle Lawry for raging at him, as if his love for her was filthy abuse. He loathed the fact that Belle Lawry lived locally, further along Barnicoat Way past Sunny Corner, and he loathed her teenage son, Sam, who had abandoned Tilly's cousin, Jenna Vercoe, after making her pregnant. 'But things can often appear peculiar at night, sweetheart. Cathy was probably half asleep and was spooked by her own shadow.'

'It wasn't like that, Finn,' Tilly protested, vehement and anxious. 'What do you think, Mrs Resterick?'

Dorrie's gentle common sense manner led so often to her becoming a confidante or mentor, the one with the answer to someone's problem. She had been going over the layout of Meadows House in her mind. 'I think, dear, that Finn could be halfway right.'

'Oh?' Tilly sighed a pent-up gasp of relief and was immediately comforted. No one doubted Mrs Resterick. She was never wrong. 'You don't think there's a ghost, that there's some other explanation for what's been going on? The creepy footsteps and everything else?'

'I think it's very likely,' Dorrie said. 'Has Cathy been anxious about anything lately?'

'Well, yes, anxious about making sure everything is right for the new mistress, even though Mrs Verity is never bossy but always generous and thankful, and fun at times. Cathy says it will be different to when Mrs Lucinda was alive. She relied on the staff to run the house in every way and took her meals wherever she happened to be at the time. She inspected nothing and took no interest in anything other than herself and her dolls and things. Me and the Kellands believe Mrs Newton will be a lovely mistress, but Cathy is, well, she's a bit of a fusspot really, always has been, even when we lived with Uncle Denny and Aunty Jean as girls. I've told Cathy not to be so silly. We're already used to having Mrs Verity in the house, and any changes she wants made have been more or less done already.'

Dorrie nodded wisely. Eloise Veronica – her second name was in honour of Dorrie's late daughter who had died at fifteen months from croup – plonked down on her lap and started playing with Dorrie's blue and white crystal necklace. 'There's a full-length mirror as one turns the corner from the foot of the stairs, isn't there? I think it's likely Cathy has been sleepwalking and getting back into bed without even knowing it, but this time she opened her eyes and saw her own reflection in the mirror. Unless her nightdress was very dark it could appear to be white. Naturally her reflection was screaming too and when Cathy fled and looked back she saw from the different angle her own horrified face in the mirror. It's easy to become startled and alarmed at just about anything when one has been terrified, don't you think? Especially after listening to people voice macabre tales, as Mrs Kelland does. Yes, I would say Cathy has been sleepwalking out of anxiety for some time now and it's been her, without her knowing it, creating those odd noises, and that's the reason for the strange occurrences since Verity and Jack's engagement.'

'That's it,' Mrs R,' Finn concurred with enthusiasm to further reassure Tilly. 'It's daft to think of the dead woman haunting the house. She brought about her own death. She couldn't wait to leave this world so why on earth and heaven would she want to come back? She didn't care about the house when she was alive, so why should she now? Apparently she didn't see Jack as a real husband. Why should she care if he marries again? She's dead and gone for good. Mrs Kelland shouldn't prattle on with all that morbid stuff. Tilly, go back and tell Cathy all this. I'll bet she'll be relieved and the sleepwalking will soon stop. Happier now, sweetheart? Not going to feel there's a spook round every corner? Remember how you loved the peace of the house when you first went there to work, that's all you have to do.'

Tilly smiled and tittered, making her dimples show, something Finn adored about her. 'I feel a bit silly now. Like you mentioned, Mrs Resterick, there's a lot in the power of suggestion. It's a shame that Mrs Lucinda is buried in the grounds though. It would be easier for all if she wasn't, for a completely fresh start.'

'Yes indeed,' Dorrie said thoughtfully. She had an idea about that, but there would never be an appropriate time to have a word with Jack about it. He had doted on Lucinda, had formed an unbreakable tie to her. Jack might find the mention of removing Lucinda's remains from the grounds of his house to a public cemetery deeply offensive.

Six

Verity Newton was swept up in her husband's strong arms and carried across the threshold of her new home. She kissed Jack. She had barely stopped kissing him, and he her, since they had left their wedding reception. She was in love, deeply in love, and rapturously happy knowing that Jack loved her back with every ounce of him and drop of his blood.

Their wedding day had been full of such joy and bliss, followed by their first night of loving (already long anticipated) as husband and wife, gloriously active through every intense sensual moment. They were born to be together, in body, mind, soul and spirit. Verity had thought the biblical meaning of marriage between two people becoming as one was unattainable, particularly when engaged to her former cold-hearted fiancé, who had made her feel useless and unattractive. She was blessed to be on the same level as Jack in every way. She loved Jack so deeply at times it overloaded her heart and it hurt. A hurt she welcomed and embraced, and in the deepest quietest moments she feared losing Jack, losing even the tiniest part of him.

They had laughingly used indulgent imagery throughout their safari honeymoon, Verity starting off with, 'You're the Romeo to my Juliet.'

'The Mae to my West.'

'You're the glittering diamond to my gold ring,' was one of Jack's tender affirmations, dreamily whispered, and Verity had felt his love for her flowing up from his heart.

'You're the glorious golden sun in my perfect blue sky,' she replied, and wrapped her body protectively round him, adoring him, kissing him again and again. 'And you'll be the best father ever to the baby inside me.' She and Jack had been strolling under the never-ending mantle of African sky outside their honeymoon bungalow and the mention of a baby had come out of her mouth as if by magic. She was already longing to have a baby with Jack, to have a large happy family with him to expunge the horrors of his childhood forever. A new and happy generation would live at Meadows House, and would be tempered wonderfully and aptly with Jack's sister's squad of children living close by. Verity had spoken to Stella Grey over the telephone and felt that she already knew and liked her.

'You think you're pregnant, darling?' Jack had gasped in wonder, sweeping her up in his arms and dancing around with her, making puffs of ochre-red dust under his feet. 'It's too soon to tell yet, isn't it? Unless it happened before our big day.'

'I think that must be the case, darling.' She had placed her hands, fingers pointing together, over her flat tummy and rested her head against Jack's warm neck. 'I missed the signs with all with the excitement going on. I have your baby inside me. Nothing can ever hurt us.'

Lowdy Kestle was washing up a small mountain of dishes in her back kitchen when she felt the first twinge. It was strong and sharp and caused her to catch her breath and stay still for several moments. 'Darn.' She banged the soapy dishcloth on the side of the deep cloam sink. 'Why did I leave last night's supper dishes to add to the breakfast ones? The only time in my life and this happens. And why now at the weekend when all the kids are home?'

'What's that, maid?' Teddy Kestle yelled from the kitchen. He was tying on his boots, a fag clamped between his lips, about to go out to the back garden. He had sent eldest son, Tony, to the shed to fetch the ladder and tools needed to shore up some loose gutters – launders, as they were called locally.

Demobbed three years ago in 1945 from the Infantry to live again in his tied cottage, he had resumed work as a farm labourer on Meadows Farm. Stubby in stature, before the war he had been cheerful and noisy. Now he was subdued and inclined to be nervy and watchful. His eyes would take on the merriness of old, but at odd moments they would cloud over with tears and he would hasten off to be alone. On his return, Lowdy would make no mention of his red-rimmed eyes, the tremors of grief and horror obviously haunting him. Teddy had seen his cousin blown up by a German shell – not even a bootlace left of him – and his best mate blinded and a boy of eighteen rendered limbless, that much

Lowdy had gleaned from overhearing Teddy talking numbly to Jack Newton. Moments of panic took hold of him at night and he'd sit bolt up in bed, and Lowdy would hold him and reassure him until his body at last softened and the flashback was over, and she would cradle him to her and soothe him to sleep.

Lowdy was thankful to have her husband back in his rightful place as head of the family, the still generous-hearted man she had courted fresh from the school playground, although there were times Teddy now doubted he was any good to her or anyone else. Her husband had returned home intact in body but the bloody war had destroyed a vital part of him, left him partly in torment, and Lowdy cursed Hitler and his evil cohorts to hell every day.

To help Teddy come to terms with his losses and to feel loved and needed, Lowdy encouraged him to make love often, and nine months after his homecoming he had been delighted when Lowdy had given birth. In addition to Tony, Shirley and Eric, twelve, eleven and nine years respectively, there was new baby Denise. Teddy loved babies and he was delighted there would be another one any day soon, although Lowdy would have preferred to stop with Denise. But never mind, every child was a blessing and brought with them their love. Teddy would pick the youngest of the day out of its cot the moment he arrived home and washed his hands, then gather his clutch of kids round him, and speak the words Lowdy had longed to hear again throughout the hostilities: 'What are 'ee putting on the table then, maid? My belly thinks my craw's been cut.' He was still her good old Teddy, just a little haggard and old before his time, with touches of raw sensitivity.

While wiping her hands on a thinning towel as she came into the kitchen, Lowdy, her hair up in a knotted scarf, in a blue and green floral print smock and a saggy grey skirt, short socks and slippers, a bit careworn and harassed, said calmly so as not to panic Teddy, 'I sent Shirley to the shop to see if she can get some marg. Got the coupons but don't know if Soames Newton will have any in stock yet. Any day now, he said a couple of days ago. I'll need her to watch over Denise when she's back. Can you keep the boys out of the house all day? You'll have to ask Nurse Rumford to call, Teddy, but give it a couple of hours yet. I'll get everything ready then go next door and tell Mrs Grundry. She's going to help out this time. Can't very well ask Jean Vercoe to do the usual, she's overdue, and poor young Jenna is heading near the end of her time too. That poor maid, it won't be a happy occasion for her, dumped by the father. Never see her out in broad daylight any more. That Sam Lawry's got a lot to answer for. He's not much more than a boy himself but he should have stepped up to the mark. I'd be ashamed if he was my son. Belle Lawry's too protective of him; she won't make much of a grandmother.'

Teddy had not heard a word beyond Lowdy's mention of Nurse Rumford. He went straight into a petrified panic, as he always did for some minutes at these times, even when his pre-war children were about to be born. Then he jumped up and grabbed his wife to him and hugged her across her bulge. The love for his wife was the one thing that had got him through the long times of separation, and the bombardments and blood, and the debilitating fear of death. His Lowdy was still lovely with hair the gold of honey and eyes of sincerity and simplicity. Teddy and their family and their ordinary terrace home in Nanviscoe were enough for him. She was fuller in the figure now, even allowing for her condition, and time had etched a few lines here and there and sometimes she looked tired, but she was still as lovely as a summer dawn.

Teddy drew his wits to order. 'God bless you, my love. Right, right, right then, you got everything you need? You sure? Right, Nurse Rumford it is. I'll go now to forewarn her, don't want her to be unreachable when you'll need her most. I'll tell her two hours sharp.'

A cascade of pink-stained water gushed down from between Lowdy's legs and puddled round her feet. 'Better ask her to come as soon as she can, Teddy.' She clutched the sideboard and grimaced as a hefty contraction took hold of her body. 'This one's in a hurry to come out.'

'I knew you and Uncle Greg would do something like this, Aunt Dor,' Verity exclaimed in sheer delight, giving Dorrie a rib-crushing hug. 'A little welcome home do; thanks so much. Stella and her husband are expected soon, you say. I can't wait to meet them, and at a later date their family. We've brought gifts back for everyone, even something for the school and a painting to put up in the village hall, if the committee votes to accept it. Jack is going into Wadebridge tomorrow to get the wedding photos, I can't wait to see them. We'll put them in those beautiful polished wood frames you and Uncle Greg gave us. I expected to see Uncle Greg hobbling about. I laughed when you told me over the phone what a terrible patient he was for you, but how much he seemed to enjoy Nurse Rumford looking after him. He's an adorable old rogue! I shall put photos of the wedding, and us on honeymoon, all over the house to remind us of such wonderful times.'

Glasses of champagne in hand, they were in the drawing room, filled with new boxy line furniture and Art Deco lamps. Verity's eyes went to the piano, and she felt as if she had been dealt a hammer blow as her stomach convulsed.

It was back!

Until a month before the wedding, standing with the photos of Jack as a boy, his mother and Stella and Tobias, there had been a picture of Jack and his child-wife, Lucinda, wearing her signature white dress and pumps, and white ribbon in her raven-black hair. Fairy-tale beautiful, short and waif-thin, the girl's eyes seemed to bore back at Verity; large, guarded, secret eyes that had always given Verity the chills. Tentatively, Verity had asked Jack if the old photograph could be put away. She had not wanted to start here as new mistress under the shadow of its former one, albeit one incapable of taking the full place of running the house and being a wife. Lucinda on display would provoke unwelcome questions and musings about her. Verity had heard in her mind, when showing some friend about her new home, 'Tell me about Jack's first wife, she was rather peculiar, wasn't she?' Stella would want to know about her brother's past but she and Jack could discuss that privately.

Verity would not have minded so much if she had not seen Lucinda's maniacal destruction of so many of her dolls and belong-ings, with the hideous daubing of red paint. Only an insane person – or worse, an evil one – would do such a deliberate, catastrophic thing. It had left Verity with the feeling that Lucinda had wished her artificial victims were real people, and it might even have been so if Kelland hadn't locked her room at night when Jack was away. To Verity's belief, Lucinda had been a perturbing presence in the house. It sat uneasily with Verity that the girl's body was buried in the grounds. Murmurs from Mrs Kelland reinforced the chilling religious belief that the dead did not rest if interred outside sacred confines. Jack, furious and resentful of the vicar for resigning Lucinda to an unblessed, undignified burial, was still protective of his first wife's memory. Jack had encountered Lucinda as a forlorn, lost little thing, clutching her tiny white poodle, while he was taking a lonely holiday in Italy. To save her from an existence of being locked away by her disinterested guardian, Jack had married the English-born unworldly girl and kept her as she'd wanted, in comfortable seclusion, with Cathy and the Kellands to wait on her.

Verity was glad she wasn't aware of which tree Lucinda had hung herself from, but she did know where her grave was. Verity had wandered the grounds imagining what a pleasure it would be to do so in the future. As she walked along the gravel garden paths, circled the pond and strolled up and down the narrow descending stream, she had intentionally shot off from various spots into the woods searching for Lucinda's resting – or un-resting – place. She believed she would feel easier to know its location rather than to imagine it was *out there somewhere.*

How wrong she was. After several attempts of forging deeper and deeper into the woods, following path after path, she had finally come across a little-used track leading shortly to an over-hang of ivy-tangled branches and tall holly. She knew at once that the natural obstruction concealed the grave. In other circum-stances she would have felt deep sympathy for the girl buried out here, all alone except for her beloved poodle who had swiftly pined itself to death for her. Instead she was overcome with chills and horror. But she had to see the grave, to see how Jack had inscribed the headstone, what his last feelings had been for Lucinda.

Rounding the thick green drooping foliage, Verity saw what she had sought with increasing urgency. Lucinda was down under-neath the earth of a small natural clearing. Her grave was closed in by low green-painted picket fencing and kept meticulously clear of fallen leaves, grit and debris. Jack sent Kelland here often to tend the grave. Verity had wondered how often Jack still came here. She couldn't expect him not to come here at all but she hoped it was rarely. The headstone was white and bore just two words. Lucinda. Polly. It could almost be the grave of two beloved pets. It was what a stranger might believe if happening across it. So Jack had not really seen Lucinda as a Newton. He had loved her, but not with a man's love for a woman, a husband's love for his wife. Perhaps with the love of a doting uncle, sad and mystified over her peculiar behaviour.

If Lucinda had not been deranged, Verity would have whispered softly, 'Hello Lucinda. I'm Verity, Jack's fiancée. I'm so sorry about what happened to you. Rest in peace. You're safe here.' Yet despite all the reason she could muster, Verity felt she was an interloper on this little piece of Jack's property, and that when she was inside the house that she had no right to enter Lucinda's old room, now a guest bedroom, decorated, as almost all the house was now, to Verity's taste. Verity had made this bedroom plain and masculine, not a clue at all that it had once been a child-woman's outlandish nursery.

Verity had crouched beside the pathetic little grave. 'I wish you weren't here at all. Stay wherever you are. You might as well stay for I'll *never* let you or anyone else come between Jack and me. He's mine, and I'll never let him go.' It was irrational, even silly, to say that to someone who no longer existed. Verity did not care. She had not wanted her pitiless former fiancé's children straight away, as he'd demanded, but she wanted Jack's babies with a passion. Jack was her soulmate, the love of her life, her breath and her very essence. God help anyone who tried to hurt him or mar the life they had planned together.

Lucinda had been past news to Verity until this moment of setting her eyes again on the wretched photograph on the piano. After all the joy and bliss and pleasure she had experienced in the last few weeks it was unimaginably difficult to keep her anger and dismay in check. Whoever was responsible for this act, this obscene act, had insulted her and it was unforgivable.

In a flicker of a second she wondered if Jack had instructed the photo be put back. No. How could she think that? He had readily agreed with her that it should be removed. 'Sorry, darling, I should have done it ages ago. Lucinda hated being exposed. I only kept it there because I felt, as I've told you, guilty that I couldn't have protected her more.' Jack had taken it away there and then, but Verity had no idea where to. Someone had known, must have watched Jack do it, and she would root out that someone and read them the riot act for taking such a liberty and demand to be told what point the guilty party had intended to make.

Smiling widely, she shifted to the piano and, glancing round to make sure she wasn't being watched she stealthily knocked the photo down and pushed it behind the others.

Dorrie had noticed the offending item seconds after Verity did, and she was saddened to see Verity's aggrieved expression. Why would anyone want to hurt Verity, who was so natural and carefree and understanding? It was a malicious act against someone so undeserving.

The matter was swept aside when Cathy announced Stella and Oscar Grey had just arrived. Laughingly grabbing Verity's hand, Jack rushed her outside to meet them.

Seven

'You haven't changed the slightest bit. I'd have picked you out anywhere.' The joint statement of utter delight from Jack and Stella was followed by them clinging together in several emotional embraces. They shook and laughed and let tears run away freely. Those watching them knew bittersweet memories assailed them and the pair would need time on their own to talk through their old life.

Releasing Stella from his arms at last but keeping a tight hold of her hand, Jack ushered Verity forward. 'Stella, meet my darling bride, my Verity. Do you remember each other?'

'Yes, we do,' the new sisters-in-law agreed, and they exchanged a kiss on the cheek.

'It was a wonderful surprise for Jack to get your telephone call at the hotel,' Verity said, the shock of the reappearance of Lucinda Newton's photograph temporarily forgotten.

'And this is my wonderful husband, Oscar,' Stella said with pride, hugging Oscar in his wheelchair, then glancing at Dorrie and winking to convey how joyful this reunion was. Smart in a tweed jacket and natty cap, Oscar, although confined and at a disadvantageous height, was a considerable presence. Dorrie was satisfied to see an instant gelling of the two couples.

'You didn't bring the children,' Verity said with disappointment. 'I'm so looking forward to seeing them and your friend Philly, Miss Lucas too. Talking about them with you over the phone I feel I know something of them already.'

Oscar laughed. 'It's something of organised chaos at our new Olivia House, having only been there a couple of days. Stella and I thought it better to let Philly and Nanny Lucas get on with settling the children in.' Stella almost always let Oscar speak first and all the while he did so, she smiled at him with love and respect.

'They're all very eager to meet their Uncle Jack and Aunty Verity,' Stella said. 'You must come over tomorrow. Just roll up at anytime. We're early risers. Philly doesn't sleep beyond a few hours, and one or other of the children often keeps us up. You'll get a noisy welcome from the dogs, Rags, Cosmo and Basil, and we've also got the lop-eared rabbits Dixie and Loppy, and the hamsters and tortoise. The girls are now asking for kittens, and Stanley is demanding a parrot. He's a right little character, they all are, and they keep us very happily busy.'

Verity felt a burning desire to see the children, but more than that she suddenly wanted to get away from her new home. Although having just arrived here after her blissful honeymoon she suddenly did not want to settle in yet. Swimming before her eyes was *that wretched photo*. Someone was trying, at the very least, to disconcert her, by making the point that Lucinda was once here with Jack, and perhaps should still be in his memory. 'Why don't we go inside and have a quick glass of champagne and a bite to eat, then all go over to Olivia House?' Verity said gaily.

Getting to the bottom of the mystery could wait until she and Jack returned, but she would not bother Jack about the occurrence. She would be strident in her inquiries. She had determined on the day he had proposed to her that she would ensure his home would only reflect calm and happiness. She would quickly sort out this matter of the unwelcome photo and forget about it and put all her energies into raising a family. There were four people on the staff, Sidney and Coral Kelland and Cathy and Tilly Vercoe. Only one of them, not an outsider, could be responsible for the monstrous insult to Verity. The Kellands and Cathy might not want her as their new mistress, holding some sort of allegiance to Lucinda, but it seemed so unlikely. They had always seemed so pleased to have her in the house, mentioning often how good she was for Mr Jack. They had been interested in all of her plans for the future. There was young Tilly, but Verity could never bring herself to believe Tilly would do such a spiteful thing. Tilly had only worked at Meadows House a few months, starting after Verity and Jack's engagement, taken on when Esther Mitchelmore had left Petherton, and Tilly was an absolute little sweetheart. Verity believed Kelland was as honest as a saint and without a nasty bone in his hearty body. So the offence pointed either to Mrs Kelland or Cathy. Verity was confident of finding out the culprit. Mrs Kelland was a chatterer and hopeless at keeping secrets and confidences. If she had not done the deed she would mark out the path to who did. Verity already had a storm to face in her new home but she would soon establish herself as the rightful mistress and rule the roost her way.

'We'd love for you all to come over to Olivia House today, if that's what you want, Verity,' Stella replied, always eager to show off her brood.

'We can dish out the gifts we've brought, and bring Tilly with us. We could all pitch in with the unpacking. It'll be fun.' Verity reached up and caressed Jack's face tenderly. 'Won't it, darling, to see the children today?'

'It's a brilliant idea, darling,' Jack said, and kissed her lips.

'Are you fine with that, Aunt Dor, Uncle Greg?'

'We certainly are,' they both agreed.

Before the gathering left for Olivia House, Verity swept into the kitchen where the female staff were busy at the table. Verity stood stiffly with one hand imperiously on top of the other. 'We're all getting ready to go off to Olivia House. Could you pack up the remains of food to take with us, please? Tilly, dear, you'll be joining us to lend the Greys a hand in their unpacking.' Before leaving the room, Verity shot Mrs Kelland and Cathy a hard look. They could think of it what they may.

Eight

Belle Lawry had got Newton Stores open and ready for business. Eight years ago, in 1940, Soames Newton had fortified the door against the threatened German invasion, and Belle had unlocked and unbolted the hefty front door in a series of heavy clicks and rasping clunks then turned the CLOSED sign over to OPEN. Next she had carried the news-stand outside, fronted today with the headline MOUSEHOLE WIDOW REACHES 100th BIRTHDAY! *Crumbs*, Belle thought. *I'm not sure I want to live to be that old, not unless I've still got all my faculties anyway. And not unless the neighbours who disapprove of me don't change their attitude.*

Belle had lugged boxes of non-perishable goods outside. It was mainly ironware – nails, bolts, screws, curtain rings, and so on – as well as beeswax polish, scrubbing brushes, mop heads and laundry products, which she put under or beside the long fixed outer shelves. She had stood up buckets, brooms and mops. On the shelving she had put baskets of wooden toys, clothes pegs, candles, primus mantles and sewing items, plus a box of cheap white crockery. Before the war other boxes would have overflowed with fruit and vegetables but they were not so easy to come by now. Much of the precious produce Soames was able to supply came direct from The Orchards, owned by Belle's husband, Charlie, and it was kept inside to prevent it being stolen.

Belle had gained the qualification to serve behind the diamond grille of the little sub-post-office counter. She had stood in for Soames Newton before, as since his wife's sudden death last year, he sometimes treated himself to weekends away. The nagging, nasty Delia Newton had become weak from some mysterious illness, assumed to be a sort of self-induced hysteria, and she had plunged down the stairs snapping her neck in two. It had been a double tragedy for Soames. Delia's cousin, the mouse-like and much put-upon Lorna Barbary, had just returned from the village Summer Fair held at Petherton, and had been struck down when

Delia's body had hit an umbrella stand and received a mortal head injury. It was rightfully assumed that Soames did not miss his supercilious, strife-making wife, but he was lost without the hard-working presence of Lorna Barbary running his house and seeing to his meals. Young housewife Lowdy Kestle had been charring for him three mornings a week.

'Just as well Soames is taking a fortnight away this time,' Belle thought, unlocking the ornate Edwardian cash register and drop-ping the float into the compartments. Soames had been struggling on his own since Lowdy had given birth several days ago, although his tubby frame was well supplemented with stews and pies eagerly handed in to him from the widows and spinsters interested in stepping up to become the second wife of the well-off parish councillor and church warden. Lowdy's baby girl, although born big and healthy, was feeding poorly, and Teddy was rumoured to have declared Lowdy would not be returning to skivvy for the storekeeper. A happy healthy family was more important to him than the weekly ten shillings Lowdy earned.

In a blue and white striped pinafore over her wide-shouldered dress with nipped-in waist, Belle looked rather out of place behind the counter. Her shining jet-black hair, presently neatly pinned up in victory rolls, her iridescent brown eyes, and her lithe, perfectly honed, trim figure made her supremely gorgeous. Greg Barnicoat referred to her as 'the ravishing gypsy-like woman, a being suited to the wild'. She was luscious, with an easy warm smile and given to a slightly arrogant air, a striking creature that drew constant admiring or envious looks from men and women. She returned her husband's unveiled sensual adoration with equal zeal. Last year she had ruthlessly sided with her seventeen-year-old son Sam's decision not to marry pregnant Jenna Vercoe and it resulted in her losing some of her popularity. This annoyed Belle and she had railed at those people, considering them two-faced. Sam had sworn to faithfully support his child. Sam did not love the girl, she was part of a rough and ready family, and Sam was far too young to settle down anyway. Charlie and Denny Vercoe had come to blows, watched by an indignant Finn Templeton, who had also stormed at Sam. The false-hearted Templeton boy had made friends with Sam and later shunned him. Belle, previously infuriated by Finn's lustful infatuation with her, seeing it as a possible threat to her happy marriage, had reproached Finn over his hypocrisy. And as far as Belle was concerned, those who considered Sam a louse for not wholly standing by Jenna Vercoe were also hypocrites; none of them were likely to want a son of theirs, especially if he had Sam's prospects of inheriting a thriving business, to marry a girl from her background.

Taking a duster to the counter, Belle sighed regretfully. Sam's baby was due to be born very soon but she, the baby's grandmother, would be excluded, through her own fault, she conceded. She should have shown sympathy towards Jenna's plight. Jenna was just a girl who had made a mistake. The Vercoes stamped away from her now. On the times she had asked how Jenna's pregnancy was progressing she had received some very choice words. They had refused the baby's layette she had knitted and taken to the door of their scruffy property, after she had first picked her way through a lot of scrap metal and weeds, with their little mongrel Tufty yapping at her heels.

Jean Vercoe, herself big with child, and a lump of a woman anyway, had bawled, 'We want nothing from you! Not now, not ever, and not a single brass farthing from that rotten son of yours. You can all go to hell. Scoot!'

Belle had tried a humble smile. 'I'm trying to say sorry about the quarrel, Mrs Vercoe, to make amends. The baby is my flesh and blood too.'

'It's too bleddy late to be sorry. Your beastly son used my poor maid. He seduced her then threw her over like so much rubbish. Well, she's too good for him, not the other way round, as you as good as said about Jenna. Had to get married yourself, conveniently forgot that, didn't you? Where would you have been if Charlie Lawry hadn't married you, eh? You'd have given birth in a home and had the baby taken away. Didn't take that into consideration, did you, when you was running down my Jenna. Now bugger off and don't darken my doorstep again, you high 'n' mighty bitch. Show your bleddy face round here again and I'll set the dog on you proper!' Jean Vercoe had then slammed the door in Belle's face.

At least working in the shop at this time meant Belle would soon hear if Jenna went into labour. News swept through

Nanviscoe faster than a wind-blown fire. Belle would see her grandchild; she was passionately determined about that. Jenna was a pleasant girl. Belle felt guilty about not taking that into consideration before. Jenna was an expert seamstress and worked from home with Jean, so Jenna would not be an impoverished unmarried mother. Home, at By The Way, was where Jenna had stayed hidden away for the last few weeks. Rumour had it she was happy about the baby, looking forward to bringing it up alongside her expected brother or sister. Those who thought Belle had been too harsh with Jenna had thrown it in Belle's face that Jenna had chosen names for the baby, Gary-Mark or Anna Kay. Belle hoped if she came across Jenna out with the baby in a pram that Jenna would allow her to take a peek at the child, and perhaps even allow some access to it. Charlie was not the slightest bit interested in the baby. He had set aside a goodly sum of money in case Jenna Vercoe ever asked for maintenance from Sam and Charlie had made it public. Sam had bought stuff for the baby, if Jenna desired it, and Charlie had made that known too. No one could say the Lawrys were shirking their responsibility. But Charlie was a man and he did not understand the pull Belle felt to see their first grandchild.

Going to the door to shake out the duster, Belle looked up and down the village then across to the church to see if anyone was about. At a short distance St Nanth's stood solidly on slightly raised ground more or less in the middle of the sprawling village, all roads and lanes tracing away from it. A watchful rook was perched invader-like on the three-stage, seventy-five-feet tower. The majority of villagers considered the aged disinterested vicar 'wasn't much cop', but they drew comfort from the sight of the spiritual masterwork, where so many of their forefathers were buried, and they were proud of the memorial cross to local dead from two World Wars, Denny and Jean Vercoe's two eldest sons among them.

Belle was pleased to see a weary-looking Rebecca Rumford in her district nurse's uniform freewheeling on her bicycle, coming from the direction of the school. Belle rightly assumed Rebecca had come from Beech End, the grand name for a solitary humble cottage set back, at a fair distance on each side, between the school and the empty, languishing Petherton manor house. It was known that yesterday at Beech End first-time mum Florrie Westlake's waters had broken. Belle was interested in news about Florrie, but if she asked Rebecca carefully Belle might just glean a little information about Jenna.

Rebecca saw Belle waiting for her. It looked like Mr Newton was taking another of his breaks. It was assumed, by some of a mucky mind, that his breaks were to gain him some female company – in other words sex. Rebecca never entered into gossip or offered opinions – people's private lives were their own concern, and to Rebecca's mind nothing went on that hadn't been happening under the sun for centuries. Rebecca had returned to Nanviscoe, the village of her birth, as midwife and district nurse after five years as a midwife in the women's hospital at Redruth. She also served the outlying hamlets. Her parents were dead and she lodged with elderly Mrs Agnes Pentecost with whom she had a daughter-and-mother relationship.

Tired after attending Florrie Westlake, daughter-in-law of the landlord and landlady of the Olde Plough, through a long and difficult labour, which had been touch-and-go for a while in regard to the baby, Rebecca had finally left Florrie gratefully cradling her pinched-faced, seven-pound girl, impressively named Florence Rebecca Mary Rose. Proud father, local postman Derek Westlake, would be late on his rounds today and would take longer than usual, planning to knock at all the addresses in his postbag and announce his happy news. Rebecca had been fortified with a breakfast of porridge, tea and toast laid on for her by proud grandma, Margaret Westlake. Now Rebecca was longing for a few hours' sleep but she'd forego her bed a little longer and enquire if her recent order at the Stores had arrived.

Soames Newton, who was a second cousin to Jack Newton, was a wizard at getting hold of just about anything in these lean times – in Rebecca's case, two pairs of the thick black lisle stockings she wore all year round. The portly, heavy-breathing storekeeper was suspected of contact with the flourishing Black Market, no doubt enthusiastically abetted by the rough and ready, but thoroughly likeable Denny Vercoe. Rebecca was expecting to be called to deliver Denny's tenth child any time now and his illegitimate grandchild quite soon, too.

'Good morning, Rebecca.' Belle waved to her, knowing

Rebecca would stop for a moment at least. She was satisfied when Rebecca dismounted and rested her bicycle against the shop's whitewashed wall.

'Good morning, Belle.' Rebecca straightened her uniform's starched cuffs and hat with its upturned brim. 'Mr Newton is not laid up, I hope?' She meant this sincerely, caring about the villagers and never resenting the hard work. The women were in contrast, Belle like a sleek pedigree cat to Rebecca's homely tabby.

Belle explained Soames Newton's absence. 'He came to The Orchards the instant he closed the Stores yesterday. He'd been down for the last few weeks, I'd noticed, I'm sure you had too. He told Charlie and me that he was lonely – well, we'd all guessed that – but also he was feeling slighted that he wasn't invited to take a prominent part in Jack Newton's wedding or invited to his homecoming. Jack's father Randall always scorned Soames, hated being even distantly connected to someone in "trade". Soames said he's tried to get close to Jack, but while Jack was always glad to buy him a pint in the Olde Plough, he'd never sought anything more. Soames had made it plain, you know, that he did not agree with the vicar's harsh refusal to allow Lucinda Newton's body to be interred in the churchyard. So Soames has gone away for longer this time, not far away, just to Polzeath to enjoy the sea air. Charlie and I got the feeling he might be considering retiring.'

'A fresh start for Mr Newton might be just the thing for him, but we'd all miss him if he moved away. He's one of our village characters,' Rebecca mused. Movement across the village caught her eye. 'And there's another one. I've never thought of Mr Evans as an incomer. There he is out looking for the milk cart for his breakfast porridge.'

The women waved across to the Welsh pensioner. He waved back and lifted his cap to them. His little home, like most village dwellings surrounding the church, had no front garden and his door opened straight on to the cobbled pavement. He was wearing his habitual brown waistcoat and gaiters. On cue appeared the Meadows Farm cart with its clip-clopping big brown workhorse bringing the fresh milk.

Mr Evans, good-hearted and knowledgeable, stooped and pale

and burdened with a troublesome cough from the long years grafting down a Welsh coal pit, left his doorstep holding the large blue and white striped jug for his daily pint. He got a shock when young, burly farmhand Gerald Nance drove straight past him and headed the nag round to the Stores.

'Nurse, nurse!' Gerald yelled before closing in on the surprised women. 'I've just seen Denny Vercoe. Nearly ran into me and old Glory, he did, with that wreck of an old van of his, gave us a right bleddy fright, begging me language. Shouted at me to fetch you to his place right away, both his missus and his maid have gone in labour. He's gone back to the house. If I couldn't find you or heard you was tending another patient, Denny asked me to ask Mr Newton, well, it'll be Mrs Lawry now, to ring Mrs Resterick and ask her to come.'

'Jenna's baby is on the way? My grandchild!' Belle gasped, wringing her hands. 'I wish I could be involved. Rebecca, will you please tell Denny and Jean I'm sorry about my behaviour and that I'm worried about Jenna. If I can do anything, if Jenna needs anything . . .' She ended on rising plaintive notes.

'If I get the right moment, Belle,' Rebecca said understandingly. Bang went her much-needed sleep. If she found the mother and daughter's labours had not progressed far she might be able to slip home and take a bath and snatch a couple of hours to put her head down. 'I would be grateful if you phoned Mrs Resterick anyway. I could use another pair of hands, having two women in labour. I'll run in to Mrs Pentecost and tell her what's happening.'

Hector Evans plodded round the curve of the churchyard holding up his jug. 'What's the matter with you this morning, Gerald Nance?' Pique was in his melodic Welsh valley voice. 'Didn't you see me standing there? You gone blind or stupid? Now can I have my milk?'

Nine

All through the previous night Jenna and Jean Vercoe had taken turns to use the downstairs indoor lavatory. After the umpteenth time of pulling the flush, Jenna had seen Jean waiting outside, arms holding up her pendulous bump, hopping from foot to foot and wincing with the obvious urgency to pee yet again.

'Out of my way, maid,' Jean had cried, dragging Jenna aside. 'I'm about to burst.'

And burst Jean did, there and then, her waters gushing out of her and soaking her legs and nightdress, and Jenna's feet and slippers, as well as her own. Jean couldn't help giggling and this had started Jenna off. Scared as Jenna was about her own forthcoming confinement, childbearing was as much a part of this household as the cooking and cleaning, and the Vercoe home, with extensions to shelter the growing family, was scrupulously clean. It was cluttered and things lay about not put away, but By The Way was a family home, a cosy home where little in the way of soft furnishings or anything else matched, and that was the way the Vercoes liked it. It was their safe haven away from the big wicked world. Quarrels and squabbles abounded here as in any other home but disagreements were settled quickly, and resentment and lack of forgiveness was not the norm. Although many called the family scruffs and looked down on them, the general peace and comfort and loving support within the family was greatly envied. The Vercoes tended to be happy with their lot, supporting themselves through Denny's wheeling and dealing, shoe-mending, blade sharpening and labouring wherever work was to be found, along with Jean and Jenna's sewing. Jean's constant childbearing had ruined her figure but she gaily accepted it. Lumps and bumps and saggy breasts meant lots of babies who brought their love into the home, and she loved having little ones about her feet.

'I've been waiting for this to happen,' Jean had said calmly so as not alarm Jenna. Jean usually had problem-free labours. ''Tis the same pattern every time with me. Niggles in my back for a good forty-eight hours and peeing like a dripping tap. Then me waters break like a dam, always on the bleddy floor, never conveniently while I'm perched on the pan, and a few hours later the baby pops out like I'm shelling peas. About ruddy time on this one; if I get any more overdue I'll go into next year. Had a good dose of Epsom salts yesterday; done the trick.'

'I hope my baby comes out like shelling peas, Mum. This peeing all the time is making me tired. Like you said the other day, the baby must be pressing on my bladder. Stay there, I'll get the floor cloth.'

'Thanks, my handsome, then we'll get cleaned up. I'll send someone for Nurse Rumford when the time is right. Don't feel sleepy now, do you? Let's make some tea and toast and share a quiet moment before everyone's up and bustling about.'

Mother and daughter lolled on the overstuffed chairs in the front room, a room not kept for special occasions but lived in every day, to be enjoyed. Denny and Jean had no time for stiff formalities. Jenna crunched her toast and sipped her tea. She kept her soft dark eyes away from the settee. It was there that she had lost her virginity to Sam Lawry, he also a virgin. Then the bloody horrible swine had dumped her. Said he was too young to settle down yet. What he had meant was she wasn't good enough to settle down with, only good enough to practise on before going on to sow more wild oats. Sometimes she hated Sam for rejecting her so casually. Even if she was not carrying his child the fact remained that he had merely broken her in while Jenna believed he cared for her deeply. He had left her as used goods. Something from which a decent young man she might meet in the future would run a mile. She would be considered used goods for the rest of her life, second-hand, like the stuff her father bought and sold; an inferior prospect as a future bride. She couldn't bear the thought of meeting another man in the future who seemed gladly to offer her marriage, a little respectability, but who would leave her to wonder all the time if he resented his stepchild and thought her a whore. She would stay single and devote her life to her child. As for Sam Lawry, no matter if he changed his mind and begged for contact with the child, he would never, *ever* get a look in. Hell was where he could go and where he could damned well stay, he and his nasty, snobby parents. Jenna would never forgive Belle Lawry for looking at her like she was scum, shit beneath her shoes, the day Denny hurled Sam's rejection of her at Sam and the Lawrys at The Orchards.

Jenna was still astonished at the vicious way Belle Lawry had gone at Finn for being infatuated with her. Many an older woman would either have been amused or flattered. Had she protested so much, Jenna wondered, because she was attracted to Finn too? Besides that, Belle was what Denny called 'a right sexy piece'. Backalong, Jenna had watched Belle and noticed how she hung on to Charlie, touching him, smiling for ages into his eyes, holding his hand and rubbing her thumb into his palm. At the time Jenna had not had dealings with Sam but she had been shocked to recognise Belle Lawry's blatantly sexual signals. Belle Lawry was loose and fast, and a superior, spiteful bitch, and Jenna didn't want her anywhere near her baby.

Jean wetted her finger pads and used them to mop up the last of her toast crumbs. 'Everyone will have to get up early today. I'll make the pot of porridge in a mo. Maia and Sadie can feed the twins, then get them washed and dressed, and push them over to Mrs Pentecost's. Kind of her to offer to have them when this day came. Then the girls can take Meg to school with them. Adrian can run over to Mrs Resterick. She's offered to help out too, bless her.'

'Yes, Mum,' Jenna said. Jean had rehearsed all this two or three times before. She followed the direction of her mother's eyes, to the huge rustic mantelpiece, to the studio photographs of Jean's war-dead eldest sons, handsome and smart in their military uniforms. Two heavily built likenesses of Denny, called Gordon and Alan. On either side of the photos was a small pottery vase of primulas. Not a day went by, Jenna knew, when Jean did not stand silently and gaze sadly and proudly at her eldest boys. Jenna missed her funny, hard-necked brothers too. Her heart heaved at the thought that it should be one of them, decently married, who was giving her mother her first grandchild. Her nerves were edgy now with the reality of her mother being in labour and she was frightened they would get the better of her.

Jean spread her hand over her bump as the first significant pain ripped and dragged at her body. 'Let's get on then, my handsome. Now, I don't want you to get worried if you hear me yelling out later on. It helps to keep things going that's all. If you want to, you can go to Mrs Pentecost's as well.'

'No, Mum, I'll be all right here. I'll keep the hot water going.' Jenna did not feel as brave and unconcerned as her reply sounded. She needed to be constantly near her mother. She was scared at the very thought of her labour starting while not in close prox-imity to the house. She had no idea when she would pluck up the courage to show her face again in public. If she did not have good and loving parents she could have had her baby taken from her for adoption – she had heard the dreadful tales of some girls being dragged off to an asylum for 'moral degeneration'. She had learned that appalling fact from a malicious neighbour who lived further along By The Way lane, and she had not left her home since. She was used to the idea that she would soon have a baby. She wanted her baby and already felt the love and an expectant mother's concern for its health and safety, but she also wanted to scream out how much she hated Sam Lawry for putting her into this disgraced situation.

The sight of Jenna's swollen middle made Jean's eyes prick with tears of sorrow and raw emotion. *My poor girl*, she thought, *this shouldn't be happening to you now*. Jean had planned a big white wedding for her eldest daughter. Denny would have seen to it that Jenna would have had a do to rival Verity Newton's. Now here she was up the creek without a paddle, cast aside by that weak-willed, pathetic piece of Lawry shite – it helped a lot that Sam Lawry was despised locally for refusing to stand by Jenna. He would never prove himself a man. Here was Jenna, fearful of childbirth, as all first-time mothers were, wanting her baby, looking forward to it even, but it did not overshadow the shame that would be thrown her way for the rest of her life. Jenna was without her old spark and verve, but she had a mature determin-ation to still make something of her life. Jean was overwhelmed with a new love for her hardworking, uncomplaining daughter. Pride burst through Jean's heart. Jenna had as much dignity as the Queen.

Heaving herself up, Jean went to Jenna and hugged and kissed her. 'Oh, we're going to have such a lovely time bringing up our babies side by side. We'll walk them out together, little Frank and Jake toddling beside the double pram, as proud as punch, our heads held high. You're a wonderful, decent girl, Jenna Vercoe; don't you ever let anyone else say otherwise, you hear me?'

Jenna felt her mother's warm arms and her loving emotion. It was Sam Lawry who should bear all the shame. He was a coward, a nothing, a failure. Jenna loathed him all the more, and she would make sure her child would loathe him too.

'Let's get weaving then?' Jean said, helping Jenna to struggle to her feet.

Jenna felt something stir inside her, a trickling sensation that fell in waves from under her breasts to her pubic area. The sensation turned into a twinge, a powerful tightening that she knew instinctively would last for several seconds. For a moment she was thrilled about the sign of her baby coming into the world, then she was consumed with panic. 'Mum! I think something's happening. What do I do?'

Jenna sat up against the pillows on her bed in her own little downstairs room, next to the lavatory, cradling the tiny new baby on her chest. Jean. Little Jean Vercoe. Her new sister just one hour old, with a fluff of fair hair and dry flakes on her dull dark pink skin, a strange little thing really, but every bit a Vercoe. She stretched inside the white lacy knitted shawl worn by all Vercoe newborns, including Jenna, yawning then turning her tiny, tiny mouth into a moue, having Jean's round chin and Denny's strong nose.

'She's beautiful, Mum.' Jenna kissed the baby's delicate cheek to hide her fear after the sounds of her mother labouring away with grunts and yowls and pants loud enough to compete with a dozen old dogs. It was little comfort to her that her mother was already up and dressed, smiling and claiming that the instant the baby was out that the hard side of giving birth was completely forgotten. It was no comfort to Jenna that her own labour was progressing so slowly that Nurse Rumford had gone home to grab a few hours' sleep. 'Relax, walk about, do what ever you feel like, Jenna. Baby might not even come until tomorrow,' the weary nurse had said.

'What? But I want this baby out now!' Jenna had yelled.

'Babies don't oblige that way, I'm afraid, Jenna. Your baby will come when it's ready, never fear.'

Fear. That dreadful word had surged through Jenna's already frantic mind and she had ended up fighting to keep her breath. As Nurse Rumford put on her cardigan and prepared to leave, the only thing that helped Jenna was Dorrie Resterick's calm presence. She had held Jenna's hand, patted it and smoothed her forehead. 'It's natural to be scared, Jenna dear. I was when my Veronica was born, but I just kept telling myself that every pain was one less to go. My midwife advised me to concentrate on my breathing, to imagine I was resting in a meadow and time was passing in a dream. It helped a lot. There were times I felt like I was floating. My mother also told me to remember that although the pains were God's will for women, he also intended the glorious result, an achievement denied to men. If a man climbs the highest mountain or makes the greatest discovery of all time he can never crown a woman's triumph of producing new life.'

'Thank you, Mrs Resterick, that helps.' Jenna had rallied quite a bit.

'Call me Dorrie, or Mrs R., if you like. We're friends.'

Jenna found comfort in the little modest ginger-haired woman, still pretty in her fifties. People called her the mainstay of the village. She was that and more, wonderful and generous to be readily here at this time, a woman who had lost her only child as an infant. Mrs R. wrote poetry and she had read some to Jenna, happy verses, soothing rhymes. She was presently making a rabbit pie and a rabbit stew to feed the family for the next two days.

'In fact I'm ready to go again,' Jean chuckled. 'Your dad's tickled pink. Our little Jean. 'Twas a shock to see the little bit of a thing, never had a baby so small even though she was overdue, but she's a healthy five pounds. I think she'll always be known as Little Jean. Ah, she's starting to fuss, I'll take her and give her a feed.'

Jenna watched Little Jean suckling on her mother's large droopy breast. 'I hope I can feed as successfully as you, Mum. Does it hurt?'

'No, love. You might feel a bit sore at first. You'll sail through it. Any problems, well, I've always got plenty of milk.' Jean kissed her newest child. 'She's my tenth but I never get over the wonder of it all. To think that very soon I'll be a grandmother.' She came over teary. 'When did you have your last pain, sweetheart?'

Jenna had been watching the little travelling clock on her night table; she had saved up for it from her own wages. Now joining the clock were towels, maternity rags, nappies and a white baby vest and gown, and some of Nurse Rumford's things. All the baby linen, blankets and a shawl were Vercoe worn and Jenna liked that. She felt lucky to have a little room to herself. She had shared an upstairs bedroom with Maia but her parents had said she must have a place for herself and her baby and she had taken over the playroom. She had a single bed with a pretty homemade patchwork quilt, a single walnut wardrobe procured by Denny in his dealing, the chair her mother was sitting on, and a good second-hand baby's cot. The window ledge was wide and served as a dressing table top, with a three-sided mirror and typical feminine items.

Jenna sighed impatiently, crossly. 'Fifty minutes ago. Mum, is this ever going to end?'

Ten

While events were unfolding at By The Way, Verity was following an example of Stella and Oscar Grey's she had learned while helping with the good-natured organised chaos of the unpacking and settling-in at Olivia House. Verity had been impressed at the way the Greys had let all the various demands of their children's disabilities and their individual characters wash over them. Their wonderful children, Verity had taken to all of them. The Greys were unflappable, seeing only what was really important when problems cropped up. No hot water, a door that wouldn't close, ornaments broken in a removal crate, grime left by the tradesmen who had made the alterations the Greys had ordered on the house plans. This had got damp; that was missing; Stanley's case of clothes could not be located. The list was endless. Verity thought she would soon be tearing her hair out in frustration if all this were happening to her. She had arrived home from honeymoon to a perfectly run house – the only blight the malicious placing of a certain photograph.

The air in Olivia House had grown thick with suggestions to the problems and offers of help from the returning honeymooners and their welcome home party, except for Verity's astute Aunt Dorrie who had correctly worked out that in truth Philly Lindley and Noelle Lucas had everything in control. The list of wants and needs they had given to Stella and Oscar, after the round of introductions, had not fazed the Greys one little bit. Stella had popped on her pencil and notepad on a chain and had quietly added lots of jotting.

Oscar, who had picked up tiny Libby from the nest of cushions she was on, playing with her toy cat, had raised a hand and his commanding voice stopped the hubbub instantly. The children, Philly and Nanny Lucas looked at him expectantly, all at ease. It was obvious to the visitors that Oscar was a kind and good master of the house and had the total respect of those he loved and was responsible for. Verity and Dorrie exchanged rueful looks, conveying that they had been feeling sorry for Oscar over his crippled legs but they had had no right to do so. He was in control here, and lived a happy, fulfilled life. He was not 'less' because he had lost the use of his legs, but a man of great depth, intelligence and capabilities.

'One thing at a time,' Oscar began, and his household chipped in with a loud, 'and first things first!'

'And the first thing is drinks all round, and the scrummy welcome home party food Uncle Jack and Aunty Verity have brought with them.'

Verity was taking a leaf out of Stella and Oscar Grey's book, Chapter One: Take Things In Your Stride. It was what she was doing concerning the offending photograph, behaving as if the insult had never happened, and it was made easier after having had a whale of a time with her new nieces and nephews, finding them all delightful in their own ways. She thought happily about the baby inside her womb. Her child would be joining in the fun with its cousins at Olivia House.

Verity wasn't going to allow some stupid woman to undermine her by an insidious act, in effect declaring she wasn't the rightful mistress in her marital home. That woman, Verity was convinced, was Cathy Vercoe. It could not be the pleasant and obedient Tilly and nor was it Mrs Kelland, for Verity had considered the cook-housekeeper to be honest and proud of her position at Meadows House. She would not have perpetrated that spiteful act – and it *was* a spiteful act, not merely a stupid joke.

When Verity had returned from Olivia House she had gone to the piano. The photograph was still in the place where she had pushed it down. Picking it up, she had slipped it into a bureau drawer. Next day, after Jack had kissed her passionately before going over to Meadows Farm to consult his manager there, Verity had taken the photo up to the loft and hidden it under some old maps and stuff in a wooden box. She had then filled her hours with what she should be doing, enjoying herself as a new bride and running her new home exactly how she wanted it. While speaking to the staff kindly – extra kindly to Mrs Kelland to make up for giving her a hard stare – she had watched Cathy, keeping aware of everything Cathy did and where she was. Inevitably, a strained atmosphere grew between her and Cathy.

Verity joined the other women in the kitchen where they were taking morning coffee, Camp Coffee from a tall oblong bottle. 'I've got news for you, Tilly and Cathy. My Aunt Dorrie's just phoned. She's going over to By The Way. Both your Aunt Jean and cousin Jenna are in labour.'

'How wonderful!' Tilly shook with excitement, and then raising her shoulders she clenched her hands. 'Must pray all goes well.'

'New little cousins for you, Cathy,' Coral Kelland said. She made a point of making a fuss of Cathy nowadays, as the new Mrs Newton seemed to have turned against Cathy for some strange reason. 'It's very strange,' she had mentioned to Kelland. 'Miss Verity and us here got on like a house on fire from the very start. Now Mrs Newton's at odds with poor Cathy. Can't think why, unless it's something to do with her being pregnant. Mr Jack is like a dog with two tails. He can't wait for his child to be born. Hope nothing spoils it for the dear of him. It's wonderful to see him happy at last, 'specially now Miss Stella's back. Only needs some sort of word about Mr Tobias to be the icing on the cake. Even if that dear boy has passed over, at least they would know.'

Suddenly, Cathy threw her head down in her hands and ruptured into a wail of sobs. Startled, Verity jumped in her skin. 'Cathy, what on earth is the matter?'

Cathy did not answer but leaned towards Tilly, who was sitting next to her, and wept on her shoulder. After giving Verity a withering look, Mrs Kelland reached out and patted Cathy's hand.

Dark colour crept up Verity's neck and face. Embarrassment and guilt. She had been chilly towards Cathy from the return of her honeymoon, judging Cathy as culpable over that wretched photograph without the slightest shred of proof. Instead of being 'clever' with her attitude she should have tackled these women outright. 'Cathy, what's wrong?' she squeaked.

Cathy kept crying and shaking.

'Tilly?' Verity was not far away from tears herself. The beginning of her marriage had been tainted and she herself was almost as responsible as the person who had insulted her.

With a mix of unease and resentment, Tilly looked levelly at Verity. 'It's you, Mrs Newton. The way you've been treating her. Offhand and cold, like she's done something unforgivable. Cathy's

the senior maid here and she should be the one given first choice
to do something more responsible, like going over to Olivia
House, not me. Cathy don't know what she's done to offend you
but she's really, really upset over it. Perhaps we should both look
for new positions . . .' Tilly was trembling with nerves but she
kept her head high.

Verity crumpled, mentally and literally, and she flopped down
on a chair. 'I . . .' She held her hands out helplessly. 'I'm the one
who's done an unforgivable thing. Cathy, I'm so sorry, please
believe me, I really am. I'm sorry too, Tilly and Mrs Kelland. It
was that wretched photo . . .' Hot tears of shame sprang down
Verity's cheeks.

Cathy looked up, still weeping silently, sniffing, gulping and
dabbing at her wet pickled-red face with her hanky. Tilly pulled her
sister's head against her collarbone and gazed at Verity in wariness
and avid curiosity. Mrs Kelland, plainly shaken, uncomprehending,
spoke up. 'What photo, madam?'

Verity was dismayed with the elevated title. *Madam.* Her own
actions had fractured her relationship with the staff, Jack's loyal
staff, two of them who had been with him for many years. Why
had it not occurred to her that by giving Cathy the cold shoulder
it would disturb Tilly and Mrs Kelland too? Coming to mind
now, Kelland's responses to her of late had been frosty. *Stupid,
stupid woman!*

Spilling hot, miserable tears, Verity told the women in halting
tones about her discovery of the replacement of her predecessor's
image on the piano, standing with Jack as his wife. 'It was . . .
as if I was being told I h–had no right to be here, t–to be married
to Jack. I'm so sorry, so very sorry. I don't know what to think
now, w–what to do. I've ruined everything. Jack will be so cross
with me. Please don't leave, girls, this is your home,' she ended
on a wail, wishing she could call Aunt Dorrie to come and
comfort and advise her. Aunt Dorrie had mentioned she had
noticed the photo and asked Verity how she felt about it, and
Verity had laughed it off. 'I'm ignoring it, Aunt Dor.' If only she
had totally ignored the whole wretched bloody thing.

'It's not your fault, Mrs Verity.' Suddenly, Mrs Kelland was
there at her side, clamping a hand on her shoulder. 'It's that
demon from hell! That Lucinda herself, not resting in her

un-sacred grave. We didn't want to mention it to you and Mr Jack, spoil your homecoming, but we – 'specially poor Cathy – have been plagued by her. It's she who did the deed, and put it into your mind that Cathy was at fault. She's trying to break up the happy home.'

'Yes, that's it, Mrs Verity,' Cathy whimpered, mopping her face. 'I see it now. Don't you, Tilly? That's what this is all about, isn't it?'

'What's been happening?' Verity was wide-eyed, and heartily relieved the awful circumstances she had caused had been over-turned. She wanted more than anything to make a happy home for Jack, anything less would be a thumping failure.

'This calls for a fresh cuppa,' said Mrs Kelland, all motherly and defiant smiles. 'Then if I may say so, we all need to take a deep breath and put our heads together about how to get rid of her evil presence.'

Eleven

Dorrie felt as if every bone in her hand was being crushed as Jenna gripped it.

'Poor dear child,' Dorrie thought, then prayed, her lips moving silently. 'Please Lord, bring this labour to a safe end soon.' It was late afternoon on the day following little Jean Vercoe's birth, and Jenna was still in the first stage of labour, her cervix opening very, very slowly, as was not unusual in a first-time mother, and her womb had been contracting painfully since about midnight. Dorrie and Jean had been at either side of the bed for hours, taking turns to wipe the heavy beads of sweat off Jenna's face and neck and encouraging her to take sips of water, and to breathe as Rebecca was dictating. Jean only paused to allow her own hungry baby to latch on to her breast.

'It's been ages and ages, Mum,' Jenna blubbed, her small face screwed up like a gargoyle's in pain and distress. 'I can't stand it. I can't do this any more. It's agony. I never knew it would be this bad. Oh God, I'm going to die!'

'Don't you worry, you can do it, my handsome.' Jean had been encouraging and soothing Jenna but it was no longer working and, steeped in anxiety, she glanced at Rebecca.

'Jenna, Jenna dear,' Rebecca raised her voice in the small bedroom, now hot and stuffy and claustrophobic despite the window being open wide. She was down at the end of the bed, looking between Jenna's bare legs. 'Listen to me. You're doing very well, I promise you. Stop tensing up. You're making it more painful and harder for yourself. Listen, I've got good news. You're fully dilated, that means you're all opened up. You can now push. When you feel the need to push, you push, dear, but don't push hard until I tell you to.' Rebecca knew how many a mother-to-be began to panic at the transition into the second stage of labour. Jenna was so near exhaustion and sometimes when that happened the woman's body would compensate by easing off the contractions and that could be risky for both mother and baby.

'You hear that, maid?' Jean said loudly, putting on jolly tones to disguise her obvious anxiety. 'You're really close to the end. Won't be much longer now and you'll be holding your little baby in your arms. Think of that, my handsome.'

'I don't want it!' Jenna shrieked. 'And I hate that rotten effing bastard Sam Lawry for doing this to me. I'll kill him as soon as I can get out of this bed. I'll make him go through pain like this. I'll make him suffer. I'll cut his dick off! He won't do this to another girl.'

'Jenna!' Jean was aghast, but like Dorrie and Rebecca she couldn't suppress a laugh.

Jenna's rage and the women's laughter made her laugh too and she relaxed then yelled, 'I want to push!'

'Good girl, Jenna,' Rebecca said firmly. 'Take a deep breath and give a small push and let me see how things are.'

Partially propped up against the pillows, her bottom flat on a draw sheet covering a rubber sheet, Jenna did as she was told. She pushed but it also felt as if her body was working without her. A couple of these and it will all be over, she told herself. The pain was different now, a little more bearable because it was productive.

Smiling across at Jean, Dorrie mopped Jenna's brow. Dorrie felt her heart punching against her ribs and her stomach constricting with Jenna's effort. Dorrie was excited as a child about to be shown all the wonders of the world. Last year, when she had been plunged into the situation of delivering Eloise Templeton, she had been given no time but had just had to get on with it. She had been fearful, having to take on the responsibility and safety of a depressed, disinterested mother and an unborn baby, but instinct had kicked in. She had urged Fiona Templeton in what to do and quickly the tiny girl had slithered out of Fiona's body and into Dorrie's hands. Next to the birth of her own baby, her precious late Veronica, it had been the most amazing experience of Dorrie's life. Now she was sharing the privilege of being present at the first moments of another new life.

Minutes ticked by. Twenty minutes. Half an hour. Jenna pushed and groaned. Rebecca used her metal listening aid on Jenna's bulbous stomach to hear the baby's heartbeat. Perspiration sparkled on Dorrie's face and Jean's as well as on Jenna's. An hour. Rebecca was sweating now. She didn't like her mothers pushing any longer than this.

Jenna was almost totally worn out. Her cries of: 'I can't stand this!' were becoming shrill but rather weak.

Rebecca took her blood pressure and listened to the baby's heartbeat. 'Jean,' she whispered. 'Ask your husband to fetch the doctor. They've both had enough. I'm afraid it will have to be a Caesarean.'

'No!' Jenna bawled and burst into tears. 'I don't want my baby cut out of me!'

Twelve

Dorrie was in shock. There was no other way she could describe it. For days now she had been overcome with strange shivers, which had been hard to shake off and she had often shed a few tears. Without knowing it she would tense her hands and frown so hard it would bring on an intense headache. One moment she would feel cold and clammy, the next she would be horribly feverish and feel prickly all over. At night sleep relentlessly fled from her. She knew if she didn't keep a grip she would succumb to the shadowy claws of depression, as she'd endured first when Veronica and then Piers had died. She took comfort in not going far from home, letting people visit her for a change rather than rushing off to those who needed her. Greg only popped out for a short while at a time to fetch anything that was necessary, and dear faithful Corky never left her side.

Jenna and her baby had almost died during the Caesarean section. Jenna first, under the anaesthetic, her body fully opened up by skilled Dr Alistair Tregonning; she had just stopped breathing. Jean's primeval savage scream as she collapsed to the floor, her guttural sobbing and bitter lamenting had frozen Dorrie's already anxious heart. She had been standing by in a sterile mask and apron, holding a boiled clean white towel, nervously waiting to be handed the baby, having received instructions from Rebecca about how to clear its airway and get it breathing, if needed. Rebecca was passing the surgical instruments and keeping one eye on the anaesthesia. Dorrie hadn't prayed so much and so fervently since she had begged for her Veronica to be spared.

'Keep your places,' Alistair Tregonning, a former Naval medic, full-bearded, with an unshakable air, had ordered Rebecca and Dorrie, military fashion, above Jean's racket. Denny had charged into the room. 'Out, Mr Vercoe!'

The command had overridden Denny's strong bond to protect his family. Out of the room Denny had gone, his big whiskered face as white as a ghost's.

Swiftly, Tregonning had pulled the baby boy out into the world, the baby floppy and unresponsive, a dark pink and blue, bruised-looking entity. He passed the baby to Rebecca rather than to Dorrie and she had gone to work on it. He had done the same to Jenna.

Dorrie remembered Tregonning barking orders at her. The rest of what happened was a blur, a flurry of movements, muffled sounds of an indeterminate time. Whatever the doctor and Rebecca did, and perhaps Dorrie herself, had worked. Thank God it had worked. Jenna and her baby boy were alive, still not very well, but getting better every day.

Dorrie wiped away a single tear from each eye and leaned over in her chair to pat squat-legged Corky. Through the open window, she listened to the fluting of the blackbirds and the robins, rivals for the sweetest, harmonious tunes. Birdsong always gave Dorrie a big lift. She knew she would get better. She had before in circumstances far worse, when she had lost Veronica and Piers; nothing would be as bad as that. She would be all right again, in just a little while.

'Come along, Aunt Dor,' Verity said brightly, appearing from the kitchen. 'I've made mock lemonade. Let's go out into the garden and drink it.'

'Thank you, dear.' It was good being waited on for a change.

Thanks to Stella and Oscar's organisational skills, all at Olivia House were settled in their owns rooms with their own familiar and much loved things and everything was running smoothly. When Oscar had the time he was a prolific reader, and he and Stella had chosen the marble-effect floored library to use as their ground-floor bedroom. He enjoyed unpacking his multitudinous books, of diverse subjects and authors, and lining them up on the lower shelves. Stella followed his lead on what he wanted up on the higher shelves. His second favourite pastime was to order books from catalogues and visit auction rooms and bid for job lots of books and trawl through junk shops for gems and oddities. Denny Vercoe had obliged him by bringing over boxes of books he had procured in his deals and the pair had spent a convivial afternoon drinking beer, while Oscar sifted through the titles. Half a dozen books had been added to Oscar's collection and

Denny had left satisfyingly patting his pocket. The room, on the cool side of the house, had French windows that opened on to a flat paved terrace and a tree-lined path leading to the front and the rear, perfect for Oscar to wheel himself outside and reach his family wherever they might be.

In the next room, formerly a sitting room, was Stanley, with his elaborate train set and dead insect specimens. Next, but also facing the back of the house, was the schoolroom, where the Greys and Miss Lucas taught the lessons. There was a large adult desk and blackboard on an easel but instead of desks four low tables were pushed together with the children's chairs dotted round them. A cushioned highchair was for Libby. As well as the usual three Rs the children were taught a lot through play. There were lots of toys and a dressing-up corner. One wall was crowded with bookcases. A huge globe of the world aided geography. A piano and percussion instruments were set in another corner. Pictures painted in the former Olivia House were pinned on a corkboard and already new ones were proudly displayed. While the twins, Timmy and Daisy, were unduly reserved and balked at acting in the little plays Miss Lucas wrote, they were good at art, drawing, painting and making clay and Plasticine models. Timmy's balsa wood aircraft and ship models joined their best efforts on the windowsills. Cuddly Pattie tried hard at needlework and cross-stitch and her attempts were also up on the craft board, as were tiny adorable Libby's scribbles when someone helped her hold the pencil and crayons. No one got sent to a corner or humiliated by being made to wear a dunce's cap. This was a happy room. When the children made friends, the friends invariably asked if they could leave their school and join the Greys for their lessons. Teddy and Lowdy Kestle's three older children, invited over to Olivia House for tea some days ago, had already given out that plea.

While the children were having a music lesson with Miss Lucas, Stella mentioned to Oscar, 'Jack is coming over for lunch today.' They were in the office adjoining their bedroom, going through accounts.

'Verity too?'

'No, she's spending the day with her aunt. Dorrie Resterick is still deeply disturbed by witnessing the near deaths of Denny

Vercoe's daughter and her baby. I hope things don't get maudlin. It won't be good for Verity now she's expecting.'

'From what I've seen of the worthy Mrs Resterick it won't come to that. Any more news about Jenny?'

'Jenna,' Stella corrected her husband affectionately sitting next to him at the huge basic desk. Wherever possible the couple stayed close. 'I asked the paper boy – you remember the little chap, Tony Kestle, who came to tea with his siblings? His mum has not long had a new baby too, and also the son and daughter-in-law of the pub landlord – quite a baby boom in the village. Anyway I asked him about Jenna and her baby, and as far as young Tony knows they're doing well. Proper chatterer, he is, small for a twelve-year-old but as bright as a button, a people-watcher. He's told me lots about the locals, including stuff about Jack's late wife. If Tony had it right, it seems Lucinda Newton was very peculiar indeed, more than just a tragic figure. Apparently, she haunts the house and has scared the wits out of the staff. I can well believe my former home is haunted. My father's rotten-ness must have seeped into the very fabric of the place.'

Stella dropped her chin on to Oscar's shoulder. The taint of her unhappy childhood still had the power to wound her.

Jack Newton laughed heartily as his gaggle of nephews and nieces pitched forward to meet him with the dogs, Cosmo, Basil and Rags tearing ahead. Stanley, sporting his Captain Blackbird rigout, his magnificent beard made from long ragged snips of old blackout material, bowled along at a fair rate despite his leg irons, and was second to reach Jack after Timmy. The children were on the front lawn enjoying their mid-morning playtime. The new nursemaid, curly-haired Gladys Geach, a granddaughter of an acquaintance of Dorrie's, was on duty with them, holding Libby in her young, lean arms. Philly was there, in her apron and pannier pockets, smoking a cigarette, with a mug of something muddy-dark in her hand.

'Uncle Jack! Uncle Jack!' The eager chorus went on and on and Jack found his waist grabbed and his legs clung on to by the children, and boss-eyed Pattie reached out to be lifted up. Such was the love and security Stella and Oscar provided for their family that not even the wary twins thought their new mummy's brother, their uncle, could be a threat. Jack had loved them all in the first instant as if they were his own flesh and blood. Overjoyed at the prospect of becoming a parent himself with his precious Verity, he felt his life was complete.

Still laughing, Jack hugged all the kids and gave Gladys a bag of dolly mixtures to be dished out. The children gathered round Gladys with their hands out and mouths open like hungry baby birds.

'Good morning, Philly, how are you?' Jack asked, lighting up a cigarette for himself and giving Philly one for later on. 'How do you like your new home and the area?'

'I'm right as ninepence, Mr Jack,' Philly answered, puffing away nasally and noisily. 'I love the house and the area's fine with me. I'm happy to be wherever Stella and the babies are, and Stella couldn't be happier now she's reunited with you. You'll hear no mithering from me.'

'Hide and seek, Uncle Jack,' Stanley chirped up, chewing on the soft sweets. 'Pl . . . ease, I'll be hiding with my pirate's treasure. We'll all hide 'cept for Libs. Count to fifty and come and find us. Eh? Eh?'

'Off you go then,' Jack happily obliged the persistent appealing boy. He turned his back and started counting out loud, joyfully imagining the day when his own child, although quite a bit younger, would join in with the games of this happy tribe.

Cathy climbed the steep stairs that led up to the attics at Meadows House. She made her way to a dark corner then slipped in behind a dusty rug she had hung up over a length of rope, like washing on a line. Mr Jack was never known to venture up here, and so far his new wife had, apparently, shown no interest in what was stored in the upper region of the house. Cathy hoped Verity Barnicoat would never do so. She did not think of the other woman as Mrs Newton, and now addressed her only as Mrs Verity, the woman who had pushed her way into the house and taken over the man Cathy had always desired more than anything, and always would.

Going to a mahogany chest of drawers, badly scratched and kicked in by the late Randall Newton while in one of his beastly rages, Cathy opened the middle drawer, the only one that would open now. With light fingers she lifted out a long white muslin and lace dress and held it against her body, gloatingly. She had made it herself from old curtains and had worn it to flit through the grounds, successfully frightening Kelland into believing he had seen Mrs Lucinda's ghost. Her own tales of haunting, and creating an increasingly dark creepy atmosphere had been laughingly easy to do.

Cathy had not minded having her first mistress in the house, the lunatic child-wife. There had been nothing remotely sensual about Lucinda. Jack would never have wanted that pitiful creature in his bed. Cathy did not want Jack as her husband or even lover. She knew as Jack's mistress her position here would probably be short-lived, and even if the virtually impossible happened and Jack fell in love with her and offered her marriage, she could never effectively mix with Jack's class, those snooty women who would inevitably look down on her and make her feel worthless. She didn't want to live in a position that would give her abject misery, and she certainly didn't want to have children – the very thought of childbearing terrified her. Cathy had a need simply to serve Jack and adore him from afar. For him to feel satisfied that she, the Kellands and Tilly, were caring for him in his home. He deserved that, for he was a kind, thoughtful and generous man; the very reasons why he had married nutty Lucinda, to protect and shield her against the world she could never have coped with. Cathy had been truly horrified when Lucinda had hung herself; an idiot mistress had suited Cathy, even though Lucinda's behaviour had been unsettling and she'd needed a lot of watching. What Jack did when not at home had not concerned Cathy. He could bed any number of women. One day, Cathy had hoped, when the Kellands retired she would move up to be his housekeeper, Tilly would marry the Templeton boy – they were made for each other – and Cathy would finally have Jack all to herself.

Jack had always tired of his amours – until Verity Barnicoat had turned up in his life. Cathy had not been too worried about the engagement; she had thought wrongly that Jack was scared of commitment to a vital, normal woman and Cathy had been appalled when the wedding had actually gone ahead. It had not occurred to her to try to cause trouble and prevent it. She wouldn't have done anything that would inevitably hurt Jack. But once the couple had left for their honeymoon, Cathy had hated and resented the thought of them returning to establish their life together and probably raise a family. She had slipped up – the fool – not starting her campaign sooner. With Mrs Kelland's daft talk about Lucinda haunting the garden and grounds, it had set Cathy to thinking that she could do something to make it seem that the first wife, although dead and gone, was maliciously haunting the second wife. The second wife needed pushing, one way or another, out of the house and out of Jack's life. It would be unlikely he would try for happiness with a third wife.

As far as Cathy could tell, Mrs Verity had not mentioned to Jack the tales of the 'haunting' that she had been told about on the day Cathy had put on a tearful breakdown. It seemed Mrs Verity was playing it down and not wanting Jack to be upset; admirable in a young besotted wife, Cathy thought scathingly. But Mrs Verity wasn't the type to let things go if there was further malevolent activity by 'Lucinda'. She could be tough. She had showed her anger over the photograph incident. Cathy could not be sure whether her mistress believed the photograph had been placed on the piano by ghostly or human hand, but Cathy had noticed Mrs Verity glancing over her shoulder, looking searchingly into rooms, and pausing to listen as if wondering if she was hearing a natural sound or not.

Cathy had let time pass, and then the near tragedy of her cousin and her baby had happened, and Mrs Verity was out again today supporting her usually undaunted aunt, giving Mrs Verity something to be concerned about outside the house. But now it was time to make Lucinda rise up from her unconsecrated grave again. Cathy must get on with it. The woman she wanted rid of was pregnant and Jack was being even more attentive to her.

Damn it! Cathy snarled, unaware of how crazed it made her look, a look glutted with bitter slyness. Verity Barnicoat must be driven to rail against Lucinda, to demand her body be dug up and buried elsewhere. It should not be too difficult for Cathy to achieve. The other woman would want to protect her expected brat, a brat that must not be born here. Jack was keenly protective of his late wife. He would almost certainly shun the idea that she was haunting the place and object to her remains being unceremoniously disturbed.

Inside the small space Cathy danced about with the dress. She had used the dress, and the photograph she had secreted away after she had watched Jack remove it from the piano and followed him and witnessed him put it in the top of a wardrobe in his dressing room.

She went to her secret drawer. Now it was time to use something else.

Thirteen

'You're a coward, Sam Lawry! Don't think it's an honourable thing you're doing, leaving to help out an elderly relative until you're old enough for National Service. You're running away from your responsibilities, that poor maid who nearly died giving life to your baby, the poor mite that was forced to struggle for its first breath. You should be in jail. She was under age when you did the dirty deed. Bugger off for good. Your sort's not wanted in Nanviscoe!'

Belle shuddered every time she recalled the animosity that saw her son off as he had boarded the bus taking him away from her for the next two and a half years, first to Belle's uncle's farm in Lanivet, then at age eighteen on to Dartmouth to train as a naval rating. The terrible truth was that Belle would have been saying the same sort of thing to another mother's son for shunning his pregnant girlfriend, for his total disinterest in his baby. Sam, Belle's only child, once so friendly and full of life, now turned sullen and insular, had left two days after Gary-Mark's birth, and Sam had taken Belle's heart with him, for she was certain he would never return to live at home again. Smashed were Charlie's dreams of his son inheriting The Orchards, which generations of Lawrys had planted and produced from for over a century.

It was horrible and humiliating working in the Stores now but Belle could not – and would not – leave Soames Newton in the lurch. It hurt her terribly to think that she deserved some of the self-righteous flak aimed at her.

'As bad as your wretched son, you are too, Belle Lawry. Instead of encouraging your boy to shun that poor maid and his child you should have made him step up to the mark.'

So she was stuck here until Soames' expected return at the weekend, suffering the coolness and the snipes over her ban from seeing her grandson, even from some locals she had once considered her friends.

She wiped down the counter after serving Dorrie with her

weekly ration of sugar and margarine. Thank goodness this kind and sympathetic woman was not the sort to turn against her friends so lightly. Dorrie had just come from By The Way and had answered Belle's tentative questions about how Jenna and Gary-Mark were progressing.

'I'm so relieved they are coming along nicely. I was so worried that day and have been ever since. I asked Rebecca how they were but I didn't expect any more than: "As well as can be expected." She has the confidentiality of her patients to respect. I told her how grateful I was to her and Dr Tregonning. She said she was sorry for me; that was nice of her, a bit of a comfort, like you are yourself, Dorrie. I hear Denny and Jean are angrier than ever with us Lawrys since Sam left the village. I don't blame them. Charlie and I took a high-handed, uncharitable stance right at the beginning, as you yourself had witnessed, when they raised their fists. Now Charlie and I feel ashamed of Sam and of ourselves. My son hasn't got the integrity that Finn Templeton showed last year when he fully supported his baby sister and depressed mother. Sam might well find that one day he bitterly regrets what he's done.'

Belle's eyes filled with tears. 'I wrote to Jenna and sent another letter to Denny and Jean explaining all this. I can only hope one day they will relent and allow Charlie and me to see our grandson.'

Margaret Westlake entered the shop and overheard Belle's plaintive wish. Belle hoped when the gossiping landlady, whose husband was loosely related to the Vercoes, inevitably passed on this snippet she had overheard, some people would think better of Belle and Charlie. Perhaps even the Vercoes themselves would find some forgiveness for the Lawrys.

'The Vercoes may well come round in time, Belle,' Dorrie said, smiling at her with understanding. 'They are a good-hearted family.'

'They are that,' Margaret Westlake interjected as she strode through the open doorway, the heavy door stoppered to allow in some cool air on the stuffy grey day. She was a woman of everyday looks and ways. Right now her nose was tilted upwards. 'Despite some folk only seeing them as rough and ready and unworthy.'

Sniffing back her tears, Belle asked politely, 'What can I get you, Mrs Westlake? Mrs Resterick has already been served.'

'I'll take two ounces of Gold Flake for my husband's pipe please,' the landlady replied, keeping her sloping shoulders raised.

Belle was grateful to have Dorrie remain with her until Margaret Westlake had left the Stores. Again, she was near to tears. 'I don't think I can stand much more of this, Dorrie. People are treating Charlie and me like we're pariahs. When really we're two concerned parents who acted badly, granted unkindly, over the fix their son had got himself into. If Sam had married Jenna the girl would have been whispered about too, and the Vercoes accused of loose morals. Some people have called them a rabble. Others have done far worse things than us Lawrys but they haven't been treated as harshly as us. Johnny Westlake's brother deserted at the front in the Great War. Mrs Pentecost had a relation sent to prison for rape.'

'People will come round, Belle. Indeed some may even think the Vercoes are being too hard on you. Human nature has a way of suddenly changing sides. If that happens you will be able to point out that you only want reconciliation with the family,' Dorrie counselled. She had seen so many ups and downs with people throughout her life and saw almost all situations in shades of grey. 'Try to keep a bright outlook, dear.'

'Thanks, Dorrie.' Belle smiled wanly, a little light sifting into her gorgeous brown eyes. 'It's so hard. Jean sends her boy Adrian in here most days with a bluntly written shopping list. He doesn't say a word except for "thank you" when he's ready to go. I've seen his reflection poking his tongue out at my back. In the old days the little ones used to pop in often, for a chat with me as much as anything, or to show me things they had made. Dear little souls, they are, a bit cheeky but I like spirit in kids. They don't come inside any more but they make faces at me through the windows or open door and mutter unpleasant things.' Then Belle wailed, 'If Soames doesn't return soon, I don't know what I'll do!'

At that moment there was a loud honking of a motor vehicle approaching, a honking jovial in sound. Dorrie swung round to see what the commotion was and Belle stared outside from across from the counter.

'Is it?' Belle was hopeful. 'Yes, it is, it's Soames in a huge brand new car! Oh, thank God.'

Dorrie saw her friend visibly sag with relief.

Belle scrambled to the other side of the counter and ran out of the Stores. Dorrie followed her. Soames waved to them from inside a shiny black Jaguar, a beauty in motoring. He sprang out and slipped round to the passenger seat and helped a woman in real silk stockings and dangerously high heels to alight.

'Welcome back,' Belle squealed like an excited child.

'What a delightful welcoming party, ladies,' Soames beamed from his chubby face.

Dorrie and Belle noted he was slightly less portly; in time they were to learn that he had stopped breathing in the heaving snuffly way that had so annoyed his self-important, sour-tongued late wife. He was wearing a new slickly tailored pinstriped suit and his receding greying hair was left naturally rather than oiled down. He looked younger than his fifty-odd years. Dorrie and Belle traded quick glances, both assuming rightly that the cause of the storekeeper's new youthful style had everything to do with the well-rounded, chic woman at his side. Dorrie admired her new dress, flared from the waist, and her perky hat. The woman whipped off her sunglasses and smiled toothily. She was wearing full make-up in the manner of a film starlet. She even had the obligatory pout, but this did not disguise her age, which had to be at least fifteen years older than Soames. She would have been beautiful still if she had not lost her freshness. Was she a gold-digger sort? both Dorrie and Belle wondered, worried about Soames. Had she been getting him to spend his retirement nest egg?

'Allow me to introduce to you my wife,' Soames drawled, something he had never done before.

Oh dear! Dorrie thought, and she knew Belle was sharing the same anxious sentiment.

'Mrs Ford-Newton,' Soames continued, quite the proudest man in the world. 'Cassandra, this is Mrs Belle Lawry and Mrs Dorrie Resterick. I've told you a lot about these two special ladies.'

Cassandra Ford-Newton swept out a gracious hand to be shaken. 'Pleased to meet you both, dear ladies, I'm sure.'

The 'dear ladies' were stunned to hear Mrs Ford-Newton was an American.

'Shall we go inside for coffee? We've brought a fine rich blend with us,' Soames suggested happily, taking charge. 'Ah, here comes the taxi. It's carrying my new store manager and his wife, and Cassandra's maid, so you can take off your apron, Belle. They'll be happy to start straight away. Then I'll be taking my dear lady wife to Petherton. She's just bought it.' He punched the air for emphasis. 'And as soon as we're refreshed I'll be taking her there to look it over.'

In unison, Dorrie and Belle's mouths sagged open.

Fourteen

Verity eased herself into the bath, lay back, closed her eyes and breathed in the evocative scents of rose and orange blossom. The warm water was soft and silky with the oil from a seductive gilt-top bottle; a wonderful surprise gift that Jack had sprung on her the night before.

Verity drifted back to her honeymoon, under the millions of diamond-sharp stars of the untamed veldt. She felt so relaxed and sensual she soon wanted Jack like she never had before. But Jack had risen early to play golf at St Merryn and Verity was left in a kind of desperation of wishing he were in the house and she could call him to come to her. To dampen her need and passion she turned her thoughts to her other love, the baby forming inside her. As she did a hundred times a day, she gently spread her hands over the perfect swell of her tummy. She had had some of her skirts altered to wear with three new maternity smocks. She loved to dress in these mother-to-be clothes, loved the way her tummy grew every few days.

'William Gregory, if it's a boy,' Verity had said to Jack last evening. Thinking up names for the baby was their usual pleasure over dinner. 'I'd like to honour my darling uncle.'

'Or Thomas Gregory, or how about Jeremy as first name?' Jack had laughed in return.

'Or Hugo. Stephen.'

'Miles or Giles.'

'Robin's nice, don't you think? It sounds gentle and kind. Claude – no. Clive. Archie, I quite like Archie.'

'Me too. How about Ignatius?'

Verity had got the giggles. 'Ignatius? Where did that come from? Come along, Iggy, time for your beddie-byes.'

Roaring with joy, Jack had paused over the summer pudding. 'If it's a girl, I rather like Alice.'

Verity was thoughtful. 'Yes, I really like Alice. But we couldn't have Alice Dorinda. Aunt Dorrie has insisted we don't tag our baby with her name. I'm glad about that; there will only ever be one dear Dorrie. Yes, Alice, let's agree on Alice, shall we, darling?'

If their baby turned out to be a girl her first name was definitely decided. Getting carefully out of the bath she dried herself, put on her silk robe and fluffy slippers, and with possible girls' second names going through her mind she opened the adjoining door to the master bedroom. Cathy had hung the clothes she had chosen to wear on the wardrobe door and over a nearby chair. Verity padded across the room.

She froze.

She swung round.

Hideous thing!

It was on the precisely made bed, resting against the pillows in their sea-blue quilted satin shams. Vile thing! A china doll with long fair ringlets, dressed in red velvet, trimmed with black braiding and white fur. It was one of Lucinda's dolls, definitely. Verity recognised it from its broken left pinkie finger and a stain on the hem of its lace petticoat. Verity felt that wretched hammer blow in her insides again but she was not scared or fazed. The obviousness of the situation would be laughable if it wasn't so malicious, so pathetic. When Cathy had been in the room earlier she had smelled of the comfortable warm smell of being in the kitchen. That smell lurked here heavily, along with sweat, Cathy's sweat, for she had a bit of a problem in that respect. Verity had not wanted Jack to know about the haunting fiasco, but by God, he would know now, and he would know who exactly was responsible for this new insult. Cathy was mad herself if she thought she would get the better of Verity with her cheap tricks.

Verity slipped quickly to Cathy's room in the back quarters. It was empty. Perfect. She went to a small top drawer. In this usual place for keeping small items she found what she was seeking, a handkerchief. On the way back to her own room she crumpled the square of cotton, monogrammed with a capital C, probably part of a gift set, then she dropped the handkerchief on the floor at her side of her bed. Next, almost smiling grimly but as angry as hell, she let out a bloodcurdling scream – she had been very good at them while playing fantasy games with her brothers and cousins in her childhood. She left her room still screaming, as if in terror and the greatest anguish. Then she floated down on to the landing and arranged her limbs carefully in a twisted fashion as if she had fallen. It would be worth the temporary discomfort, and the pain of banging her head across the wall to produce a bruise and sizeable lump. The thump against the wall really hurt and it was easy to fake tears and begin some convincing sobbing.

'My baby, oh no, my baby!' she screamed and screamed again and again.

Fifteen

Gary-Mark Vercoe was two months old. Today, the third Sunday of August, he and his aunt, Little Jean, were to be baptised. They would wear the parachute-silk gowns Jean had made for the twins, Frank and Jake. From a scrawny five pounds and two ounces at birth, Gary-Mark had put on little weight and was still bony and wrinkly, his skin jaundiced. Denny and Jean had put it about that he was thriving. He wasn't. He was restless and colicky and cried for hours, and Jenna could barely look at him. He meant nothing to her. He looked too much like his rotten absent father, fair-haired and dark-eyed.

Fate had intervened for Jenna in an ignoble way but Jenna was glad of it. Sacked Cathy was now sharing her room and Cathy was caring for Gary-Mark in every respect except his feeding. Jenna allowed her baby to suckle off her, and he demanded milk often. But she fed him with utter revulsion, never holding him snugly, and the tiny boy fed poorly and fretted constantly throughout the day and night. Cathy cared for Gary-Mark wearing a pained, regretful expression, as if she was bitterly sorry for her perverse actions against her new mistress, the last one having nearly brought on a miscarriage in Verity Newton. In truth, Cathy showed Gary-Mark no affection or interest unless someone else was present and the only thing she was sorry about was that Verity Newton's brat had not leaked out of her body.

If she could get away with it, Cathy let Gary-Mark cry in a soiled nappy before she reluctantly changed him, and she did not bother to handle him gently or cleanse him thoroughly. So he had sore nappy rash and cried over that. Jenna did not love Gary-Mark because of his traumatic birth and his father's rejection of them both. Cathy loathed the baby because she was stuck here having to sleep in the bedroom with the 'squell-ass', unemployable without a reference and with nowhere else to go. After facing Jack Newton's wrath she had been sacked without pay. Her malicious deed had been rumbled through her own fault, although she couldn't remember taking that particular handkerchief out of her drawer that morning.

After stealing up the main staircase to the master bedroom and placing the doll on the bed, Cathy had silently returned to the drawing room and sang softly as she had resumed the dusting. It wasn't long before the Newton woman's screams had reverberated round the house and Cathy had halted and smiled. She saw herself in the mirror over the mantelpiece. A satisfied cat-creature had looked back at her, a cat that had caught a sparrow and ended its reign twittering in the highest tree. Cathy ensured she raced upstairs just ahead of Mrs Kelland and Tilly so she could feign concern.

'Not you! Not her! Get her away from me!' The hysterical woman lying twisted on the carpet had grabbed at a frightened Tilly. Mrs Newton had stabbed a finger towards the bedroom then at Cathy. 'Doll . . . on the bed . . . you did it. My baby!'

'But Mrs Newton, I didn't do anything!' Cathy had squealed, playing the card of shocked innocence. Her face was flushed with excitement but she painted hurt on it. 'I–I'll ring for the doctor.'

Spinning on her heel she had belted downstairs, working up a few loud sobs.

'Dr Tregonning was taking surgery but he's coming straight over,' she had announced at the bedroom door. The near hysterical Newton woman was lying on the old-fashioned day bed. Mrs Kelland was kneeling beside her holding her hand and rubbing her wrist. 'What doll was Mrs Newton talking about?' Cathy had not looked in the direction of the bed so as not to readily incriminate herself.

'There girl, there,' Mrs Kelland jerked her head towards the source of the fright.

The red-dressed doll was in the exact same place where Cathy had carefully placed it. Tilly was standing near there with something in her hand, her small face drained of all colour. 'Cathy, this is yours,' Tilly had whispered, appalled.

'What is it?' This piece of evidence against her had truly surprised Cathy and she had been unable to deny the incriminating handkerchief was hers.

'So it was you all the time,' Mrs Kelland had gasped, clearly horrified and in a state of miscomprehension. 'You wicked, evil wretch, Cathy Vercoe. You'd better pack your things and clear your heels before the master gets back. Whatever has Mrs Verity done to you? I can hardly believe it. There'll be hell to pay for this.'

From the manner in which Jack Newton had battered on her uncle's door and demanded to see Cathy it seemed he had brought all the vengeance of hell with him. Cathy had hid in Jenna's room and she had peeped out of the small window and saw her former master's handsome face contorted into an ugly rage.

'Let me speak to you outside, sir,' Denny had spoken contritely – and loudly, as Cathy knew he had wanted her to hear. 'Do you really want to see that shameful young bitch, sir? We've taken her in for a time but only because she's blood, and to forbear with dear Tilly, whose heart is as pure as the driven snow. She's not worth wasting your breath on, Mr Newton. She didn't even tell us the truth when she turned up here with her tail 'tween her legs. Sidney Kelland came after her with a few bits she'd left behind and told us everything and why you'd been sent for from your golf. Me and Mrs Vercoe are bleddy ashamed of her, ashamed, and after us taking her and Tilly in when they was orphaned. We asked why she done it and all we could get out of her was she didn't know. I don't think you'll get any more out of her, sir, just a load of tears like we did. We don't think she knows she did it cos she's mazed in the head. We've given her a month then she's got to move on. Begging your pardon telling you what to do, sir, but as word's got to us that Miss Verity and the baby are going to be all right, why bother to see her miserable face again? She's too scared to show herself out and about. Why not forget about her, sir, and just look after yourself and Miss Verity?'

Jack had stayed rigid and menacing, his hands clenched and white-knuckled and Cathy was sure he'd like to spread out those fists and tighten them again round her neck.

'You don't deserve to have *that* under your roof, Denny, any more than my dear wife had to suffer her in our home. I'll let it rest for your family's sake, but take caution. She's a viper. I want to tear her limb from limb; if I ever see her again I might very well do just that.'

As he had stalked off in his boiling wrath and indignation, Cathy had scowled. *The bastard.* Why had she ever wanted him to herself, even if only to serve him? She must have been as mad as batty Lucinda. Jack Newton was a weak, pathetic little boy still living in the past and whining about it. Cathy had overheard him and his irritating superior sister, who thought she was a saint for taking in a few underprivileged brats, lamenting over their childhood facts. Randall Newton may have beaten Stella Grey, terrorized her even. But she had not suffered the beastly sexual abuse that Cathy had at the will of her evil father. Stella Grey would never know that shame. Stella Grey had never had to offer her body like a seasoned whore as Cathy had to her own father to save her younger sister from suffering the same vile crime. Cathy had wailed to her outraged uncle and aunt that she didn't know why she had done those spiteful, dangerous things to Verity Newton and in a way Cathy had told the truth. Now she knew why she had wanted only to adore Jack Newton from afar. She did not want intimacy with him or any other man. It hurt and it was dirty. Jack Newton in his former aching loneliness had not been a sensuous, desirable man to her. He had never bedded a woman under his own roof and the only wife he'd taken had been a disturbed eternal child to whom he had sought only to be a kind father figure. Although Cathy had resisted thinking about it, the normal husband and wife's loving relations between Jack and Verity Newton had been unnerving to her. Cathy had resented it, hated it. Verity Newton had needed to be punished and got rid of. If Cathy explained this to her Aunty Jean she might receive some understanding, a little sympathy perhaps, but Cathy's secret was too shameful. She couldn't bear a soul to know about it and look at her in a different way, maybe wondering, imagining what had happened to her, especially sweet, innocent Tilly. Tilly was the only one she loved. It was paramount to her that Tilly was kept untainted. Thank God that because of his humiliation over his infatuation with Belle Lawry, Finn Templeton treated Tilly as the innocent sweetheart she deserved to be. If he ever did otherwise, if he left Tilly in the same straits Sam Lawry had left Jenna in, Cathy would kill him.

She had only a few days left now before she had to move out and leave her family behind for good, all her family except Tilly. Tilly had come to her the following day and they had cried together. Precious Tilly would forgive Cathy anything. 'But why did you do it, Cathy?'

'I can't explain it really. I suppose I just fell for him and was jealous of his new wife and wanted to drive her away. Please, Tilly, I don't want to talk about it. All I care about is you. Are they being funny with you? Will they treat you right? That's my worry.'

'Mr and Mrs Newton called me in and they both said all will be the same as always, but that if I felt it was difficult they would give me a glowing reference and send me my wages until I got a new position. Mrs Kelland begged me to stay on. I said I'd see how things go, but I do feel awkward, Cathy. I'm going to miss you so much. Where will you go?'

The answer to that, Cathy still didn't know, but she had re-assured Tilly she would keep in touch and once she was settled somewhere Tilly must come and see her. She had a little savings but it would take a lot more money to make a good new start elsewhere. She couldn't wait to leave here now, except for Tilly, and the village people were even more against her than they were the Lawrys.

'I can't face the christening, Mum,' Jenna whined miserably. 'Do you think people will come out for a look? I couldn't bear being stared at and whispered about.'

'You've got nothing to worry about, maid. We'll be in chapel, just us and a few others. The Kestle and Westlake babies are being christened in the church, remember? Just about the whole village will be there.'

'But someone's bound to come and see what Gary-Mark looks like. They'll think me a piece of dirt. If we were church and not chapel, the vicar wouldn't want to christen my baby.'

'Dirt? You're nothing of the kind so you can stop that talk right now, Jenna Vercoe,' Jean replied crossly, but she was worried over the girl's skinny frame and deathly white face, the lack of her usual attitude that all problems can be solved. They were in the kitchen, and once again Jenna had left her baby alone with Cathy. 'Jesus would never turn an innocent baby away, and if that bleddy vicar's got something to say he can keep it to his snobby self. He's no better than us, no one is. Christ says we're all sinners. It's just that some, like you, Jenna, are found out. God knows what that old hypocrite – and everyone else come to that – has got up to in private. No one's perfect. It's not your fault Sam Lawry ran out on you.

'Show the world you're proud of your little one. He needs you.

His father's parents won't be in the chapel, we've told them not to come near the place, and Cathy can't go, not after the terrible things she's done. I used to be so proud of that girl and never thought she could do something so vicious. Gary-Mark needs his mother more than anything, the dear of him. You got to pull yourself together for Gary-Mark's sake, or what sort of life is the poor little soul going to have? You should stop relying on Cathy. I don't trust her. Think about it, Jenna, for goodness sake. How can you trust her with your dear little baby? She did those wicked things against Miss Verity, who never did her any harm. The sooner she goes the better. Gary-Mark's my first grandchild and I'm worried sick about him. Now will you please wash your face, get out your chapel clothes and cheer up. Try, will you? This whole thing is bringing this family down and we don't deserve it. Go and get Gary-Mark and bring him here to me. I'll keep an eye on him until his next feed.'

Feeling guilty about her mother's anxieties rather than for the neglect of her son, Jenna said feebly, 'Sorry Mum,' and set off for her room, from where Gary-Mark could be heard beginning to bawl. Jenna knew he was sore and in pain. She would force herself to wash and change him and slather on the soothing cream Nurse Rumford had recommended for his nappy rash, and she would give him a cuddle. She would try to.

'And Jenna . . .'

'Yes, Mum?' Jenna turned wearily round.

'Can't you just call him Gary? Gary-Mark stands out like a sore thumb. Surely you don't want that for him. He's going to stand out differently as it is . . .'

'Because he's illegitimate?'

Jean nodded, numbed and distressed. It was something that had not struck her before, that her grandson's illegitimacy would be a disadvantage to him all his life. She had thought life could go on happily with little Gary mixing in with the family as if he was one of her own. But reality had just leapt up at her and scored a direct hit. Gary would have to endure a certain amount of name-calling and rejection over his unfortunate beginnings and it might knock his confidence or make him feel resentful and lead to other problems. It wasn't fair on the dear little mite. It was his father Sam Lawry who was the true bastard. If Jean could get her hands on him . . .

'All right.' Jenna merely shrugged. 'Gary will do. Mark can be his second name from now on.'

The door banged shut as the last of the family trooped off for the small stolid Methodist chapel a good deal further along By The Way lane. Cathy sat still on Jenna's bed staring but not actually seeing the rolled-up mattress she slept on at night. Her head and shoulders were bent over, suddenly heavy with the weight of miscomprehension. Her mind felt as if it was dead. She certainly didn't feel anything, no emotion anyway. Was she mad in the head? Why had she ruined her perfect live-in job at Meadows House? She would have had a good position there all her working life and the generous Newtons would have provided something, she had no doubt, for her old age.

She curled herself up in a ball on Jenna's bed and felt the lump of self-pitying anger, but she herself had been cruelly used and abused. Her evil father was responsible for her plummet into hateful behaviour. He had damaged her so much she was afraid to make a real and loving relationship. 'It's not fair!' she wept into her hands. 'Not bloody fair.'

Cathy's actions had left her damned inside her old home and outside of it, doomed for the time being to look after her cousin's scrawny fretful baby.

'Poor baby,' Cathy said in a huff, turning over on her back and staring up at the low white ceiling. 'They think badly of me here but Gary's mother doesn't care tuppence for him. Gary will be another one who'll turn out bad. Stupid Jenna. Should have got rid of it while no one knew. Or put him up for adoption. It's selfish to keep a kid you don't want, who could have had a good life elsewhere.'

Cathy did not really care about baby Gary. Her last words about him kept circling in her mind. She sat up straight and slipped on her shoes. 'A good life elsewhere . . . I might be able to help him out with that and do myself some good at the same time.'

Sixteen

'Do you think she'll like it?' Soames Newton asked his new wife. 'Your daughter-in-law?'

'Oh, Nancy will revel in it – for a while. She's never satisfied for long,' Cassandra replied as if gall was stuck in her throat. She and Soames were taking a tour of the cleaned through and functional but otherwise undisturbed Petherton manor house. 'It was the worst day's work my poor dead boy ever did marrying that uppity cinch. She hid her origins from him, made out she was an English lady. She was English born, but she used the details of the real lady she worked for as secretary. She pulled the wool over Eugene's eyes. Eugene had nothing to show for the marriage; he never had a proper home life or got children out of it. All she ever thought about was going up in the world, but Nancy was a terrible Senator's wife, and my boy Eugene Howard the third! Sadly, I promised Eugene on his deathbed that I'd see she was all right. Eugene wasn't very good with money, so it's been up to me to fund Nancy's latest wont, which I've done for Eugene. Eugene did care so about Nancy, he was a sweet, caring boy.

'Now she fancies becoming an English lady of the manor, somewhere rural and quiet. Huh, back to her roots as a village girl. When she came across the owner of this place,' Cassandra used a throwaway gesture, 'this antiquated, lifeless old place, Mrs Esther Mitchelmore, in Switzerland, she leapt in with both her silly feet and agreed to Mrs Mitchelmore's terms – not changing a stick of furniture in it or removing a single painting. All counting on my money, I'll have you know.' Cassandra was full of sighs. 'But it would have made my Eugene happy, so as usual I've pandered to her wishes and bought this place for her.'

'I can hardly wait to meet this Nancy,' Soames said in an ironic tone. He was so besotted with his wife he already thoroughly disliked Nancy Howard. The woman was a sponger. They were upstairs in the unimpressive picture gallery overlooking the unrefined hall. The house's foundations were pre-Georgian, a little of it crumbling in a lazy manner, but the interior affected a Jacobean gloom despite its early-Victorian furnishings. A house at odds with itself, Soames thought, one would expect to find it parading suits of plain armour and Puritan plate. All through his life he had thought Petherton forbidding. He had never enjoyed the stiff dinner parties he had attended here in his capacity as parish councillor and churchwarden. There was a smell of stifling antiquity. The lack of windows in this spot afforded little light but dust motes, seemingly as big as snowflakes, could be seen clearly drifting about in invisible sources of draughts, and Soames kept twitching his nose, one podgy hand continually roving towards the breast pocket of his sports jacket while he expected to break out into a round of heavy sneezing. 'I'd hate to live here with a lot of stuffy-looking, gaunt-faced people staring down at me every day. The whole place is pretty grim. It smells of dead things. Don't know why Esther Mitchelmore is so intent on keeping the Mitchelmore family in focus. She wasn't born a Mitchelmore. Her husband was the last of 'em, they're all dead and gone and forgotten now. Betterfit this old house was pulled down and four nice modern bungalows built here instead. Would have done it myself and lived in one if I'd had the funds.' Soames came over sheepish and starry-eyed. 'But of course, meeting you, my dear, would have cancelled that out.'

Cassandra's wink at him was risqué.

Soames pushed his hands into his trouser pockets and shuffled about in his shiny new shoes. 'Belle and Charlie will be here soon. They must be a bit baffled why we've asked them to come here of all places. I feel bad about lying to everyone that we intended to live here.'

'Well, I wasn't a hundred per cent sure I would close the sale for Nancy until I'd seen the place. I had to describe it to her over the telephone in every last detail. She didn't quite trust Esther Mitchelmore's glowing account of how much she was respected in the village. Nancy doesn't trust anyone. I'm not surprised after the string of unsuitable lovers she's had after Eugene died. Lounge lizards every one, relieving Nancy of her last bean, the silly bitch. If I hadn't made that promise to Eugene I'd have told her to fend for herself long ago. But this is the last time. I've made that plain to her. I'm settling a sum on her that will see her out if she's thrifty and I'm going to break all ties with her. You and I, Soames, darling, will be off round the world and we won't ever be coming back here. Although I must say, I've found it a lot of fun squeezing into your little place for a while.'

'We'd better go down and wait for Belle and Charlie. At least the place feels a little alive with Mrs Teague glad to come out of retirement and cook and housekeep here again. I'll ring for tea. It will be fun to play a country squire for a few minutes.'

Sticking out his thick arm, Soames took his wife down to the south-facing drawing room, one of the few rooms Esther Mitchelmore had used during her lone habitation, except for her three servants, which had included Tilly Vercoe. This room did not therefore seem as forsaken as the rest of the house. Its thread-bare pink and cream carpet was in keeping with the shabby elegance. A spaniel or two, or Labradors perhaps, Soames considered, making the room smell of that comfortable doggy smell. Would Nancy Howard care to have a dog? Judging by the one snap Cassandra had shown Soames of the woe of her life, Nancy would go for a small breed, if she tolerated dogs at all. Of the haughty expression he had seen she was unlikely to tolerate much. So why should she desire a place like this, depressingly old money, draughty, comfortless? To pretend to herself that she was someone of high breeding, with a history of people who had mattered? The Mitchelmores had only mattered locally; no great hero or politician had issued from their dreary ranks. Soames wasn't one to think beyond the outward impression of people, but now he felt in Nancy Howard there was a person of low self-worth from a struggled background. He almost felt sorry for her. Nancy Howard's description was as a snobby madam, but Soames doubted if she was anything like her mother-in-law, a force to be reckoned with. The one person who would really be able to see through the new lady of the manor was Dorrie Resterick. Soames would have enjoyed having a private chat to Dorrie about Nancy, but that would never happen. His wife would want to go with him. She was the motivation in their marriage, the boss. He didn't mind that, after the soul-breaking lonely months of his widower-hood it was so good to have some company, at the very least. And to relax and have the decisions made, to have money lavished on him and to drink fine wines, to soon be off seeing the sights of the world – to be doing things he had never even dreamed of. And to cap it all he was enjoying the best sex of his life.

The Lawrys arrived and Mrs Teague, short, apple-cheeked, quick-eyed, wearing her old uniform, her greying hair flattened under a puritan-style cap, gaily showed them in and went off to make the tea tray.

Again, Cassandra was struck at how beautiful, how stunningly gorgeous Belle Lawry was. She was a Vivien Leigh, and her husband was a Tyrone Power with a touch of Laurence Olivier's belligerent Heathcliff thrown in, although Charlie was tow-haired, and not a restless soul, at the moment. They were a passionate couple, intensely passionate about each other; it seeped out of them. They were ideally suited. Their curiosity at being asked here today was etched in their watchful eyes. Cassandra was sad to note their aura of cheerlessness. Apparently, both were missing their heel of a son. Cassandra had liked Belle from the first moment, as she had the charming darling little Dorrie Resterick when she and Soames had pulled up at the Stores. After a couple of subsequent meetings, Belle had confided to Cassandra how sorrowful and hurt she was to be denied a part in the life of her first grandchild.

'I can understand that in every way, my dear. I feel bereft that my one and only child was never given any children by his ineffectual wife.' Cassandra had been a little shocked at the bitterness that had crept into her heartfelt declaration. She had never particularly wanted to be a grandmother; carrying on a family line had never seemed crushingly important to her. But she loathed Nancy for taking prominence in Eugene's life.

'I'll come straight to the point.' Soames smiled at the Lawrys, pleased with himself in a benefactor kind of way. 'It's not Cassandra and I who are going to live here in Petherton, but her daughter-in-law, Nancy Howard, the widow of Cassandra's son. Cassandra and I are leaving Nanviscoe to tour the world and we'll finally settle down in the States. So I'm selling the Stores and surrounding property and I'm giving you lovely couple first refusal.'

Sitting side-by-side, and sipping from Mitchelmore second-best china, Belle and Charlie gaped at one another. Always on the same level, going through both their heads was the question: 'Do we want to own a store?' This was totally out of the blue.

Charlie said, 'Have you offered it to your three sons, Soames?'

'I rang them and they're all of one mind. They said for me to sell up and enjoy the money. I'll make no bones about it, I like you two, always have, and Belle has done me proud every time she's stepped in at the Stores for me. I'm offering you my business and old home at eighty per cent of the market value. We'll be leaving in a fortnight, plenty of time for you both to think about it and seal the deal, if that's what you decide.'

'Well, thanks for thinking of us, Soames. I've never thought about taking on another business. The Orchards has always been enough for me. But what do you think, darling?' Charlie draped his arm round Belle's waist and pulled her in against him. 'Shall we think about it?'

Charlie was met with tears, quiet tears that were to wrench at his heart. 'I'm happy with just The Orchards, but there would be no point in thinking about the Stores even if we wanted to take it on.' Belle dabbed at the corners of her glimmering eyes with shaky fingers. 'The people of Nanviscoe hate us over our former attitude to Jenna Vercoe, for our Sam leaving her in the lurch. You don't know what it's been like, Soames, serving in the shop while you were away this time, and having to put up with open hostility. It got worse when Jenna and the baby nearly died. Now people are talking about how ill Jenna looked at the christening and how the baby looked sickly. I just know they think it's our and Sam's fault. Thanks, Soames, but I'd rather not show myself in this damned village!'

Belle was showered with sympathy, understanding and apologies from the other three and more close physical contact from Charlie. 'I didn't realise how much all that was affecting you, darling,' Charlie, in horror, sincerely voiced his regrets.

Belle did not want any of it. She had as good as lost Sam and could no longer feel any pride in him. She wanted to see Sam's son, to at the very least see Gary. She *needed* to see him, because according to the letter she had received yesterday from the underhanded, viperous Cathy Vercoe, Jenna was wilfully neglecting Gary. Jenna apparently, had no feelings for him and did not care how much he cried and went hungry.

Cathy Vercoe could not be trusted any more than a hot-handed thief, but she had given Belle something to hope for, to cling to.

Part of her well-written letter had stated: *I think that you as his grandmother should be allowed to see Gary. If I'm allowed to I'll take Gary for a walk in his pram along By The Way tomorrow afternoon and wait by the old bridge.*

In normal times, Belle would have been taking a turn as a volunteer in Faith's Fare, next to the Stores. The large hut, built on the site of a long forgotten tithe barn, had been thought up during the war by stalwart Esther Mitchelmore, to offer refreshments and a thrift niche, to raise funds for the war effort, and now for the village. Belle could not even face going into Faith's Fare now. Whoever she was on the rota with, Dorrie or Mrs Pentecost usually, the customers invariably snubbed her and asked the other women to serve their tea or coffee. Small-minded wretches!

Never mind considering whether she and Charlie wanted to take on another business in Nanviscoe. If things didn't get better soon she would be talking to Charlie about selling The Orchards and moving away. When respect for you turned to loathing it was absolutely horrible. She now understood how Finn Templeton had felt about her hostility with him for being infatuated with her. She had hurt and crushed him and he still loathed her for it. Now she had to pin her hopes on an obnoxious, greedy, calculating young woman, someone who deserved her banishment from the ranks of the well liked. Belle knew Cathy Vercoe was only trying to help her because she was after money.

Seventeen

Jack was building a scarecrow.

'I didn't know this was one of your talents,' Verity said, impressed that he was enjoying this simple pleasure. They were with Dorrie and Greg in Sunny Corner's huge back garden where Jack was making a replacement scarecrow to stand in the long straight rows of the vegetable patch.

His tongue laid on his bottom lip in concentration, Jack was too absorbed in his task to answer. An elderly farm labourer had taught him to do this as a boy. One of Jack's few pleasures back then had been to slip away to Meadows Farmstead, on the other side of the woods to his home.

'Us chaps are multi-talented,' Greg said, lolling in a wicker sun chair. Corky was curled up snoozing on his lap. His slightly lame back leg meant Corky had to be lifted up.

Verity and Dorrie were sitting either side of Greg. The circular garden table was covered with a white, daisy embroidered cloth. A low basket tray had tall glasses empty of iced mint tea and plates with the crumbs of scones. The wind was a little brisk and the women were wearing shawls over their cardigans and Greg a linen jacket. Jack had his shirt sleeves rolled up showing the crisp dark hairs on his arms. A lock of his dark hair fell often across his eyes but he didn't notice it.

Jack was working at a bench brought out from the shed on which Dorrie had put a bundle of old clothes.

While smoothing over her expanding middle, Verity asked, as if she was watching something as serious as Shakespeare's best, 'Which clothes will you choose, darling?' She traced a light fingertip over her bump. 'See what Daddy is doing, darling?'

'Watch and learn,' Jack said, without looking away from his work. He had a long sturdy garden cane and a shorter cane to hand, and had already stuffed a pillowcase with straw for the scarecrow's head. Pushing the long cane into the head he used string to bind it on. Choosing an old, buttoned-up shirt of Greg's he cut a chunk off each arm. 'You don't need a big scarecrow for a garden,' he told Verity in the manner of a schoolmaster. He threaded the shorter cane through the arms of the shirt then bound it to the longer cane and the head. He tied off the arms then, laying the fledgling scarecrow down on the bench, he stuffed the upper body with straw. He pulled on a pair of women's dark trousers that Dorrie had bought long ago at a jumble sale, pushing the longer cane down through a hole he'd cut out of the crotch. Then with the greatest of pleasure he stuffed the trousers from the waist down and bottoms up then tied off the trouser hems and waist, first pushing in the shirt. From his trouser pocket he produced one of his own ties, of maroon and grey silk that he had never liked, and used it as the scarecrow's belt. Jack had brought paints with him. While he cheerfully painted on smiley features, Verity, Dorrie and Greg got up and crowded round him.

'Don't make it look like Dorrie,' Greg instructed. 'It wouldn't scare away a ladybird let alone a crow.'

'It doesn't look anything like Aunt Dor,' Verity laughingly protested.

'I'd rather have a pleasant face. Scarecrows should have character not menace,' Dorrie said.

'She wants something to read her poems out loud to,' Greg said, nudging Verity. 'And she'll name it. The last one was called Albert. She wants them to feel at home.'

'Oh, Aunt Dor.' Verity squeezed Dorrie affectionately.

'Albert, that's a good name for our baby if it's a boy. What do you think, Jack?'

'It's a prince's name, and the King's real first name, very fitting. Bertie – maybe,' Jack said, pondering over which old hat the scarecrow would have. This more than anything would define the scarecrow's character. He was at the happiest of his life, and it was why he had drawn a smile and not his usual straight red line on the scarecrow's face. He knew Dorrie had noticed, giving a satisfied nod. So this scarecrow should have a careless hat, the floppy felt scarlet one, after Jack had fashioned its straw hair.

The telephone rang.

'I'll get it.' Dorrie hurried inside through the sitting room's open French windows. 'It might be Soames. He's promised to let us know when he and Cassandra plan to depart. Apparently they aren't going to stay and wait for Cassandra's daughter-in-law to arrive.' Rather unkind, Dorrie had thought, but then she had decided that of course she didn't know the reason behind it. It had been easy to gather there was no love lost between Cassandra and Nancy Howard.

'Hello Dorrie,' came Stella's voice after the operator connected them. 'I understand Jack and Verity are there with you. Can you tell them to come here immediately? Someone has arrived and Jack will want to meet him as soon as possible.'

'And Stella refused to say any more than that?' Jack said, as he reached for his car keys.

Verity had wanted to stroll to Sunny Corner but Jack insisted she was driven everywhere, so afraid was he she would miscarry. Verity's counter-ploy had successfully got rid of the insidious Cathy Vercoe and Meadows House had taken on a new calm, but Verity's convincing fibs that she had had a little back pain had worked against her by making Jack overprotective. But it was worth it. She would never let go of her happy life with Jack.

'Jack, Stella stressed that there's nothing to worry about,' Dorrie said, swapping curious looks with Greg.

'We'll let you know if it's anything interesting,' Verity said, expressing avid inquisitiveness herself.

In Belle's hands was the second letter she had received from Cathy Vercoe and the contents detailed everything she had asked Cathy to put down in black and white.

Evidence.

Evidence that Gary was being neglected, even ill-treated. It was exactly what Belle wanted.

She had been utterly disappointed to meet Cathy in the arranged spot, the old wooden hump-backed bridge past the Vercoes' home, past their distant neighbour's little cottage. Belle had crept warily past the bitter and reclusive Pauline Rawlings' shabby premises. Her daughter Mary had been brutally murdered, with her lover, after a failed blackmail attempt against a person or persons unknown a few years ago. Belle had served Pauline Rawlings in the Stores and received a hard stare and curt thanks, and all the while Belle had felt the other woman judging her as if she was vermin and had no right to be handling food. Belle had been glad to see no sign of the woman who had hated her rather tragic daughter and had not even gone to her funeral. *Why am I thought of so much more badly than this woman is?* Belle had thought miserably. Her shoulders dragged her down as she'd trudged along, her mind under siege with unwelcome images of Finn Templeton. He was being hailed as God's own saint again for supporting his girlfriend Tilly over her sister's notorious disgrace. She could imagine the handsome youth's new disdain with her if he knew she was on her way to meet the offensive Cathy.

As long as little Gary was being well cared for and grew up hale and healthy it was all that mattered, Belle had told herself. Sam had exiled himself and she didn't know when she would see him again. Life seemed so unfair.

The small wooden bridge, a popular meeting place for lovers, was concealed by willow and hawthorn. Emerald green algae crept over most of the weather-blackened wooden slats that rose a few feet above a stone bedded stream that was deep in some places. Belle had looked eagerly for signs of Jean Vercoe's pushchair or her double pram. Perhaps Cathy would have baby Jean with her too.

Belle's heart had tumbled down in disappointment at seeing Cathy waiting for her in the lane alone.

'I'm sorry,' Cathy had said sweetly. 'But Gary had settled down for a sleep and Aunty Jean said I shouldn't disturb him.'

Belle marvelled that she had not noticed something cunning and not quite natural about this girl before – but then nor had Dorrie and she could usually put the spotlight on the truth about a person in two ticks. And Belle had not really seen much of Cathy before. 'Does Mrs Vercoe trust you with our grandson?' Belle had asked bluntly.

She had seen a darkness flick behind Cathy's eyes. 'Oh, she does, honest,' the girl had rallied, 'much more so than she does Jenna. She couldn't care if poor Gary wore the same nappy for a week and she hates having to feed him, poor little soul.'

'Let's get straight to the point. Are you saying Jenna is a bad mother?'

'Not exactly,' Cathy had been wary too then. 'She went through a bad time giving birth. But Gary is suffering. He won't sleep for long, he's probably fussing already and he won't get seen to unless Aunty Jean picks him up. He deserves better.'

Belle eyed the girl for a moment then said carefully, 'Are you saying Gary could have a better life with me and my husband? Is that what this is all about, Cathy?'

'I suppose I am really,' Cathy had replied as if a momentous thought had just occurred to her. 'You could give him everything. He's your flesh and blood too. It isn't right that he's being denied all contact with you. How's he going to feel when he's aware he's got his other grandparents on the other side of the village? People who are well off and want to help give him what he deserves. I could help you . . .' There was an unmistakable shifty gleam in Cathy's expression. 'If you get my meaning. I'm sure you only want what's best for Gary.'

'I do, more than anything,' Belle had cried out with all her emotion. Then she grew serious. 'And you want money from me for this? What sum were you thinking of?'

'I want enough to enjoy life far away from here. I won't be able to get much of a job without a reference. What's your grandchild worth to you? Shouldn't be too hard for you to get custody of him, that's what you want, isn't it? Jenna has played straight into your hands with her neglect. I'm sure the authorities would prefer the baby's brought up with you and Mr Lawry with your much better circumstances.'

'I'll need evidence, written evidence preferably. Here's the deal, you write down for me in detail how Gary is being neglected in exchange for a hundred pounds, and not a penny more, Cathy Vercoe. You're desperate for money and that's a very generous deal.'

'I want the money as soon as you've got the letter,' Cathy had demanded. 'Then I'll be off and no one round here will ever hear from me again.'

'I'll need to go into town to get that much money. I'm not prepared to give it to you until I'm satisfied with the wording of the letter. Put down all the facts and make it plain what's been going on and sign it clearly. Send the letter through the post. The authorities will take more notice of it that way. I'll meet you here again at the same time the day after tomorrow.'

The letter said everything Belle hoped she would need and she was now on her way along the lane. However, she was early and she did not walk as far as the old humpback bridge. Instead she went to By The Way and straight to the front door.

In a little while it was opened by Denny, curious about who had come to his front door and not to the side kitchen door as everyone did, and Belle quailed for a moment in her shoes. Denny could bellow like the fiercest storm and it was highly disturbing. 'Please hear me out, Mr Vercoe,' Belle cried, as Denny opened the cavern under his monumental moustache to yell at her. 'I'm here on the greatest importance. It concerns Gary's immediate safety and your niece Cathy.'

It was enough to pull Denny up to listen to her. 'What do you mean, woman?'

'Read these.' Belle proffered Cathy's two letters. 'It will show you just how sick-minded and calculating Cathy is. I could have used the contents of these letters against Jenna but I would never mean her any harm. I only care about her and Gary. I've been trying to prove it to you all these last months and I hope this will let you see I genuinely mean it, and to finally forgive me for my attitude towards Jenna last year. *Please*, Mr Vercoe.' Her words trembled on a tear-choked whisper.

Denny regarded her for a moment. He said gruffly, 'I'll read these first. Come inside.'

He led the way down the short passage over the coconut matting and into the large kitchen. It smelled homely of cooking odours and babies, and a whiff of tobacco. Jean was sitting beside the window stitching at a treadle sewing machine. A second machine lay unused, Jenna's, at where she earned her living, but there was no sign of her. The toddler twins were sitting on the floor absorbed playing with wooden building bricks, jabbering away to each other in baby talk, self-contained and oblivious to all else. Belle smiled apprehensively at Jean and then winsomely at the twins. Then her heart lurched with the same unending depth of emotion as it had at her first glimpse of Sam after he had emerged from her body. The double pram was in the room and she saw two tiny babies in white knitted bonnets tucked up and sleeping soundly. The slightly larger baby was Gary. At last she had seen her grandson and he was so much like Sam had been as a baby.

'What's she doing here?' Jean demanded antagonistically while hefting her wobbly self up from the sewing machine. 'Why have you let her in, Denny?'

'She's brought these letters—'

Denny did not get to finish. Cathy came out of the walk-in larder and hurled herself at Belle, her clawed hands reaching for Belle's hair. 'You bitch! You've betrayed me. I'll kill you!'

Taken completely by surprise, Belle was propelled backwards by Cathy's talons and body weight until she was smacked against the sideboard. Ornaments, papers and cups were sent toppling, but before Cathy could inflict serious scratches on Belle, Denny yanked Cathy away and dumped her on the floor as if she was a rag doll. 'Stay put you!' he roared at his niece while pointing a warning finger.

Instinctively, Cathy curled herself into a ball, hugging her legs at the knees, but she glared up at Belle and spat at her.

Jenna ran in from her room, where she had slipped away and brooded dejectedly. She stared in bewilderment from face to face and down at Cathy shaking in rage on the floor. Her better feelings coming to the fore, Jean led Belle to her vacated chair.

'Right, let's read these letters then,' Denny said. Belle had written on the envelopes Letter 1 and Letter 2. Denny started by reading Letter 1 out loud, his gruffness growing louder and angrier throughout Letter 2.

Cathy put her head down and snivelled low sobs. 'I only wanted to get hold of some money to get away. She,' she screamed, 'was only too pleased to hear from me. She suggested how much money she would pay. She's just thought better of her part in it and has come appealing to you and Aunty Jean direct. She'd do anything to get her hands on Gary.'

'No, I would not,' Belle bit back. 'I'm a mother and I wouldn't do anything to part a child from its own mother unless it's sorely neglected or in danger. Jenna is obviously suffering from post-natal depression and it's no wonder after the rotten time she's been through. She'll come round in time and Gary will mean everything to her. It's you, I'm sure, who hasn't been caring for Gary properly. You've taken advantage of Jenna's present state of mind. It was clear to me that Mrs Vercoe didn't trust you and had started keeping Gary with her own baby. I did not go to the bank for the money and I never had any intention to. I'm happy to prove it. You're warped in the mind, Cathy Vercoe. You nearly cost Verity Newton her child and you had no conscience about helping to take your own cousin's baby away from her and causing her more distress. I'm here today to protect my grandson and his mother and my hope is that the outcome will allow me to be a part of Gary's life.'

In the last minutes a new and powerful feeling had built up in Jenna, the love and the primeval desire to at all costs safeguard her child. A piercing animal cry escaped from her throat and she leapt forward and slapped Cathy across the face, the sound of skin against skin resounding like a thunderclap. 'You vile bitch! Go near my baby again and I'll kill you!' She ran to the pram and picked up her son, now whimpering and frightened by all the noise, and she held Gary lovingly against her breast and rocked him, soothing him with gentle words, and he quieted and his startled blue eyes turned peaceful. 'Thank you, Mrs Lawry, thank you so much for coming here today.' The invitation in Jenna's smile drew Belle to her, and Belle went to her, shedding grateful tears of joy and put her arms round Jenna and Gary.

'You were planning to leave today so I take it you've got your things packed ready,' Denny said with disgust to the girl on the floor who was now struggling to rise to her feet. 'Get them. I'll drive you to Wadebridge and put you on a train. I'll buy you a one-way ticket to somewhere well away from here. I'll tell Tilly what you did. I daresay that, like us, she'll never want to hear from you again. From now on you're dead to us.'

'Why, Cathy?' Jean appealed to her. 'Why did you turn out like this? What happened to you? Your uncle and I helped to rear you; we used to be so proud of you.'

'You wouldn't understand . . .' For a moment it was on the tip of Cathy's tongue to tell her family about the abuse she had suffered, but she knew she did not care about any of the people here – not even Tilly, bloody Goody Two Shoes Tilly. Cathy leered at Jean as if she wanted to spit at her, but then she gave an indifferent shrug and whirled round out of the room to get her belongings.

When Denny had driven her away in the van, Jean sighed in a mix of sorrow and happiness, and then she was smiling. In one single day Gary had got his mother's love and his other granny in his life. 'Well, there's nothing for it but to put the kettle on, eh?'

Eighteen

Greg was in the village hall placing the table and chairs for the July monthly meeting of the Gardening Club. It was exclusively a men's club, nine at present after the recent demise of an octogenarian, and all the members were keen never to allow women into their ranks.

'You lot have the Women's Institute and the Embroidery Circle and your homes to run,' was Greg's stubborn stance when Dorrie had questioned the Gardening Club's apparent misogyny. 'And you like to run Faith's Fare and the Thrift Niche all by yourselves. You've never asked a man to help you out there, unless you have something heavy to lift,' he tagged on a trifle bossily.

Dorrie had only been teasing him. If her beloved Piers had not tragically perished he would have joined in the Gardening Club and 'good old Dor' would have been happy for him to have an interest that didn't include her. It was good, she had said, for couples not to spend every minute together. But other women weren't happy about it, Verity for one.

'What gives you the right to say gardening is just for men?' she had challenged Greg in a maddened fighting mood. 'Women are not inferior to men.'

'I have never thought they were,' Greg had replied sincerely. 'A chap likes to toil away and bring in a nice plump cabbage or a lovely bouquet of perfect flowers to his better half. If you feel so strongly, darling, why not start a women's gardening club? And you can include flower arranging.'

'Typical male comment delivered with condescending tosh,' Verity had stormed.

She was also unhappy about something else, resulting from the day Stella had called her and Jack away from Sunny Corner's garden. Verity had given an account to Greg and Dorrie.

Stella had introduced a schoolmaster from a boarding school in Cardiff to Jack and Verity. They were seated, with Oscar, in the drawing room. 'This is Mr David Garth. He went first to

Meadows House and Tilly told him you were out. She told Mr Garth about us so he decided to come here. Jack, you'll hardly believe it. Mr Garth knew Tobias!'

The impression Verity had got of David Garth was of a young, rather eager-to-please sort, of a rangy build, casual posture and drooping tweed jacket and dusty shoes. In a pleasant lilting Welsh accent he had rummaged for the right words.

'I'm very sorry to have to tell you that Tobias is, well, I'm afraid he died.' David Garth had then waited sensitively for the sorrowful exclamations to pass away.

'How long ago?' Jack had asked, hushed and regretful.

'Nearly four years ago, the same day our Lancasters sank the battleship *Tirpiz*. It was in a nursing home in Shrewsbury, Shropshire, where I was teaching at the time, my very first post at a grammar school. You probably won't be surprised to hear it was drink that played the largest part in Tobias's death. I'd met him a few months earlier, and Tobias was, I'm sorry to say, homeless and begging to get by. I think I'd given him a few pennies to buy a cup of tea. I really met him when he came to my aid after a pickpocket snatched my wallet. I admit he intrigued me with his refined voice and good manners, and he allowed me to take him for a meal in a nearby café. I liked him and gave him food every day. I knew he had a drink problem and I gave him only enough to buy a cup of tea. Sometimes we would go to the park, where he slept mostly, and share a picnic. After a while he grew to trust me and allowed me to find him a room. It was pretty grim really but the rent was very cheap. Tobias let me pay the first two months' rent on the condition he paid me back.

'It was during those months he shared with me something of his past. I realized then that he was a lot younger than he looked.' Any more about Tobias's physical appearance David Garth had left to his listeners' imagination. 'He talked about you, Jack, and Stella a lot and your mother. "My dearest mother", he would always say. And his face would take on a softer appearance. I think he was happy during those times he spoke about you. He told me about the games you'd devised to cope with the tyranny of your father when he was at home. How you pretended your father was the evil Sorcerer Randall and you were princes and a princess and your mother was the Gentle Queen, bravely awaiting the next time the sorcerer would go away and how the minute he did his evil spell would be broken. In other games you had shortened names for each other, Jay and Ste and he was Ias. You had a hideout in the woods, and one day you took food and lemonade there and then led your mother there and you all enjoyed a feast.'

As Jack and Stella had wept over their brother's ignoble fate, Verity had cried piteous tears for Tobias. Verity had pictured him, as Jack and Stella must have done, shabby and haggard, as he recalled the happy times of his childhood.

David Garth had coughed apologetically and dipped his head. 'You may know this, although Tobias thought you probably didn't, Jack and Stella, that it was in your hideout that your mother had gone to be with the man she truly loved. Tobias had glimpsed them kissing goodbye once and your mother swore him to secrecy in fear of her life.'

'My real father! It has to be,' Stella had broken in. 'What did Tobias say about him, Mr Garth? Did he know the man's name?'

'Only that he was a bit like himself, down on his luck, and that your mother saw through to the real man he was. When your father came home again and realized the baby girl's date of birth meant he couldn't be the father, your mother decided to never meet the man again, for his sake. She would often say to Tobias, "Never, ever give away our secret or it would be the end of us." She tried to content herself with the fact that she'd had her true love's baby, Tobias had thought.'

'Did Tobias say what my father looked like, anything else at all?' Stella had been desperate to know. Verity had felt sorry for her. She knew Stella was glad that Randall Newton wasn't her real father, but the mystery man might be alive and she might come across him one day.

'I asked Tobias about that. I had a feeling, you see, that I might be passing on information about Tobias to someone one day. I could see him thinking about it as if wondering if it was important. Then his expression changed while he seemed to search his mind. Tobias said the man was quite young, tall and shabby and had likely been in the Services because he was straight-backed, but he didn't notice anything else. He heard the man call your mother his pearl. Tobias said he had liked that, and that every time he saw a woman wearing pearls he thought of your mother.

'I suggested to Tobias that he get in touch with you both. I pointed out that you were a grown man and woman now, and that even if your father was still alive he couldn't rule you all in the same cruel way. Sadly, Tobias insisted he was too ashamed of what he had become; that it was better he stayed away. I also pointed out how close you all had been, that you'd probably be delighted to hear from him, but sadly I couldn't sway him.'

'You must know more about Tobias,' Jack said, 'but I'd like to move on for now. I take it you arranged for Tobias to go into the nursing home, Mr Garth?'

'Yes, I did, when things were getting really bad for him I just couldn't bear to see him die in that squalid room. Tobias would have objected to my intention. He had such a low opinion of himself, so I had to wait until he was no longer aware of anything. He was in the nursing home in a comfortable clean bed in a room of his own, and I was with him when he passed away. He didn't suffer. He died in his sleep. I lied to the nuns that I was his half brother and I had him buried in the nearest churchyard. I couldn't bear the grave to be unmarked so there's a simple cross with his name and the date of his death on it. I've brought the death certificate with me. I'm sure you would like to have it. I can't tell you how pleased and . . . comforted I am to find that all Tobias said about his brother and sister is true, how you had all loved one another. I'm so very sorry about the cruelty of your past. I'm sorry too that I didn't try to get in touch with you both while Tobias was alive, but I felt I couldn't go against his wishes and betray his trust in me. I sensed it had been many years since he had last trusted anyone.'

'And speaking for myself and Stella, we can't thank you enough, Mr Garth, for coming all this way to tell us about Tobias. We'll travel up soon and visit his grave. Now, Mr Garth, the least we can do is to offer you our hospitality. I hope you're not planning to travel back yet. You're more than welcome to stay with one of us overnight or for as long as you like, come to that.'

David Garth had smiled, a handsome smile, Verity had noticed. 'I'd very much like to see the house where Tobias grew up and see the places where he had been happy.' It had been agreed he would stay for a couple of days at Meadows House. He was on sick leave from the boarding school, having suffered a bout of bronchitis. It would be just the ticket, David said, to set him up for the return to his post.

'But wait, I haven't told you everything,' David Garth had continued, with the glowing mien of someone about to spring a wonderful surprise.

'Oh?' Jack and Stella had replied together, leaning eagerly towards him.

'While I was packing up Tobias's things I discovered something important about him. He had been married briefly, I was to learn, and he had a son.'

'Oh, my goodness!' Verity cried. 'How old is he? I mean, do you know where he is, Mr Garth?'

'Yes, I do, I made it my concern to track him down, to a back street in Shrewsbury, not many miles from Tobias's stamping grounds, as it happened. I'd wondered if Tobias stayed close to his son to catch a glimpse of him from time to time. He's called Louis and he lives with his mother Renee, now widowed after Tobias's death, and the man she had taken up with and his four children. They welcomed me bringing news of Tobias. Renee was very sad to learn about Tobias's death. It had been love on her part, but she said she knew Tobias had trouble coping with the past, something he'd never talk about, and he was always drinking heavily. He stayed long enough for Louis's birth, but told Renee he had to go because he was afraid of being a father, that he'd taint his son's life as his father had his. He'd sent a little money to Renee twice but the postmark was a different area each time so she had no idea where he might end up next. She was pleased she and Isaiah Turner could get married and she invited me to the wedding. I was happy to accept as I was interested in seeing Louis again. That was last year and he was four years old then. I also attended the wedding to support Renee and Isaiah. Isaiah is black and they were suffering some really nasty racial attacks. Renee is expecting, so Louis will be getting a new brother or sister in a few weeks' time.

'I visited the family and told them of my intention to travel down to Cornwall to speak to Louis's uncle and aunt. Renee was apprehensive about me doing so in case Randall Newton was still alive and tried to cause trouble. She'll be delighted when I tell her how good you people here are. I've told Louis how much I'd liked and respected Tobias, how he'd had a dignified end. He didn't say very much. He's unnaturally quiet and it took a few visits from me before I gained a little of his trust.'

'I can't wait to meet Louis,' Stella said, looking for and receiving a confirming nod from Jack. 'Do you think Renee would mind if Jack and I travelled up to see him?'

'No, but not until after she's recovered from the birth of her new baby,' David Grant had said firmly. 'The Turners live in very humble circumstances and I'm sure Renee would be embarrassed if you turned up on her doorstep. I'll arrange for you to meet at a quiet hotel.'

'Thank you, that would be for the best,' Jack had said. 'We'd hate to make Mrs Turner feel uncomfortable.'

It was the arrangements after that which Verity objected to. She had complained to Greg and Dorrie. 'Stella's being so stubborn about it. She's insisting it should be just her and Jack who go up to Shropshire to see Louis. Because Renee Turner lives in a back street and might offer an invitation to go there after the initial meeting, Stella thinks that the conditions wouldn't suit me. Why shouldn't they? I argued. I went through many deprivations during the war. I know what it's like to go hungry and be freezing cold all night. I'm not going to look down on them and I certainly don't have a problem with Isaiah's colour. I shared a billet with a Jamaican girl and we still keep in touch. Just because Stella has adopted children from deprived backgrounds she thinks she has the right to take charge of the situation concerning young Louis.'

'What does Jack say?' Dorrie had asked, making a comforting mug of warm milk laced with honey.

'He's pointed out that by the time Renee's had the new baby and recovered from the birth, I'll be well on with our baby, and he doesn't think it's a good thing for me to go somewhere where there might be a risk of diphtheria and other diseases which might be passed on to our baby.'

'And don't you think he might be right?'

'I suppose so,' Verity admitted reluctantly before going on, disgruntled and pouting. 'I won't press the matter. It's Stella's attitude that's annoying me so much. Because she saw David

Garth before we did, she thinks she has the right to be in charge concerning Louis. If he's allowed to, she wants him to spend part of some of his school holidays at Olivia House every year. She's even got suggestions about his education. I told Jack to tell her to hold her horses, but he said we should take one thing at a time, and meet the Turner family first.'

'Let Stella stay in charge, darling,' Greg had counselled. 'Young Louis might turn out to be very difficult and Stella and Oscar will be the best ones to deal with it. You don't want any of that sort of worry. You concentrate on building up your home and marriage and looking forward to your baby.'

'Mmm,' Verity had murmured in agreement. Then her face had closed over as she sipped her milk and honey, and Greg and Dorrie recognised the streak of stubbornness denoting that she had something else on her mind, something she wouldn't divulge to them until she was ready, so there was no point at all in asking her about it.

Greg went to the little kitchen of the village hall and filled up a large brown kettle and put it on the primus in readiness to make tea. There was a plump metal teapot, and to go with it was a thick knitted colourful cosy that Dorrie had styled as a cottage with rambling roses. He had brought with him half an ounce of precious tealeaves. Johnny Westlake would top up the cheap white cups, donated by Soames Newton as part of a job lot of crockery, with a tot of brandy. It was Hector Evans' turn to bring a few biscuits. Oscar Grey was a new member. He was a dab hand with raised garden beds, and knew as much about mulching, leaf rot, diseases, pests, and good composting as the next chap. He was a welcome addition, and he would come with a cake tin of Nelson Squares, made by Philly from leftovers, so it would be potluck whether they would be delicious or a bit bland.

Whistling a cheery 'Pack Up Your Troubles in Your Old Kitbag', Greg was surprised and immediately territorial to be accosted by a female voice, until he saw who was behind the intrusion.

'Rebecca! I mean Nurse Rumford,' he fumbled on the words, hot colour riding up his throat to his scalp. 'To what do I owe the distinct pleasure of seeing you on this fine day?'

Did he really say that? For one thing it sounded ridiculously flirtatious and for another thing it had been drizzling with rain all day and the skies were a morose iron grey.

'Good afternoon, Mr Barnicoat,' she replied in her bright manner. If she had noticed Greg's blunder she did not show it. 'I was passing the Stores and Mr Newton called out to me. He and Mrs Ford-Newton have decided to pack and go off on their travels today. They're leaving the manager and his wife to run the shop until it's sold. They're asking everyone to pass on that they'll meet anyone interested for a farewell drink this early evening in the pub. I knew I'd find you here, and I thought it would be just the ticket for you to pass on the invitation to the Gardening Club.'

Greg was secretly pleased she was here. He was very pleased. Apart from having thought her agreeable and attractive, he had not thought much about this young woman until she had nursed him and his sore head and ankle. While she had tended to him, close up and gently, he had become aware of her breezy perfume, her delicately formed hands (she should not be doing the unpleasant tasks required of a nurse) and the gleam on her meticulously pinned-up dark brown hair, the grips every day in the exact same place, her trim feminine figure under her loose-fitting uniform. She had such shapely ankles. He particularly liked her soft unhurried voice, how her words drifted off her tongue.

He had thought about her a lot since she had discharged him from her professional care. In simple speak he fancied her. He had occasionally become involved with women since his dear Caroline's untimely death in a road accident, the same smash that had killed their five-year-old son, Gregory junior. Each romance had frittered out – Greg's fault, for he could not face committing to another woman after six years of perfect marriage to Caroline. He had quickly forgotten those other women, but Rebecca Rumford kept cropping up in his mind. He must forget her. She was about thirty-three, and would be unlikely to be interested in a man well over twenty years her senior, a man set comfortably in his life. If she did want a husband and children one day she would, and she should, look for someone nearer her own age.

'Mr Barnicoat?' Rebecca frowned and shook his arm.

To his horror Greg realised he had kept her waiting for an answer. Answer to what, he thought desperately, as he gazed into her lovely almond-shaped blue eyes. 'Oh!' He felt really silly. 'Oh yes, Soames Newton, I'll be glad to tell the members of the Gardening Club about it. Dorrie and I will pop along to the pub, and I'll phone Verity and Jack.'

Rebecca never gossiped, otherwise he might have expected her to comment that it seemed strange or unfriendly, as indeed it had to him, for Soames and his sweeping-mannered bride to be leaving before her daughter-in-law took up residence in Petherton; that there must be some sort of a rift between the two women. Cassandra Ford-Newton had made it plain she had a low opinion of Nancy Howard.

Greg ventured, 'Perhaps we'll see you there, Nurse?'

'That rather depends on the baby of my next patient,' Rebecca said. 'Well, I'd better get to it. The way the village is expanding it will need a bigger school soon.'

Nineteen

There was a light knock on Verity's sitting-room door. It was Tilly. 'Can I have a word please, Mrs Newton?'

Verity's humour dropped a little. Since Cathy's dismissal, Tilly had been overly polite towards her, had barely looked at her and was making a point of no longer being chatty with her. Tilly had quarrelled heatedly with Cathy over her wicked actions, but the events had also spoiled Tilly's working relationship in the house. Tilly had been deeply embarrassed again on learning about Cathy's mean plot to wring money out of Belle Lawry and to separate her own cousin from her baby. 'Of course, Tilly, what may I do for you?'

Tilly stood stiff and formal. 'I'm sorry, ma'am, but I'm handing in a month's notice. I happened to hear that Mrs Howard is looking for staff at Petherton to be there ready for when she finally arrives. It would be nice to go back there to work. I applied to her secretary and she's offered me the position of head maid.'

Sighing heavily, tension gripping her scalp, Verity looked at Tilly directly. 'I understand completely, Tilly. It's difficult for you working here now. I'm really sorry about that. Would it make things easier for you if you left sooner? You will be paid until the end of the month.'

Tilly's whole being seemed lighter, as if relief flowed through her from tip to toes. 'That's very generous of you, Mrs Newton, thank you.'

'Well, that was a bolt out of the blue.' Jack scratched his head incredulously in the master bedroom that night. He had been out on business all day at his various properties and it was the first Verity had seen of him since breakfast.

'Tilly's leaving us.' Verity rubbed moisturising cream into her hands and wrists with ferocity. 'It was a bit of a shock to me too.'

'Tilly's leaving?' Jack flopped down on an armchair at the hearth. 'I'm talking about the Kellands. Kelland has just come to me and said he and Mrs Kelland have decided to retire. Years ago I promised them a cottage on a peppercorn rent for their years of loyal service to me. I suppose I thought they would stay here until one or other of them was infirm. Kelland said they'd like to enjoy their retirement while they're fit and able; of course they do, why shouldn't they? Now you're telling me Tilly is leaving too?'

Verity explained about Tilly's new position. 'I was upset at first, but you know, Jack, I think it's actually a good thing, and the Kellands going too. We're soon to begin the next generation of Newtons. New staff will mean a complete fresh start. No more wittering about ghosts and haunting, no one to whisper about what Cathy did and why.' To Verity's own surprise she blurted out, 'If only that could go too, banished and forgotten forever!'

'Darling?' Jack's heavy brows raised skywards. 'What on earth are you talking about?'

Later, Verity could only think she was protecting her unborn baby to shriek out what she did next. 'That wretched grave in the woods, that's what, the source of all the talk about haunting of banshees and insanity. It's no wonder that the Kellands have had enough. I don't want tales about that creature out there in the woods to frighten our children. They should be able to play anywhere without stumbling on some creepy grave. I believe it's the atmosphere Lucinda left here that turned Cathy wicked. Mrs Kelland never stopped whispering about the aura of evil she's left, saying that she's not resting in that unconsecrated grave.'

'That's enough!' Jack cried, appalled, leaping to his feet and pointing at Verity. 'Lucinda was a child. She was harmless to everyone except herself. It was her own life she took and she probably didn't realise what she was doing. She was *not* evil. She was an innocent child who never grew up because her parents and then her guardian kept her locked away from the world in just a few rooms. She never got the chance to mature and look forward to the things a young woman should. She's not some wailing spirit. She can't hurt anyone now any more than she could have when she was alive.'

For the first time Jack was angry with her, a vein twitching at each temple, and Verity was angry with him because of it. 'She couldn't have hurt anyone? You saw the visceral way she destroyed her dolls. Lucinda was deranged and she was dangerous. If she hadn't killed herself, how long do you think it would have been before she hurt or killed someone else? Lucinda couldn't help it;

of course she couldn't, but face it, Jack, she was a lunatic. I'm sure she wasn't locked away without good reason. She might have been hurting other children, perhaps puppies and kittens. Whatever it was about her it twisted Cathy's mind. You did a wonderful thing in keeping her out of an asylum because she surely would have ended up in one, but you owe her nothing more now.

'And, let me tell you this. I want that woman's remains removed from the grounds before my child is born. I won't have my child frightened or even curious about the grave, which it will surely stumble across at some point. We've got to employ new staff. It's a new era, Jack. I simply can't contemplate having that woman kept here and dragging us back into the unhappy past. I simply won't have my baby's life tainted too.' It wasn't until she finished that Verity realised hot tears were searing down her cheeks and dripping off her chin.

Jack was staring at her, at her unappealing red puffy face, as if he had never seen her before. He had never, and could never, think of Lucinda in the same terms as his second wife, and it horrified him that his staff all did. 'Don't upset yourself any more. Lie down and rest. I have a lot to think about. Don't worry. I'll sort everything out.' He left the bedroom on the heaviest tread.

There was only one place for Jack to go, one person to see. Dorrie should be home by now following a stint at Faith's Fare, and hopefully Greg would not be there.

'I know what I have to do, Mrs R,' he said, still feeling as if his guts were ripped to shreds. He was utterly bewildered but still as angry as hell. He'd driven here wildly, just keeping his Roadster under control. He now hated to think what the consequences might have been if someone had been wandering the lanes. His sister, nephews and nieces could have been out for a walk. The fact remained that if he had seen that shockingly mean side in Verity before he wasn't sure he would have fallen in love with her.

How could Verity not have been touched by Lucinda's innocence? By Lucinda's sad story? Lucinda had not been evil or insane. She had been disturbed, a frightened young soul part of the time. There had been times she had delighted Jack, running and playing barefoot on the lawns with her little white poodle, Polly, splashing her feet in the stream, greeting the morning hello, waving goodnight to the setting sun. All the time Lucinda had been under Jack's shelter he had thought his staff had understood Lucinda and her ways, and like him, had doted on her. Now he had learned in a hostile manner that Cathy and the Kellands had betrayed him, talking about her with complete disrespect. He would give the Kellands a home to retire in, as he'd promised, but not one anywhere near Nanviscoe. He had property in Wadebridge. They could shunt themselves off there as soon as they damned well pleased. Without the nest-egg gift he had always planned for them. Tilly was innocent in the whole dreadful matter. She did not appear to have an unkind thought in her head. Jack could wish her well. It was best for Meadows House to engage a whole new staff, but Jack could not help himself having mixed feelings now about its mistress.

'I'm sorry about your troubles, Jack,' Dorrie said softly. She had got up from her chair and looked up under his lowered chin. 'What you need first is a drop of Greg's fortifying blackberry wine. It's as rich as a fine port. Then you can tell me more about it.' Dorrie was concerned for Verity, who must be worried about Jack's abrupt departure, but for now Jack needed Dorrie's attention.

Jack swallowed a mouthful of the wine, appreciating the warmth it gave to his stomach. 'I was shocked by Verity's passion on the issue. I've never really considered her full feelings after Cathy used Lucinda's situation to try to scare Verity away. I have no option now but to get Lucinda disinterred and laid to rest somewhere else, but where I haven't a clue or how to go about it. That's why I'm here, Dorrie, to ask your advice about it.' He would do the deed, for the sake of his child, but he would always resent the manner in which it had come about. He had been bullied throughout his childhood, and Verity had bullied him into what he now must do. A truly loving wife would have talked to him about her concern at having her predecessor's grave in the grounds. Damn it all! Lucinda had been his wife. She had the *right* to be buried in the grounds of her home.

Dorrie noted, with some anxiety, the burning dark emotions playing out on Jack's face. She had thought about this possibility cropping up since the time Tilly had talked fearfully about the so-called haunting while at Merrivale, in Finn's presence. She had an answer to Jack's predicament but offered it as if it had just occurred to her. 'Well, I suppose you could speak to a psychiatrist and tell him all about Lucinda's life and behaviour. If he were to conclude that Lucinda took her own life while the balance of her mind was disturbed, and she was a child, after all, the vicar might be prepared to think again about allowing Lucinda to be buried in the churchyard.'

Jack shook his head sadly, and spoke with much regret. 'It would be better if she was out of the parish altogether, otherwise her grave might become a spectacle and people would gossip about why she's suddenly been buried there. I'll do as you suggest, and if a psychiatrist does come to that conclusion I'll approach other Anglican vicars, find one who offers proper love and charity and will allow Lucinda a place in his churchyard. Failing that, I'll apply for permission at a public cemetery.'

Jack pressed his mouth into a hard line. 'I shall hate the thought of Lucinda being disturbed and removed like a dead dog. I buried her where she had felt safe, but I have to make allowances for the living. I want Verity to have a successful pregnancy. She's had troubles since we came home from honeymoon. I wish she had told me about that photograph right at the start.'

Full of discontented sighs, Jack told Dorrie about the Kellands and Tilly leaving his employ.

'So it's the end of an era.' Dorrie smiled to encourage him. 'And now you have Verity, and Stella back in your life, and even news of a son of Tobias. You'll be getting the chance to see young Louis soon and you have your first child to look forward to. It's a lot more gain than loss, Jack.'

Jack said little after that. He thanked Dorrie for the wine and left with more sighs. Dorrie knew he was unlikely to return home for ages. He had taken on his old heavy-heart loneliness again, a closed-off man. Verity had opened his heart, made him really alive, and enabled him to love her fully, but through her stress and passionate desire to protect her baby, her brash demands had slammed a new door shut on Jack's heart. Jack would indeed hate having to have Lucinda's remains moved and reinterred, a task that would be done without any thought except Jack's for the deceased in the coffin. Jack would feel he had been wronged and Lucinda heartlessly cast out by Verity, and to Dorrie's great worry it was plain he thoroughly resented it.

Twenty

Luzmoor Farm, twenty-three miles away from Nanviscoe. Hunched over, Sam trudged away from the milking shed, which he had just washed and brushed down. Every muscle and ligament of his body ached at its deepest point, his knee throbbed where he had copped an agonising kick from bad-tempered Tulip, but he hardly noticed his discomfort for all his senses were like a desert.

He hated it here. He hated his life. He hated himself for running away from his home and family. He hated the daily sweat that seeped into his eyes and stung like wicked nettle stings, and the heat that burdened him as if with malicious glee, even when a strong breeze was blowing. And he hated every one of the damned twenty cows he had to milk twice a day. They were forever spinning about and kicking out at him. How could his mother suggest he stay here with her little-known uncle until he began his National Service? Clearly, his mother believed he needed to be punished.

It was ridiculous but those black and white Friesians seemed to accuse him,

'Take that! That's what you get for running out on that girl.'

'Don't you think your baby son deserves a daddy?'

Sam knew it was his guilt reproaching him and he deserved every ruthless moment of it.

He clumped into the washhouse and scrubbed himself clean. No matter how much he lathered up with the harsh chemical-smelling slither of cracked soap, he could smell dung and acid cow pee on him. He hated his great-uncle, Milyan Jory, an ancient and wizened troll, but annoyingly sprightly and hopping about all the time. Milyan constantly smoked a chipped-rim pipe, and most evenings he insisted Sam play draughts and dominoes with him on the dirty, sticky deal kitchen table, with the radio blaring rubbish programmes. He had cracked and rotten teeth and bilious eyes. Sam had only seen Milyan once before, at a family funeral many years ago, and he had recoiled at the sight of the leering troll. The small farmhouse was filthy and smelled of mouldy food, reeking tobacco and body odour. Milyan was dirty in body and dirty in mind.

'So you knocked up some tart then, eh boy? You should learn to wear an overcoat when you're having a bit of slap and tickle.' Milyan's first question on Sam's skulking arrival had shocked Sam into the reality of what he was actually doing, running away from his responsibilities. A blaring coward.

'She's not a tart,' Sam had objected.

'Must be some kind of good-time girl if she dropped her drawers for 'ee.'

'It wasn't like that. She thought she was in love with me.'

'Ah, the old honey trap to bag herself a husband. All women are tarts; they use their minnies to get their own way.'

'They're not all like that. Are you calling my mother a tart?'

'The trick worked for her, didn't it?'

Sam was so appalled he almost thumped the lecher there and then and returned home, but once again, to his immediate humiliation, he took the coward's way out, and stayed and hid himself away. He was a heel, a louse, a big shit, not a man at all.

Milyan's only slightly better point was not to be stingy with meals, cooked by his bottle-blonde big-busted woman, Liz. She was definitely a tart, a rough, prematurely aged tart. She wore too much startling red lipstick and filled ashtray after ashtray with red stained cigarette butts. While Milyan forced Sam into the board games, Liz paced up and down the stone flags on her ugly bare legs, jigging up and down to music on the radio, with a Woodbine propped on her bottom lip, and moaning about her corns. Sam rarely had an appetite for the munificent plates of grub Liz dished out for she never seemed to wash her hands, and the old man hacked great dry coughs all over the place.

'A man's got to have a big gutful if he's going to work hard, drink hard and shag hard,' he'd guffawed. All the way through every meal he would talk luridly about sex and his conquests.

'Liz's got the best arse I ever had,' Milyan smirked over tonight's supper.

It made Sam feel physically sick and he jumped up, thrusting back his dirt-encrusted chair. 'I need some fresh air.' He stormed out under the heavens. The clouds were low and it was getting dark early. There was a touch of autumnal chill in the air. Summer was fading, and he thought wretchedly that he had not even enjoyed the spring of his life. He stumbled into the barn and hid behind bales of straw, lighting up a fag with a match. He did not smoke in the house. Liz would filch cigarettes from his packets.

It was nearly pitch dark when he stole back into the house and up to his mouldy smelling tiny room. He was furious to smell cigarette smoke quite different to his own brand. The unscrupulous Liz had been in here probably looking to steal money or anything of his she could grab. There was no electricity so he lit the oil lamp, and saw that he owed Liz an apology. There was an unopened letter on his bed. The rhythmic hand-writing on it was his mother's. Another heap of sentimental stuff about how wonderful it was now she and his father were involved in the life of Jenna's son. He had never allowed himself to think of Gary Mark Vercoe as *his* son.

Unable to face his guilt and failure again Sam tossed the letter aside. He threw himself on the bed, lying flat on his back and staring up at the low, cobweb festooned ceiling. He smoked to soothe his anguish at how he had ruined his life, denied himself of his inheritance, for he could never show his spineless self in Nanviscoe again to be reviled, to catch a glimpse of the child he had sired. He watched a fat black spider spinning more of its exact artistic web. If only he had an easy untroubled life like the spider. It didn't have to worry about ambition, financial success and personal happiness.

Sam let his mind drift. Think of nothing. Hope for nothing. Feel nothing. *God, I wish I was dead.* This life, this bloody, bloody life!

Giggles and creaking bedsprings and the most horrible animal noises started up from across the tiny square landing. *Not again!* Sam screamed inside his head. *You dirty swine. I could kill you. Why the hell am I staying here?*

More than anything else right now he needed comfort and that he could get from his mother's letter. Sitting up he retrieved it, ripped open the envelope and in his haste a photograph fell out and he was looking at the smiling face of a baby, a face not unlike his own. His baby. His son. 'Gary . . .'

He felt the most tremendous lurch in his heart and then a sort of unlocking inside it. He read his mother's letter, devouring all the new details of the progress of his son's young life. Belle always enclosed a sheet of notepaper, an envelope and a stamp. Sam reread the letter, slowly. He lit another cigarette and sat scrunched up on the narrow lumpy bed, thinking things through. Wondering. He looked at Gary's photo again.

Twenty-One

Stella was called to the telephone.

'It's David Garth, darling.' Oscar passed her the white gilt edged receiver. 'He sounds rather grim.'

Stella pulled a face. 'Hello David, how are you? Is all well?'

'I'm afraid not,' came his grave reply. 'Renee had complications giving birth. The baby was stillborn and Renee died hours later.'

'Oh, dear Lord, David, that's terrible. Is there anything we can do?' Stella nuzzled against Oscar and he gleaned the facts behind her distress.

'There certainly is, Stella. Renee knew her life was ebbing away. She told Isaiah it was her wish that Louis go to live with his relatives in Cornwall. Isaiah will find it hard enough bringing up his own four children on his own. A white stepson would be an added burden to him. He's asked me to come and collect Louis straight away. Am I right in thinking you or Jack will be happy to give him a home?'

'Absolutely,' Stella cried, her eyes moist from the overwhelming joy of having Tobias's son come to live with her family, and saddened for the tragic Renee Turner. It stood to reason Louis would be better off here at Olivia House, growing up under the care and experience she and Oscar had with children who had lost their parents, than with Jack and his pregnant wife. And it couldn't be said things were settled there, with a whole new staff needing to be engaged and tried at Meadows House, nor was it a particularly happy house now poor Jack had been ordered by Verity to dig up and get rid of his (equally tragic) first wife. Verity had been unfeeling and crass, in Stella's view. Verity should have spoken to Jack about the matter in a calm, reasonable way at the very least. Poor Jack, he had not had much luck with his wives: first a perpetual needy child, and now a bossy woman who had driven away Jack's trusted long-serving staff. How was Jack expected to purge the old malignancy in Meadows House and bring it to a happy new order if the very person who should support him in every way continued to behave so selfishly?

'There's plenty of room for Louis here,' Stella said into the phone. 'You're very welcome to stay for a few days as well, David, to see him settled in.'

David did not reply with relief, rather he thanked Stella with resignation. 'I knew you would say that; it's how it should be, although I wouldn't have hesitated to have adopted Louis myself. But of course he will be better off with his own flesh and blood and growing up in a home with other children.'

'Well, you have an open invitation to visit him and stay here at any time.'

David gave her the time of their expected arrival and, after consulting with Oscar, Stella went upstairs to air the twin guest bedroom, which David and Louis would share, leaving Oscar to ring Jack with the news.

In a while she would slip out to The Stores and pop into the Thrift Niche to buy some suitable toys and books for a five year old. David had said Louis had already grasped the ability to read. He had obviously inherited Tobias's early intelligence. Stella would ensure he had paper and crayons as well. She and Oscar would ask Louis if he would like his own pet. They had discovered while working at the children's home that this was one of the best ways for a nervous or standoffish child to settle in with a new family. These things would belong to Louis alone. Coming from such a poor background, doubtless he had very little. Hopefully he at least now had some decent clothes to wear, bought from the money she and Jack had sent, via David Garth, to Renee.

Stella danced round the room. Tobias's little boy was coming home. She couldn't wait to meet him.

'So this is what the old bitch thinks of me,' Nancy Howard whispered as her chauffeur drove her through the gateless entrance of Petherton. 'Why am I not surprised? Well, I suppose I'll just have to make the best of it, just as Eugene and I always did with her holding the purse strings. But why did Cassandra think I'd want this rundown heap? A nice accommodating house or cottage would do me fine. Seems a nice little village though.'

Petherton was the latest revenge set out for her by Cassandra Howard – or Ford-Newton as she was now – so bitter was she over her peaceful, honest and put-upon Eugene, the son she had pushed into politics against his will, for falling in love and marrying the lowly Nancy against her will. Her latest and fifth husband would soon discover that he had sunk into the lion's den. Nancy had rather taken to Soames Newton on the one occasion she had spoken to him over the telephone. She had counselled him not to be too eager to sell his business. After a moment's heavy silence he had thanked her it.

The tall granite gateposts were like a pair of protective sentinels. The terms of accepting Cassandra's (highly begrudged) 'gift' of this small rundown manor house was that she must never bring the property up to date. It was the expressed wish of Esther Mitchelmore, who had also stipulated that her late husband's family portraits must never be removed from the house. When Nancy had been faced, via her mother-in-law's lawyers, with the prospect of receiving this property and a goodly (to make Cassandra look generous) financial allowance for the rest of her life, she had shrugged her shoulders and signed the documents. Eugene would want Nancy to have some of his mother's considerable wealth, and it amused Nancy to have planned various schemes in her widowhood to get hold of some of the dollars posthumously for him. Eugene, the poor dear, had been such a pleasing, shy man, quite unable to project himself in his career unless gee-ed up by hours of painstaking encouragement and huge quantities of liquor. His office team had written his speeches for him, every word. His death had come about from a simple infection in a scratch from a fishing hook, received at their holiday cabin in the mountains. Eugene had not showed the scratch to her but instead had allowed it to fester. When he was rushed to hospital with breathing difficulties he went downhill rapidly. Nancy was certain he had lost the will to live, dreading the forthcoming re-election campaign.

Nancy had met Eugene during a house party weekend in Manhattan attended by her English employer Lady Daniels. The young Eugene Howard the third, she had noticed, seemed out of place and was terribly uncomfortable around the politically attached women, socialites and glamour pusses, and he had been drawn to Nancy in her capacity of an underling, loving her English top-drawer accent and her polite, charming ways.

On the third occasion they had met he had begged her to marry him. 'My mother is funding my bid – well, her wish – to become a senator. She insists I find myself a suitable bride. A statesman must have a good wife. Please, you mustn't be cruel and let me down, Nancy. Save me from the fur-wrapped, bejewelled tigresses.'

Immediately fond of Eugene, and grown bored of being at her ladyship's beck and call, bored of spending long hours in hotel rooms or mostly keeping out of sight in grand mansions, Nancy had obliged him. Cassandra's fury over her nerve to secretly wed and bed Eugene, and her refusal to be bought off and sign an annulment, had not fazed Nancy one little bit. And the sweet thing was that Eugene had fallen deeply in love with her and in their private moments he was a fun-loving, sensuous husband. Nancy had loved the part of the man that was exclusively hers.

If she married again she would have to give up all rights to Petherton and her allowance. But if Nancy were to fall in love again she wouldn't care a jot about losing this old place or Cassandra's allowance. She wasn't an extravagant woman and had been saving all her adult life and would continue to do so. She had a tidy nest egg. New love with a poor man would not leave her struggling. It was love and integrity that counted to Nancy.

As for keeping Petherton in its Georgian-Victorian time capsule with the Mitchelmore portraits, Nancy would comply, in her own way. It was not as if the dreadful Cassandra would ever bother personally to inspect Petherton or to send anyone else to. She had declared in hostile terms that she had now finished with Nancy and would cut her out of her life.

Hooray! Nancy could not be more pleased.

Nancy had travelled with her secretary-cum-personal maid, Marnie Cabe, the daughter of her chauffeur, both of whom had come over from the States with her. Most importantly, in its splendid wicker travelling basket was her new beautiful glossy white cat, Romola. The cat's exotic looks matched Nancy's, who had striking bone structure and stunning lake-blue eyes, a fine nose and slightly curving mouth. She wore flattering new-look clothes, nothing vulgar or fussy, and a little make-up. She looked nothing like a former secretary, or a politician's wife, or even English born, but with her frost-white skin she appeared more of a Nordic beauty. Nancy knew she was going to stand out in this greenfield backwater. She rather liked that. She wasn't at all shy.

The first impression Nancy gave to the staff – the reinstated Tilly, the short, apple-cheeked Mrs Teague, and grumpy old part-time gardener Ellery – was that she was mysteriously refined and exuded a graceful self-assurance. They were soon to learn she could display a sense of fun and be stubborn to an intense degree. She was good to her staff if they showed her absolute loyalty. The servants new to Nancy soon grew to like her as much as her old ones did.

Within days, the mournful, condescending, and few stout-hearted faces of the long-dead Mitchelmore clan were banished to a small, shady, never-to-be-viewed gallery at the very top of the house. The most tarnished, scratched and barren-looking furnishings received a similar unceremonious fate, all resigned to languish under dust sheets. 'Effectively gone and altogether forgotten,' Nancy had cheerfully pronounced on the unwanted pieces, smiling secretly at getting more than one up on her voraciously nasty mother-in-law and the inconsiderate, living-in-the past Esther Mitchelmore.

She quickly filled up the vacated spaces with joyful items found in antique shops and auction houses. Assured by Tilly that the best and wisest person in the village was Dorrie Resterick, she had at once claimed Dorrie's friendship and had asked her to join her in what she called her treasure hunts. For such an ordinary little woman, Dorrie had a surprising eye for old things – and the not-so-old that were uplifting as well as functional and decorative. As for Dorrie's charming brother, Nancy took an instant shine to Greg Barnicoat, although he clearly had an eye on the District Nurse.

When alone and all was quiet, she occasionally gave way to her unedifying childhood, stuck in a dull middle-class life where her stilted parents believed girls should aspire to marry a man in a white-collar position, or higher. They had been furious when she, their only child, had defied them to train at a secretarial school, and they had been hesitant about her prestigious job with the marquis's daughter which had taken her to Washington. They had delightedly approved of her marrying Senator Eugene Howard the third, however. Nancy had loved her parents, and she had been sorry for distressing them by going her own way – that was until Lady Daniels declared that women were wired to feel guilty in just about all regards and they would do well to ignore that unfair emotion.

Wandering through her new, more warmly composed home, Nancy grieved for her parents, both killed in the Blitz. They would have been so proud of her now living as a lady of the manor. She would have asked them to join her, offer them a posh home to end their days in, and they would have been delighted to live in genteel surroundings and to have standing in this rambling rural parish. The shabbiness of Petherton would have been perfectly acceptable to them; it would shout of pedigree, of history.

Nancy found no trouble fitting into her (expected) status in Nanviscoe. Relaxed, and relieved to have finally shaken off the mean termagant who had overshadowed her marriage, she felt free and light in spirit and it was natural for her to show interest in all her neighbours right down to the humblest. She joined in with – but did not take over in a superior way – all her predecessor's causes: new equipment for the primary school; Faith's Fare; Red Cross collections and many others, including the quite newly formed Women's Institute. Nancy was a hit in the village. She felt thoroughly at home at last.

'And long may it continue.' She toasted herself in champagne, her thoughts once again straying to the manly dish, Greg Barnicoat.

Twenty-Two

The same day Nancy Howard moved into the village, Verity had interviewed the candidates for her new staff. She had placed a postcard in The Stores' front window and taken a box in the local newspapers, wanting to give employment to locals.

To her annoyance, Stella, the instant she'd heard about Verity's exiting staff, had rushed off a string of unsought advice.

'Verity, you should do what I did and . . . What you need to look for . . .'

What *I* should do? What *I* need to look for? Verity inwardly seethed. Did Stella think she was incapable of making a wise and considered decision in running her own home? Being a loving adoptive mother and successfully engineering a smoothly running house did not make Stella a fount of wisdom for other's circumstances. Besides, it was none of Stella's business. She should wait until her opinion was asked for. She had absolutely no right to interfere. To Verity's further outrage Stella had started each snippet of pressed advice with 'For Jack's sake . . .' Stella had clearly resented Verity's demand that Lucinda's remains be buried elsewhere. It hurt Verity that Jack now leaned heavily on Stella's sympathy. It hurt her more that Jack had had Lucinda secretly removed from the woods and invited only Stella and Oscar to Lucinda's interment in a new secret location.

Jack had slipped out of the house one day and Verity noticed on his return that he was wearing a black suit and tie.

'Jack?' Verity had hurried to him, worried about his downcast posture.

'Lucinda's gone from here,' he had replied tightly. 'Where she is now and how it came about you don't need to know, except that she's had a proper Christian funeral. Her beloved Poppy wasn't allowed to join her, however, and she's now buried on the farm. We need never talk about this again, Verity.'

Verity had felt herself shrinking under his unwavering cool gaze. She had apologized over and over again to Jack for the hard, hysterical way she had made her horror known at having Lucinda buried in the grounds. She had tried to make it up to him with her love and by attending to the meals and housework cheerily with all the staff gone. Jack had asked them all to leave the day after their resignations. He had thanked Verity for her efforts in a quiet formal way. He had made love gently and held her in his arms afterward, but Verity had been grieved that he held a lot of himself back from her. His passion and delight, so evident on their honeymoon, were gone.

'I'm sorry, Jack. I've said so often enough. I hope this will be the end of it. Shall I send your suit to the cleaners?'

Jack was still unforthcoming, but Verity hoped that once the new staff had settled in he would shake off his melancholy and they would be really happy again. Surely when the baby was born he would finally put the past behind him. First she had the daunting task of engaging a cook, a housemaid and a gardener-handyman who would be hardworking, honest and loyal.

Another thing that angered Verity about Stella was her taking it for granted that she and Oscar would give Tobias's orphaned son a home. It should have been discussed first with Jack. It had been Jack's inquiries that had brought David Garth to Stella's door and he had only gone to Olivia House because Jack had not been home at the time. Stella hadn't paused to consider what Louis might prefer. The poor child was to be uprooted from one family and plunged into another. Louis might prefer to spend time, at least at first, in the quieter surroundings of Meadows House. Jack was his flesh and blood uncle, not Oscar. Louis might relate better to Jack, while Oscar was surrounded with his own more needy children.

'Stella is very bossy,' Verity had recently complained to Jack.

'I don't see it that way. Of course Louis would be better off settling in with Stella and Oscar. The children are excited about it. They'll make Louis welcome. He'll find a lot of things to do there to distract him. We've got little to offer him at the moment. It's not as if Louis won't be welcome here at any time.'

He had said it calmly but Verity had flushed with guilt at Jack's look of disappointment in her. He obviously thought she was being churlish.

Then Verity had become vexed again, with herself this time.

She was about to have a child of her own. It was time she concentrated only on her child and Jack. From now on the other Newtons, particularly the dead ones, were none of her affair. Meadows House was her domain and she was its sole mistress and it would be run her way alone.

She had asked Dorrie to sit in with her during the interviews. She wholeheartedly trusted her aunt's wisdom and uncanny discernment. Aunt Dorrie would weed out anyone unsuitable to Verity's needs. They were in the drawing room. Verity did not want to come across as stuffy, haughty and too formal by using Jack's office or the library.

Dorrie glanced at the names Verity had neatly jotted down. 'Joan Argall – would that happen to be the Joan Argall who is one of the dairymaids on the farm? She mentioned to me quite a while ago that she would like to work here in the big house.'

'That's right, Aunt Dor. She was here asking about taking Tilly's place the instant she heard Tilly was leaving. I don't know her really. She seems an honest girl and is always hard at her work when I've gone to the farm. What do you think of her?'

'I've known Joan from her birth. She lives in Kemp Row, behind the pub, and she was in Tilly's class at school. She's straightforward and sincere. I think she would make you a very good maid. You would have to guide her through a little training.'

'Well, she's probably got the job then, but we'd better give all the candidates the chance. There isn't a married couple applying for cook and gardener-handyman. Let's see what happens.' Verity had also claimed Greg's help for the morning. She rang an ornate silver bell to alert her uncle to show in the first person.

Three other young women tried for the post of housemaid. One was slovenly with scuffed shoes and did not wait to be asked to sit down, another smelled of something peculiarly herbal – something she smoked, Dorrie deduced – and could not produce references. The third came with her mother, and the mother did all the talking while the daughter giggled and did not seem aware of what was going on. Joan Argall was the last to step into the drawing room.

'Good morning, Joan.' Verity smiled at the presentable seventeen-year-old. Verity was impressed with her homemade hat, made from old treated wool, stiffened at the cocked crown and jauntily finished with a dyed lace detail. It showed thrift and flair. 'Sit down. Take a deep breath. I won't keep you on tenterhooks. You've got the position. When can you move your things into your new room? I'm sure we'll get along very well indeed.'

'Really, Mrs Newton?' Joan's delight seemed to slap out of her, replacing her yearning expression. 'Oh, thank you, thank you, madam. I won't let you down, I promise with all my heart. If you please, I can move my things in today. Mr Faull, the farm manager, says I can leave immediately if I got the job here. My sister Norma will take over from me as dairy maid.'

'Well, that works out excellently,' Verity smiled at the bubbling girl. 'You may leave the room by the other door, Joan, with Mrs Resterick. She'll show you to the kitchen. Take a look round and perhaps you'd like to make a pot of tea. The necessary things you'll find on the table. You'll be joined bye and bye. I'll tell the other girls they weren't successful.'

A short while later, Verity, vibrant and pleased with herself, said, 'That was easy, Aunt Dor. I'm glad the other girls weren't at all suitable and they all took the news from me with barely a shrug. The ghastly mother went off mumbling about favouritism. Well, that's settled at least. I'm getting my very own staff!'

'Yes, it's a very good start,' Dorrie agreed, glad for Verity. Verity had been down in the dumps since the difficult business over Lucinda Newton's removal. It was good to see her back to her usual positive self. Pray God it had only been a blip in her happiness. Dorrie breezed over her misgivings about Jack putting the unfortunate episode fully behind him.

'Choosing the next people won't be so straightforward, however,' Verity said. Firstly, we don't know any of them at all, and secondly they've all got good to excellent references. There are two people here for the cook's position and five for the gardener-handyman. All the men are ex-forces. All desperate for work, I daresay. I'm sure I shall feel bad about those I'll have to let down.'

The selection of the new cook proved as uncomplicated as Joan Argall had been for the new maid. The first woman, in her early fifties, was looking to serve in a quieter household after the rigours with a constant partying extended family at St Mawes. Widowed, light of foot, seemingly keen to please, Gillian Rabey's culinary skills were wide and varied. She was personable in a wide-shouldered, dark green suit, the skirt pleated at the front. Bunched ribbon on her neat hat pointed to light-heartedness. She had agreeable eyes. Verity followed Dorrie's lead by looking first into a person's eyes. The other candidate would have quite easily done, experienced as she was in all the general duties required in a genteel home, but she did not match up to Mrs Rabey's attributes in the kitchen.

Dorrie took Mrs Rabey along to the kitchen to meet Joan. She found Joan making notes at the large scrub-top table, and the kettle simmering on the electric stove, the tea caddy, teapot and cups ready. Dorrie introduced them and left Mrs Rabey in charge, noticing Joan's happy relief.

When Dorrie returned to Verity her niece was sipping water and rubbing at her forehead. 'It was awful, Aunt Dor. The other poor woman left in tears and I felt she really needed the job.'

'I know it's hard, Verity, that's why most employers send out letters of rejection.' Dorrie gave her a warm hug.

'It would be easier if we lived like you and Uncle Greg, happy to potter at home yourselves and send your laundry to be professionally cleaned, but of course this is such a big house and things are different altogether.' Verity was downhearted. She had thought it would be kinder not to let the interviewees wait to learn whether they had got a job or not. Now she saw it was naïve of her. She still had a lot to learn as Jack's wife. Just for a moment she wished she was single again and living in the comfort of her beloved aunt and uncle's care. Suddenly, becoming a mother was daunting. It was frighteningly new; she knew nothing about babies, and now she thought thank goodness that Stella had charge of young Louis. She was welcome to the responsibility.

'Do you know, Aunt Dor, I think I'll write to Miss Weston and offer her the position of nursemaid-nanny. Her references mentioned she has had experience with children. It will give her a roof and a job, and I'll need a hand with the baby. I can't expect Joan and Mrs Rabey to mind the baby when I, or Jack and I together go out socially.' Verity felt so much better, as much for herself as she did for the needful Miss Deborah Weston. She pictured with pleasure the relief on Miss Weston's well-rounded face as she read the letter Verity would write shortly. As a healthy twenty-five-year-old she would have the energy to cope with a baby, and hopefully Verity's expanding family.

'I think that's a very good idea, darling. Now, shall we ring for Greg to show in the first man?'

Over an hour later Verity sagged in her chair. 'Oh Lord, I didn't like any of them. Two can be discounted because they're more labourers than gardeners, but I'll have to make a choice. I can't keep them waiting for too long. What did you think, Aunt Dor? Did anyone strike you in particular?'

'Yes, someone did. Elias Carey.'

'Him!' Verity exclaimed, astonished and not pleased. 'But he was my least favourite. He didn't wear a suit and he wasn't particularly tidy. He seemed a shady character to me. He stared right at us and came across as a bit bigheaded.'

'Granted he was a little brash but I noticed too the times he dropped his eyes. If anything I think he was the most nervous of the five, and prefers his own company. He certainly knows the seasons and plants, and about machinery and mechanics. He served in the Army. His demob suit would have looked unbefitting on his rangy frame and I think he knows it. That means he's honest with himself and rather than being a braggart it shows he's basic-ally honest. His shoes were highly polished and he had a pristine white handkerchief in the breast pocket of his sports jacket, so he did make an effort. Elias Carey was quietly spoken, and he only issues what others can expect to get from him, no facade. I think he can be trusted, and he's very fit and able.'

'Mmm,' Verity sighed in thought. 'Well, of course, Aunt Dor, I trust your judgement. It's the very reason you're here. But perhaps he's a little too fit and able. He's the same age as Miss Weston, and you can't help but notice he's extremely good looking. That, and his fair curly hair and blue eyes might turn the heads of my younger staff. I couldn't be doing with that sort of complication.'

Dorrie remained quiet.

'Oh, all right, I suppose I am seeing trouble that might never arise.' Verity rolled her eyes to the heavens. 'Elias Carey it is. Jack will be pleased there's been a decision on all counts. Would you mind showing Carey to the kitchen and ask Uncle Greg to give my apologies to the others? I can't face doing it myself any more.

And ask for a tea tray for us please, Aunt Dor? I suddenly feel exhausted and a little shaky.'

Dorrie did not like the look of the flush that was rushing up over Verity's throat and face; she was visibly trembling. 'I'll do that, darling, but I think you'd better have your tea in bed and take a good long rest.'

Twenty-Three

Jenna was back at her treadle sewing machine, facing Jean's, at the long side window of the kitchen. The kitchen was a well-constructed extension to By The Way, built with Denny's own hands, and nowhere was there a draught or cold corner. All along the wide white-painted window ledge were stacks of dress patterns, offcuts of material, bias binding and lace, small bundles of net, and a broad miscellany of sewing implements. Strewn around on the floor were boxes of old garments and curtains, procured mainly through Denny's deals, to be picked apart and made into new clothes or cushion covers, table runners and patchwork items. Jenna had just finished off a cotton blouse, ordered by Mrs Resterick, the cloth bought at a haberdashery in Wadebridge.

Proud and pleased with her precision work, finished with some tiny pearl buttons Mrs Resterick had cut off an old dress of hers, Jenna hung the short-sleeved blouse carefully on a clothes hanger. Then she set to work on the scraps of pretty blue floral print to make a ruffled suit for the stockinette clown's body she had already made for Gary. She was humming softly, and Jean, facing her daughter at her own machine, smiled to see Jenna happy after so many months of despair.

As she did often nowadays, Jenna looked across at Gary asleep in the double pram with Little Jean, two cherubs lying side by side under a white crocheted blanket. Gary was the bigger baby but he was snuggled into Little Jean and she had her tiny arm over him, as if the baby girl sensed her nephew needed a little extra comfort after his neglected earliest days. Jenna felt guilty about not wanting her son at first, for leaving him to suffer at the beastly Cathy's hands, but she did not allow it to over-shadow the new burning love she had for him, her joy at having him in her life. She would give Gary the best she could give him and if being his mummy was all her life amounted to, she was happy to accept it. She had foolishly conceived Gary and brought him into the world fatherless. She owed Gary her lifetime of love, care and protection and to support him in everything, always.

Jenna had finally been coaxed to venture out into the village by Jean and Dorrie. The new babies had been got ready, decked out in the traditional white, and Jenna pushed them in the pram while Jean took the twins crammed into the pushchair. 'We'll be with you every step of the way,' Jean had said stoutly. 'No one had better say a word against you or my precious grandson.'

'Or against my darling godson,' Dorrie had added resolutely.

Putting on her best dress, made by herself, a tight-waist, square-shoulder, front pleat creation in royal blue crepe de Chine, with elbow-length sleeves and a dainty square neck with side collars, a warm plain, light blue cardigan, and her best shoes with low heels, Jenna had sat nervously in the kitchen while Dorrie had brushed her hair back from her face to form the fashionable sumptuous waves. 'You can be proud of yourself, Jenna, and of Gary. You were the one who was badly let down. Keep your head up and look everyone in the eye. That will damn the ones who have something to say. Good people will be interested to see Gary and the others don't count.'

'Yes, maid, get this over with today and you'll be able to face anything in the future,' Jean had declared. 'We're off to meet Gary's other grandma and take a drink in Faith's Fare. Mrs Pentecost and Lowdy Kestle are on duty today so you'll be fine, and Mrs Verity will be in the Thrift Niche. Then we'll call on Mr Evans. He's said he'd like to see Gary, the dear old fellow.'

'What if someone mentions Sam?' Jenna had asked in a wobbly plea. She hated the very thought of that happening.

'Tell them the truth, that you've had a letter from him saying how sorry he is for running out on you, and he sent you some money for Gary's keep and is to make it a regular thing, and that's all you've got to say. Anyone who has a good bone in their body will see your situation for what it is, a couple of youngsters going off the rails but trying to do right by the baby. Anyone who insists on making a nasty point of it will have your father to answer to, and they won't want that!'

Every step Jenna had taken, as she and her defiant guardians walked along By The Way lane, she had done with trembling knees. What she was about to do might become what her mother qualified as a 'nine-day wonder' but it had to be got through, and she would always be a subject for gossip. During the war a young married woman whose husband was away fighting in North Africa had carried out an affair with a farmer from St Teath and she had got pregnant. It had caused outrage in Nanviscoe and the woman had scuttled off in disgrace. Jenna's circumstances were not quite in the same league but some would think she should always hang her head in shame. She would surely receive some snide remarks and jeers. Her family had always been looked down on as scruffs and her mum's constant childbearing had received many a bawdy innuendo and occasional statement of disgust. The housewives and old people tended to keep an eye out for passers-by and would whip out of their homes if they saw anything of interest. Some people might be standing on their doorsteps, and neighbours sharing a cup of tea or a chat or gossip. Jenna had felt a little scared for Gary. Scared some spiteful individual might give him a particular sneering label. She could not bear the very thought of it, that her innocent little boy would be held in contempt, and it would be her fault, hers and Sam Lawry's.

She had no intention of mentioning Sam's letter to anyone. It had been a shock to receive it. At first it had been a puzzle for she had not recognised the writing on the envelope, although she had guessed rightly that the scrawl had been a man's.

'Well, who's it from?' Jean had asked, dying to know. It was she who had picked up the post and passed the letter to Jenna. 'Open it then.'

'I don't really want to,' Jenna had muttered warily. 'It might be something horrible.'

'Give it to me then.' Anxiously, Jenna had watched Jean tearing the letter open and unfolding the two sheets of unlined paper. ''Pon my soul, it's from Sam, and he's put two pounds in it. Do you want me to read it out?'

'Sam!' It was the last thing Jenna had expected. 'No, I'll read it.' Turning her back, she had read Sam's words with mixed emotions – disbelief, a sense of relief, and anger.

Dear Jenna, I know you'll probably want to rip this letter up but please read to the end. I've tried many attempts to put down how I feel but it all sounded false. What I want to say is how sorry I am for treating you badly. I'm glad you've let my mum see you and the baby. She's sent me snaps of Gary Mark and he's nice. I'm sorry you had such a bad time having him and for all that business with Cathy. I'm glad you let Mum help you. I know you don't want anything to do with me and I deserve it. But please will you take the money I've put in for him. I'll send you two pounds for Gary every month after my uncle has paid me. One day I would like to see Gary if you'll let me. I hope you are well, Jenna. Please forgive me, Sam.

She read it out to Jean. 'What do you think of that, Mum?'

'More to the point, maid, what do you think?'

'Phew. I think that he's got a damned cheek, but I'm relieved that he's now acknowledging Gary and even hopes to see him one day. It's good that Gary won't feel rejected by his father all his life. I still hate Sam, though.'

'I s'pose that now he's away from home he's had time to think about what he's done. I mean Sam always seemed such a good person. It was a shock to me and your father that he shied away from you like he did. At least he's putting his hand in his pocket for Gary. You be sure you take his money, Jenna. It's Gary's due.'

'Exactly,' Jenna had agreed emphatically. 'I can provide for Gary's needs from my own earnings. If Sam doesn't go back on sending the money I'll save it for Gary's future.' Things were looking better for her abandoned son. It made his father's rejection of them both easier to bear and lifted off some of the humiliation. She still hoped Sam would never return to the village. She still did not ever want to see him again.

On reaching the village proper, Jean had yelled across to Jenna. 'Head up, maid. You've got someone to be proud of in that pram.'

Aware only of the tightening fluttering feeling in her tummy and the bouncing of the pram wheels, Jenna gave a start but she did raise her head. Directly ahead on its little mount the church basked in the sun, its tower seeming to float peacefully as wads of luminous clouds drifted behind it. The ancient familiar grey and light brown sanctified building seemed a welcoming friend, and Jenna felt her head lift and settle firmly upright on her neck. She did not have to spend the rest of her life looking down at the dirt. A smile came to her lips and she shared it with Jean and Dorrie.

'That's the ticket,' Dorrie had smiled back.

The Olde Plough was to their right and the excited voice of Margaret Westlake sailed towards them. 'Oh, look it's the new babies. Yoo-hoo! Come and join us. Florrie's here with baby Florence.'

The Westlakes had cooed over Gary, then it was on to Faith's Fare, the comfortable little snack hut so called because it was by faith that the villagers expected donations of beverages and snacks. Jenna was introduced to the Kestle baby, Vera-Lynn, lying in a snug basket. Verity came out of the Thrift Niche to see the babies. Lowdy asked to hold Gary and Jenna held Vera-Lynn, and Jenna felt the beginnings of being accepted as local young mother – though sadly she knew she would never feel totally at ease, thanks to Sam Lawry.

The women, and an elderly gent, Mr Boscombe, who lived near the school, sipped weak tea and munched biscuits made with powered egg but redeemed by a dark flavoursome honey, served by Mrs Pentecost from behind the narrow counter. Mr Boscombe treated his repast as he did most days, as his breakfast. He smelled of the strong herbal liniment that eased his rheumatism but otherwise he kept himself in good fettle. He was uninterested in conversation and browsed through the *Daily Mirror* and he pretended, as everyone knew, to be deaf. Notoriously unsociable, he drank his nightly two half pints in the same manner in the pub. When he got up to go he stared down at Gary, partly wrapped in his shawl and awake in Jenna's arms. He stared from narrowed eyes and scowled. 'Huh!'

Although her face flooded in high colour, Jenna met his condemnation with silent dignity.

'Good for you.' Dorrie patted her hand.

'He don't count!' Jean declared.

'The twins and the babies are so contented today,' Verity said. 'I hope my baby will be exactly the same.'

'Babies!' The call came from a cut-glass voice not yet well

known in the village. Nancy Howard entered on graceful feet, elegant in a full-skirted suit, long white gloves and a wide hat shaped like an upside-down saucer. In her arms she carried her gorgeous sleek cat. The slightly slanted blue-eyed creature, wearing a red velvet collar, with a lead, was causing a stir at how it behaved like a dog, even enjoying short walks. 'Good morning, Dorrie. Wonderful to see you again. How good to find so many people in one place. It's like a nursery, how lovely. Did I hear there is an expectant mum too?'

Jenna had felt intimidated by the new 'lady of the manor'. She had not seen Nancy Howard before and she dreaded this newcomer realising she wasn't married like the other women. Thankfully, Nancy Howard made no more references to the children. She had approached the counter with a large card. 'Mrs Pentecost, isn't it? I've just popped in to ask if you'd kindly place this in the window. It's an open invitation to a little garden party I'm holding in a fortnight, so I can get to know my neighbours. Hopefully the weather will allow it to be outside, otherwise in the conservatory. Offers of help on the afternoon will be gratefully received. Do call on me if you have any bright ideas, and please pass it on. Well, I must run along. Toodle-oo for now.'

The end of Jenna's outing had been capped pleasantly by the time spent on Hector Evans' doorstep. He had fussed over Gary, and Little Jean and the twins too. He had even pressed a florin in the fists of the babies to prosper them.

Now, while she stitched Billy's clown, she knew her mother had something on the tip of her tongue. 'Go on and say it, Mum.'

'Why not change your mind and come to the garden party with us? The kids are there already. Come on, Jenna, I know you don't want to go out where there are lots and lots of people, but Mrs Howard seems a good woman. She don't care for that rotten vicar for a start. When she paid him an introduct'ry call, apparently he was ungracious to her, said she should have phoned first to ask when he was available. Rude old sod. He won't be there today. He's getting lazier by the minute. Come on, be brave, my handsome, take the plunge; the more you stay away the harder you'll find it in the future.'

'I know you're right, Mum, and now would be as good a time as any to show my face in front of everyone, because they'll be taking more notice of Mrs Howard than me, but I just don't feel like it. I'd rather be on my own with Gary. I won't stay in and mope. I want to take him for a walk down the lane and we'll get plenty of fresh air.'

Jenna started the walk with Gary soon after her parents, dressed in their best, left with the twins and Little Jean, using the big pram. Wearing her coat she strolled along the lane with Gary lying in the pushchair all wrapped up against the autumn chill. Trotting along beside them, joining them by her own choice, was Tufty, the family's little terrier, who preferred to live outside in one of Denny's scrapped rusting vehicles. Tufty could only be coaxed inside in extreme weather and she had never known a collar or lead. Jenna knew that any moment now her yappy little companion would probably take off wherever it took her fancy.

She reached Pauline Rawling's shabby inhospitable cottage where it stood at a right angle to the lane behind the low hedgerow. The bitter-tongued, reclusive widowed mother of murdered Mary Rawling was, as usual, nowhere to seen. There was rarely a sign of her actually living here. There was never any washing on the line. The chicken run had long been deserted and broken down. The patches of ground to the front, back and sides of the cottage were jungles of dying gorse, and blackthorn, brambles and nettles, decorated prettily with lacy white cow parsley. The woman could die and her body would lie here days, perhaps weeks, unattended. She only strode to The Stores about once a fortnight to draw her pension and buy a few candles and what her food coupons allowed. Someone would eventually, and reluctantly, call to see if she was all right. Even Mrs Resterick had given up on the Rawling woman after receiving short shrift on the dirty doorstep while going up with flowers to console her over Mary's brutal death.

Pauline Rawling had raw-looking areas of skin on her face and hands. Apparently Soames Newton had taken the time to tell her about the new National Health Service, a scheme met with huge relief and excitement throughout the whole nation, and which meant she could now get free medical treatment. His poor return had been her furious accusation that he was making fun of her affliction and she had called him a bastard, and worse.

It seemed she did not have a wireless or ever read the news headlines to discover such events for herself.

'She can suffer then.' It was the general feeling in Nanviscoe. 'And serve her right too!'

Jenna smiled down at a wakeful Gary then jumped in her skin when Tufty started up a hostile sharp barking. Jenna swung her head to the side and was startled and horrified to be facing the hard stare of Pauline Rawling, over the hedge.

'So you're brazen enough to bring your brat out then?' Rawling hissed.

At once Jenna flew into a mother's rage. 'Don't you dare call my baby a brat! I'll jump over the hedge and give you what-for if you throw another insult at him.'

'Think that scares me?' The bile and total malice of the old woman made her stricken raw skin screw up into a mask of hate. She was very like a wicked stepmother Jenna had seen in a fairy-tale book. 'You're a whore just like my daughter was. She jumped at the chance of blackmail with her wicked lover and they both got their heads shot through for it. Served 'em right and serve 'em right they're now damned in hell.'

'You're the one who'll go to hell, woman. You have to be forgiving and not full of hate in order to keep out of hell. You hated your Mary. I was a child but I can remember seeing her covered in bruises from the beatings you gave her, how you always ran her down. You didn't go to her funeral and you've never even marked her grave. You're a cold-hearted old bitch and you'll die a lonely death which you'll fully deserve.'

Expelling a horrid shriek of rage Rawling ducked down out of sight. Jenna, satisfied she had got the better of the insidious crone, made to walk on and get Gary away from this hostile spot. She was feeling proud of herself. She had not been bothered by Pauline Rawling's insults to herself and she had stood up for her Gary. She felt brave enough to face anyone. And that meant anyone at Petherton today. She would slip back home, put on her best summer hat and dress and go to the garden party. She would show the small local world she was proud of her son.

As she turned the pushchair around, she was hit fully in the face by a flood of putrid liquid. Pauline Rawling had climbed on top of the hedge and in her hands was an upturned metal bucket.

Jenna was soaked with urine and a lot of it had sprayed over Gary's legs. As she screamed in horror she could taste the acrid urine in her mouth and she inhaled some up her nose. She went numb all through, petrified to the dusty ground in disgust and despair.

'There!' yelled Rawling like a lunatic. 'That's what people think of the likes of you. You're only good enough for pissing on. You're a whore and you're filth and your little bastard is filth too. No honest mother will want their kids anywhere near your brat. I've given you the stinking body you'll go to hell in. Mary and I will see you there.'

Jenna began to shake, desperate to run away, desperately wanting to protect Gary but in deep anguish because she could not move.

'Get away from them!' A dark shadow flew between Jenna and her tormentor still jeering at her up on the hedge. Pauline Rawling howled like a wild animal as she was violently pushed down off her perch. Jenna burst into tears of relief to no longer be confronted by the witch. 'Jenna, it's all right. I'm here now. I'll look after you and Gary.'

'S–Sam?'

'Yes, it's me. Your mum told my mum you were taking a walk along the lane. I came hoping that you'd let me see Gary for a few minutes. It's a good thing I did. I'll get you both home.'

Jenna could only stare at him. She had hated Sam for rejecting her and her baby but now, after his letters, she could think of no one she would rather have come to her rescue. Sam was the one person who could assuage this new humiliation, otherwise she knew she would go completely to pieces and plunge into a fresh bout of depression.

'I won't let anyone hurt you again, Jenna,' Sam said softly. 'Can you manage to walk? Shall I take the pushchair?'

She nodded. She took the handkerchief Sam offered and wiped at the vile stains on Billy's cotton leggings. 'I need to get us out of that beastly woman's filth.'

'First . . .' Sam grabbed the fallen bucket and hurled it over the hedge. It landed with a dull thud among the overgrowth. He leaned over to peer down on Pauline Rawling lying in a heap where she had hit the ground.

'Is she hurt?' Jenna asked, a little fearful now of serious consequences.

'Who cares? She looks stunned, might have a bruise on her rear end. That's her ruddy fault. Let's leave her to stew in her own venom. One thing I will say, Jenna: God help the next one who tries to put you down. Let's take our little boy home. You hold on to the pushchair handle for support.'

Sam gazed at his son for the first time as they walked off. 'He's gorgeous. I hope you'll let me make up for the rotten things I did to the both of you.'

Twenty-Four

David Garth glanced over his detective novel at the boy in the opposite window seat in the railway carriage. At the outset of their long journey Louis had been interested and even excited to be taking his first train ride. He had seemed to enjoy the change of trains at the stations and he had eagerly read the comics David bought for him. He was a clever boy eager to grasp knowledge, and David had been glad to explain the meaning of the words he did not understand. Louis had only seen scraps of discarded comics before. He had owned nothing except the clothes on his back and a buggy he had made himself from a crate and old pram wheels. Louis had wolfed down the sandwiches in the station cafes in great gobbets but David had not checked him. Louis Newton had too often known what it was like to be hungry, to hear his late mother wonder aloud where the next meal was coming from.

David had grasped that Renee had taught him a few simple words and Louis's quick brain had done the rest. He had good general knowledge for a child so young. He had been taught good manners and hygiene. He had not started school yet but had told David he'd been looking forward to it – not feeling out of place, as his mates would have been just as shabby.

With sadness, David had picked him up at the end of the street, just him in his new short trousers, white shirt and sleeve-less jumper, new shoes and knee-high grey socks. 'Where are your things, Louis?'

The dark-haired boy with a little street-wise cheeky face had turned out his lips. 'Got nothing I want to take. Can't bring my buggy so I'll make a new 'un.'

'Where are Mr Turner and your stepbrothers and stepsisters? Aren't they going to see you off?'

'Nah. He's out working on the bins. The kids and me don't get on, never have. They're all glad I'm going. I don't belong with them, said so soon as Mam died. Just want to get away from 'em. I'll miss me mates though.'

'I'm sorry, Louis. Well, you can make some new mates now and you'll certainly be able to make a new buggy. I'm sure your Uncle Jack will provide you with the things to make a really superior model.'

Now as the steam train trundled over the Brunel Bridge to cross the River Tamar from Plymouth into Cornwall, Louis was getting fidgety.

'Growing nervous, Louis?' David put the book down to engage in talk. It would be a one-sided conversation. Louis had spoken less and less as the journey progressed. David understood; Louis had lost so much in his five years. He was bound to be insular. He could not be expected to trust in fate and certainly not adults. So far those, apart from his mother, who were supposed to look after him had let him down. His mother could not help dying but in the mind of a boy so young, she had abandoned him.

'Why did Mam leave me?' Louis had asked plaintively when David had taken him on a last visit to her grave. Talk of heaven and angels had meant nothing to Louis. 'But I needed her more'n God did.'

Their last fellow passengers had got off at Plymouth and David was pleased they were alone. 'Don't be afraid to tell me exactly how you feel, Louis. I'm sure I can allay your fears.'

'Don't want to go there.' Louis pushed out his thin lower lip and his eyes pooled and he waved his small hands about. 'Want to live with you, Mr Garth. Can I live with you? Please, I'll be quiet 'n' good. I won't make a mess. I won't swear, honest. I'll polish your shoes. I do it well, done it for gents. I can run errands. I can scrub floors. I used to go with Mam to her cleaning jobs. I won't mind God having Mam if I can live with you. Please say I can.' Louis was up on his feet, swaying with the lazy motion of the train, his hands up prayer-like under his chin.

'Sit down, Louis, so I can speak to you properly,' David said kindly.

Louis obeyed, climbing up on the seat beside David, sitting with his back stiff and fingers interlocked, his toffee-coloured eyes hopeful.

Before now David had wanted only to do the best for Tobias's son, to see him leading a good life with his prosperous relatives, but he was hit by paternal feelings for this sad little boy. 'I know you must be really nervous about meeting your uncle and aunt, but you needn't be, Louis. They're kind people. They have so much to offer you. They have the right to bring you up. You'll have so much fun with your Aunt Stella's children. You'll have everything you could ever want, even your own pet. How about that? Brilliant eh?'

'Won't be brilliant!' Louis yelled. 'Don't want to meet the Newtons. My father ran out on me. He was a stinking drunk and I hate him. Glad he's dead! Left my mam crying and crying. She worked day 'n' night and got old. Then she met Isaiah and we lived with him. I had t'sleep with his kids. They hated me for it and I hate them. They called me trashy white boy and stole my food, said their father earned to get the food and I had no right to it. People jeered at me and called me tar brush and other things. Some kids threw stones at me 'n' beat me up. Isaiah couldn't wait to get rid of me. The Newtons won't really want me. Be just a ragged-arse kid to them.'

'But you won't be, Louis, I promise you. Jack Newton had been searching for your father for years. He and your Aunt Stella were delighted to hear Tobias had had a son – you. Louis, I understand your misgivings after all you've been through but please give the Newtons a chance. It's a marvellous opportunity for you. Think about all the good things you've had just lately, all bought from the money they gave to me to kit you out. There are other new things like a dressing gown, pyjamas and slippers waiting for you. I found the Newtons and the Greys to be kind and friendly, and there are some really nice people living in Nanviscoe. I'm sure you'll settle down there very soon. You can choose between going to the school or taking lessons with the children in your new home. There's a lovely comfortable warm classroom with lots of interesting things to do.'

Louis had hardly listened. 'You don't want me either, do you?' he blazed, spitting in his vehemence and his little dark face crumpled in anger and bewilderment. 'You've taken me all this way just to dump me!'

David hunkered down in front of Louis. 'I swear I'm not dumping you, Louis. I never dumped your father. I stayed his friend until the end of his life and saw that he got a decent burial. Your father shouldn't have left you and your mother but he always regretted his weaknesses. I swear on my life that I care about you, Louis. I promise I will make sure the Newtons and the Greys treat you well, but try to understand that it's up to you to give them all a chance. The Grey children will understand how lost you feel; they were all abandoned by their real parents. I'm going to stay at Olivia House for a few days and I will make sure all is well for you before I leave. Come on now, Louis, chin up, be a proud young man. Give things a chance. You have an exciting time ahead, I swear.'

Louis nodded and looked away.

David knew he wanted to cry but Louis's tough life forbade a show of feebleness. 'Better now, wobbles over?'

Louis nodded again.

'That's good. I'll always keep beside you, Louis. Even when we're miles apart I'll keep in touch with you and I shall come to see you as often as I can. You have my word. Your worries are over, believe me; you'll never go without anything ever again and that goes for care and love.'

Closing his eyes after Mr Grant sat beside him, Louis leaned against the arm of the man's tweed jacket. He felt a little less scared now. Mr Grant had as good as promised he would always be his guardian. Louis was sure he would hate living with his relatives, and if so Mr Grant would take him away and allow him to live with him.

'I can't wait to see our little nephew,' Stella said enthusiastically on the platform of Wadebridge railway station. 'From the photos David took of him he looks enough like Tobias to bring us back the good memories of the old days.'

Jack rubbed the back of his neck. 'I feel a little nervous.'

'Whatever for?'

'Well, I'm not used to having children around me. You're a natural at it, Ste, but I won't know how to relate to Louis.'

'Just make things fun for him and leave the rest to me.' Stella had come dressed motherly in a simple dress, small hat and sandals, and a cardigan draped over her shoulders. She wore a silver brooch shaped as a rose bud and white cotton gloves and carried a small cream handbag.

Stella's confidence made Jack relax. He would never see his

brother Tobias again, but when Louis stepped off the train Jack would have his family back with him for good. He had Verity, new staff in the house and gardens who worked smoothly together, and quite soon he would be a father. He would never feel lonely again.

The train was six minutes late and then the lumbering tons of steel and smoke slowed to a squealing, hissing halt. The only people to alight were David and Louis.

All smiles, Stella hurried towards Louis, who was now shuffling behind David. 'Don't be worried, Louis. I'm your Aunt Stella, and this is your Uncle Jack. We're so sorry about you losing your mummy, but you're with family now and you'll have a settled future.'

'Get away from me, you bitch!' Louis bawled at full pitch. 'I don't want to know you or him. I want to live with Mr Garth and he wants me to live with him. If you make me come with you I'll run away and drown myself in a river!'

Twenty-Five

'You should have heard Louis scream, Aunt Dor, Uncle Greg. I thought my eardrums would burst. Anyone would think the boy was being brought into a torture chamber. Mr Garth took him straight up to their room. Poor Jack was beside himself, not having a clue what to do. I just kept quiet and helped Nanny Lucas and Philly usher the other children out into the garden. Jack took me straight home. He was worried about the baby. We left Stella and Oscar to it,' Verity finished tartly. 'They're the child experts. I'm sure they soon got things under control.'

The three, and Corky, were at the side of the back garden, scattering corn and bran for the hens and bantams, and feeding swill to the pig. They had kept pigs all through the war. Wen was the last pig Dorrie and Greg would have and they would be very sad when it was time to sell her; she would be 'put away' and parts of her returned to them salted and cured.

'You started on a note of something akin to delight and ended on a rather unkind one, darling.' Dorrie studied her niece. Proudly displaying her seven-month bump, Verity was glowing from more than impending motherhood. 'Have you had words with the Greys?'

'Have they upset you, precious girl?' Greg plunged in on hearing the touch of chiding in Dorrie's tones; he as always was quick to defend Verity.

'Not "they", Uncle Greg, just Stella. She's bossy, she jumps in on every matter as if she knows best in every situation, and she is a little too condescending. She hasn't been part of Jack's life for years yet she's breezed back in and treats me as if I'm no more than Jack's secretary. I think she's quite put out that I've also got a successfully running household, that my new staff has gelled as if they've worked together for a great many years.' As Verity trilled on, Dorrie got the image of Verity's snobbish, gossiping mother. Verity had hated her mother's toffee-nosed manner but sadly, and whether consciously or not, she was taking it on. 'Mrs Rabey makes the most mouth-watering meals and her cakes are legendary. Jack rarely leaves a crumb on his plate. Joan is quite the sweetest soul and completely unobtrusive. She doesn't have to be told the same thing twice. My silver gleams like pure ice and there's not a speck of dust in the house. Miss Weston consults me on how I want my baby to be nurtured, not the other way round with endless suggestions. It was her suggestion that she double up as my dresser. My wardrobe had never been so well turned out.'

'And Elias Carey?' Dorrie interrupted before Verity began to crow about his skills and virtues. 'The chap you wouldn't have chosen and thought looked shifty. How is he measuring up?'

Verity made a tight stroppy face. 'He's adequate.' She put her pert nose in the air. 'Jack approves of him and he's the one who deals with Carey. I think they've become rather matey. Carey knows about golf, apparently. Jack loans Carey to Nancy Howard two afternoons a week to work in her grounds. Well, you must know better than I that Mrs Howard has been also employing Finn Templeton throughout the summer holiday, and with grumpy old Ellery, the Petherton gardens are being completely transformed.'

'And Louis?' Dorrie lifted her brows. 'Did you or Jack inquire about him?'

'Oh, Jack rang later, and apparently Mr Garth had managed to get him to pipe down, and to apologize. "Suitably chastised," Stella called it, indeed. "And he's willing to give us all a go. He'll be as right as rain in a week or so." She's optimistic, I must say.'

'Mmmm. Coffee time, I think, and then a spot of hoeing.' Dorrie added nothing to Verity's assertions to show her niece she disapproved of her touch of sarcasm. Small words of discontent, some unfair, left unchecked could grow into lofty ill will. Dorrie accepted that it must be tiresome for Verity to have to endure Stella's slightly overbearing ways, but Stella had a wealth of experience behind her where children of all abilities and disadvantages were concerned and Stella often mentioned how her successes had only come about through much trial and error, and that it was through the joint effort of herself, Oscar, Philly and Miss Lucas. Stella stressed that above all a huge amount of patience was needed. People of small character, in Dorrie's opinion, relished in relating others' faults and lapses while ignoring their good points. Verity had made no mention about the welcome she would give Louis when he was brought to Meadows House for tea or to play. Dorrie was sure Verity would not welcome any suggestion of Louis sleeping over in her home. If Dorrie were right, she would be disappointed in Verity. Dorrie and Greg were interested to meet Louis, but they were respecting Stella and Oscar's wish that he be allowed to settle in comfortably and presented slowly to the villagers.

Dorrie led the slow troop into the kitchen, washed her hands and put the kettle on.

As Greg washed his hands he exchanged rueful glances with Verity. Even when she was in the wrong he showed her indulgent support.

'All right, Aunt Dor, point taken,' Verity said contritely. 'I shouldn't have been gleeful and high-handed about the Olivia House situation.'

'That's my Verity.' Dorrie smiled. 'Let's sit outside. Greg, you take out the rock buns.'

'Poor Louis, I hope he will feel able to settle in,' Verity said, in kind, motherly mode. While breaking off a piece of tasty rock bun, she thought inwardly, *But if the boy uses disgusting language again he won't be allowed anywhere near my child.*

Twenty-Six

Nancy was enjoying the simple meandering life of Nanviscoe. It was a welcome change from staying in hotels or as a guest of the wealthy and influential, all arranged by Cassandra, who had sold Eugene's house within a month of his death. Nancy did not miss the cocktail parties and glitzy round with the cream of society, the political campaigns Cassandra insisted she attend so people did not forget Eugene. Nancy had often asked herself why she didn't simply tell her spiteful mother-in-law to go to hell and look for a new job. She wasn't averse to earning her own living. But somehow she felt it would be letting Eugene down by working, throwing away the good life he had striven to provide for her.

Nancy had hoped to have children and as the years had slipped by it had become a huge regret. She thought about babies a lot, especially with so many new infants keeping the pleasant nurse Rebecca Rumford so busy. Sadly, on reflection, she knew if she had had a family – a son at least – with Eugene she would never have been free from Cassandra. The witch would have sailed in and taken over and tried to rear another politician. It wasn't such a bad thing to be childless then, and she could have plenty of years left for childbearing. She had not heard from Cassandra or her to-be-pitied bridegroom. Soames Newton must have soon found out he was totally out of his depth with Cassandra.

When her neighbours asked if she had heard from Soames, Nancy answered, with smile, 'Oh, my mother-in-law and I were never very good at keeping in touch. I expect news from Mr Newton will come one day.' But not by a letter or a telephone call from someone. Nancy fully expected to see Soames again sooner or later. Having assuaged his loneliness once and for all, his new experiences and adventures turned foul on him, having endured his wife's violent temper, with bruises liberally served as side dishes, he would return cursing the day he met Cassandra. It would end something like Cassandra howling, 'Get out of my life! I'm divorcing you, you little fat Englishman. You're useless at everything. You're terrible in bed. Don't expect to get a big fat settlement out of me. I'll get my lawyers to draw up a sum of ten thousand dollars. You can take it or leave it. I've had your stuff packed and an automobile is standing by to take you to the airport. Here's your one-way ticket.' This would be thrown at him with the ferocity of a native spear engaged in tribal war. 'Don't *ever* get in touch with me again, you hear?' The bitch-witch would then swan off to her suite or cabin or the salon, and that would be that for Soames Newton. And how bloody relieved he would be. Ten thousand dollars would equate to a nice little windfall for him – but he would not care if he'd have to pay a king's ransom to get away from the iniquitous Cassandra. Nancy was convinced he would promptly return home, but not slinking back with his tail between his legs, rather he would be triumphant and eager to regale his old friends with tales of his dreadful American wife.

One of Nancy's pleasures was to take breakfast in her sumptuous, satin-sheeted new bed, brought into her on a tray by Marnie Cabe, with the morning post and newspapers. Nancy had a healthy appetite and she was blessed to be one of those people who could nibble all day long and never put on an ounce of weight or mar her marble complexion. What British rationing couldn't supply her with she sent for abroad. 'Good morning, Marnie.' She leisurely stretched up her arms. 'Ah, American ground coffee and Swiss muesli. Is Mrs Teague still scandalised by my choice?'

'Yes, ma'am, she makes a face like she's sucking on a lemon. She can't understand what's wrong with the usual fare of eggs, toast, bacon and kedgeree. Kedgeree, ugh! Young Tilly and the new kitchen maid nearly succumb to giggling at her.' Marnie Cabe was a thin, crisp woman. Keen to be stylish, she was always well turned out. She seemed to tiptoe about her duties. Deeply loyal to her mistress, Nancy knew Marnie had many times forestalled Cassandra from upsetting her. Nancy called Marnie her 'godsend'.

Nancy munched on her muesli and took a mouthful of the strong coffee. 'How do you think the new kitchen maid, Dorothy, is working out, Marnie?' She always sought Marnie's opinion. It had brought the two women to a lasting mutual respect, stopping just short of friendship, but only on Marnie's part. Nancy considered that if the two of them grew old together they would slip beautifully into becoming companions.

'She appears to be better than the last one that was tried out, Mrs Howard.' With a soft cloth Marnie buffed the pair of cross-strap cream sandals Nancy was to wear. 'Tilly says she's easier to train, this girl. Tilly has taken her under her wing. Dorothy is certainly not idle and full of cheek like the last girl. She's a bit nervous. It must be strange for her, fifteen years and straight out of an orphanage.'

'I'll give Dorothy a little pep talk later on. Oh, listen to that, will you? It's Ellery going at the Templeton chap again like a Dickensian sweatshop owner. Finn doesn't deserve it. I've observed him, he's a hard worker and he knows what he's doing. After all, how difficult is it to dig over the ground for the new flowerbeds and arbours, and the repositioning of the summerhouse? Unsurprisingly, Finn's patience is running low with Ellery. He'll clear off soon if I don't intervene. Ellery resents Elias Carey working here and hates the worthwhile suggestions he makes. I'm afraid the truth is that the old boy is long past getting up a full head of steam and just doesn't want to acknowledge it. He finds it a trek just from his retirement cottage. He won't admit it, but I'm sure he misses Mrs Teague's company because she's chosen to return and live in. Well, I'll have to grasp the nettle. I'll speak to him today, outside, on his own ground, as it were. It will be kinder.'

'Will you be giving him notice, ma'am?'

'Well no, but I shall have to find a way to suggest he should just potter in the greenhouse, that sort of thing. I'll assure him he's a valued member of the workforce. I'm thinking of offering Denny Vercoe the job of full-time gardener and handyman. From what I understand he will fit the bill admirably; he's a skilled jack-of-all trades. He can still carry on with his other moneymaking interests at the weekend. I've met him a couple of times. I think the job will appeal to him. He made me laugh and he's tough as old boots. I've noticed he's just up your father's street; they both like a drop or three. Having a chap like him about the place will send out a message that all is secure here.'

Marnie's head shot up from the silk underwear she was laying out. 'Oh, do you feel threatened here in any way, Mrs Howard?'

'Not in the least,' Nancy said gaily, finishing her muesli and picking up *The Times*. 'I shall like to feel secure. I never enjoyed a sense of security until I met Eugene, and then Cassandra was always chipping away at the edges.' She looked over the newspaper, let her half-spectacles slide down her neat nose. 'Young Dorothy must be feeling insecure. Once I've had my bath and dressed, Marnie, ask her to come and see me in the morning room.'

Lifting the newspaper high to obscure her face Nancy squeezed back the moisture warming her eyes. Old non-specific fears caught her unaware at any time. She had suffered no vile abuse or any neglect, and sympathized with those unfortunates who had, but had grown up an only child with a mother who was a little aloof and a bowler-hatted father who took his bank manager duties first above all else, and the loneliness of her single life – loving Eugene yet always being on edge over his weakness at allowing his mother to bully him – sometimes got to her. At times Nancy slated herself for not getting a job and supporting herself and for not telling Cassandra Ford-Newton to go to hell with her stipulated offering of this old house. She was happy here, very happy actually, but had she sold herself, demeaned herself? She had Eugene's photographs and portraits of him from boy to Senator in her sitting room, but did they belong here? Yes, she told herself, crying it out inside her head. Eugene only wanted me to be happy. The evil witch would never return here and Nancy and Eugene's memory were safe from her. One of her new garden arbours would feature a three-feet cross of granite and seasonal flowers, particularly scarlet red geraniums in summer, Eugene's favourite, a lasting memorial to her husband. It would be a serene place his hag of a mother would never see or sit in.

She took a deep breath and lowered *The Times*. 'The wind looks a bit keen. Look me out a warm cardigan please, Marnie.'

Twenty-Seven

Louis looked long and hard at the diagram of the long run and obstacle course, drawn by David Garth on graph paper for his two pet male mice, Bod and Bim.

'We've finished it,' David cheered, clapping an exultant hand on the boy's bony shoulder. 'It's exactly as we'd planned, lots of twists and turns, spinning wheels and things to climb over. It's surprising what can be achieved with a few lengths of hosepipe and some odds and ends. Your little chaps will get plenty of exercise and they've got a lovely cage for eating and sleeping quarters. Well done, Louis. You did the greater part of the masterpiece. Be very sure you never let them run out of water and to wash their water bottle out regularly.'

'Aunty Stella says I can take them out any time I like,' Louis said archly, cross that Mr Garth had finished on a warning note. Why did grown-ups always think kids were stupid? Over and over he had said that his whiskery mice, Bod the grey one and Bim the white one, would get his full care. He wasn't going to let them thirst to death, for goodness sake, or keel over legs up from some disease.

'Mind you keep them away from the cats and dogs,' Uncle Oscar had cautioned him.

Yah, he wasn't daft in the head. Louis knew all too well cats and terriers liked to kill mice. He had witnessed the Jack Russell of a boy he'd known, killing mice and rats with a swift snap of their necks. How he and white-haired Chalkie had laughed at the crack of their bones. 'Bod and Bim won't want to stay cooped up all day long. Don't worry, I won't let them out of my room.'

'There's no need to be rude about it, Louis. I'm only thinking about how upset you would be if you lost Bod and Bim.'

'Sorr–ee,' Louis said, without meaning it. He had not quite forgiven Mr Garth for turning on him the day of their arrival here. That was another bugger about grown-ups, he and Chalkie had agreed; one minute they treated you like a baby who had to be mollycoddled and the next they were bawling at you, 'You're a big boy now and should know better.'

David Garth's anger with Louis, the terrible dressing down he had got for calling Mrs Grey a bitch and refusing to apologise on the journey here, still echoed inside his head. Mr Garth had called his behaviour 'obnocshush' whatever that meant. It must be very wicked for Mr Garth had grabbed hold of Louis and hauled him upstairs to the room they were temporarily to share. So many stairs, it had seemed like a mountain climb to Louis. He had feared he was being taken up to the attics. He had heard stories about people, culprit children in particular, being locked up and starved in attics – high-up dungeons.

Once in the guest bedroom, Mr Garth had ordered him to stand at the foot of one of the beds, the one furthest from the window. 'I'm thoroughly ashamed of you, Louis. You've let yourself, your mother and me down very badly indeed. From what I saw of you before I'd never have thought you'd be capable of such low and disgraceful behaviour.' Mr Garth was a droopy sort of bloke but he had thrust up his chest and seemed to grow to ten feet tall.

'On the train, you begged me to give you a home. You pledged to me that if I did so, you would always show your gratitude and be no trouble whatsoever. How could I now trust your word after your dreadful performance on the station platform when you insulted the very people, your own relatives, who had so willingly come to greet you and receive you into their family, where you belong, I might add? You sulked all the way on the drive here. What you called Mrs Grey is a vile, nasty name, a word that should never ever be said to a lady.'

Mr Garth had joined his hands behind his back and brought his face right down to Louis's, bending his neck like an angry swan. Just like a bloody schoolmaster. Louis had stood rigidly, darting back equally furious looks. 'You are five years, boy, nearer to six, and old enough to understand right from wrong. Most of the boys of your acquaintance would give their eye teeth for the opportunities and privileges that you're being handed on a plate. There are masses of children all over the world who would happily change places with you, children who've been orphaned in the war and through many other tragic fates. Mr Turner could have had you put into an orphanage. Yet here you are, about to live with members of your own family who were so looking forward to meeting you, and in the very best of surroundings. Here you will never go without anything again for the rest of your life. You will have your own room all to yourself. How could you be so ungrateful, Louis? Well, what have you to say for yourself?'

Mr Garth had not shouted or raised his voice. There was no wildness in his eyes as if he'd liked to strike Louis or spank his legs or box his ears. Louis could have coped better with that, he was used to wallops even when he had done nothing wrong. It was part of life in a household of many where all too often you had to fight for your bit of space, to get some food before it was all gone. Instead Mr Garth's utter disappointment in him, and his dismay, and his smooth pale cheeks, where red spots had appeared and got redder and redder, had frightened Louis. Mr Garth was his hero. He had saved him from life as a guttersnipe and now Mr Garth was horrified and ashamed of him. He might turn on his heel and go back to Wales and never bother with him again.

When the scolding ended, Louis understood that Mr Garth had been right about his awful behaviour. Louis recognised he had got scared on the train. He got muddled in his head when he was scared. He struggled to form the right words to say he was sorry and to beg Mr Garth not to turn against him. Tears welled up in Louis's throat but the manly pride he'd gained in his street life, the jeers for any weakness he had shown back then, had made him push down hard on 'wetting his face like a lass'.

'Well, if you won't answer me, turn around and look at your bed then.' Mr Garth had sprung forward and clutched Louis's arms and turned him around. 'See there, it's a teddy bear, just for you, all of your own. Your Aunt Stella put it there because she understands that children like you who have lost so much, who have had a hard struggle all their lives, need something to cuddle. Isn't it kind of her? The first toy you'll get of many more to come. Don't you want to pick up your teddy?' The softness Mr Garth had then used was Louis's undoing. Tears had burst out of him like a bomb going off. He had wetted his cheeks, his chin and his shirtsleeves from wiping the tears away. Mr Garth had reached for him and he had wept streams in Mr Garth's arms.

Mr Garth had tousled his hair. 'I understand, Louis. We all understand. Now what do you think you should do?'

'Tell 'em downstairs I'm s—sorry.' Louis blew out his runny nose on the handkerchief Mr Garth passed him and dried his face with the sides of his hands. He accepted he deserved the telling off but he resented the fact Mr Garth had made him blub like a baby. His aunt and uncle had gladly smiled at his apology. They had repeated Mr Garth's 'we understand' thing, and then to Louis's horror Aunty Stella had hugged and kissed and cuddled him. It had been the peak of embarrassment because all the other kids were with them then and had watched him squirm. Thankfully, no one had teased him about it – he would have thumped the hell of out anyone, later, if they had.

In fact the kids were a pretty good bunch, especially Stanley. Louis had soon become his partner in mischief. Louis had never played dressing-up before, only pretending, and he loved putting on a pirate or cowboy's costume. He was fascinated by tiny Libby, and fell into calling her Libs, as everyone else did, in awe that someone could stay a baby all their life. In the next few days he had moved into his own two-tone blue painted room. So much room! And all to himself, how jealous his stepbrothers and stepsisters would be if they saw it. He had a cupboard for his things – not his clothes, for he had a single wardrobe and chest of drawers for those. He also had a chair and a small table, an unimaginable treat, where he could draw, make jigsaw puzzles and play card patience. Best of all his bed was soft and springy and he was allowed to jump on it. 'Just be careful you don't fall off and hurt your noddle,' Philly had laughed, when discovering him during his first go at this delight. Philly was great and Louis loved her. She was ugly like an old crone in fairytales but was so much fun, singing music hall songs and kicking up her legs, showing her knee-length drawers, invariably with a fag dangling on her lip. Miss Lucas was firm, but nice enough. She read stories to the kids every day. Louis loved that, and he had books of his very own too. The novelty of having a proper bath in a big proper bathtub soon wore off, and there was the bugbear of all the washing behind the ears and his neck, and his hands before every meal. Last night in bed, before snuggling up with his teddy Albert, Louis thought he was in paradise. Getting shipwrecked with Stanley on a desert island with heaps of buried treasure, and a ship they could whistle up to take them home at any time, well it couldn't be better. And he had the 'vantage of being flesh and blood to the Greys and not just another adopted kid.

Suddenly he grabbed Mr Garth round the waist. 'Thanks for everything, Mr Garth.'

David knelt down and hugged him. 'I'm returning to Wales tomorrow. It's made me very happy to know I can leave you here happy, Louis.'

Louis knew a moment of uncertainty. 'I don't want you to go!'

'I'll be coming back. I'll return before you know it, and we can talk over the phone and write to each other. Apply yourself to your lessons, Louis, learn quickly, as you're more than able to do, and you'll soon be writing me longer and longer letters with bigger words. I'm proud of you, Louis. Your mother's looking down on you and I'm sure she is as proud as punch of you too.'

'Do you think my father would have been proud of me? Do you think he'd have liked me?' Aunty Stella talked a lot about his father Tobias and the japes they had got up to as kids.

'Every time you feel the rain on your face, Louis, some of those drops will be tears of happiness from your father's eyes that you are here where you belong and will have a happy life. Your father would want you to make the most of it, and not to throw away his life as he did.'

'Did he ever mention me?'

'Lots and lots of times,' David lied. 'He very much regretted leaving you and your mother. Honour them by growing up well and God will honour you.'

Louis had had enough of 'heart and soft stuff'. He moved away and picked up Bod and Bim and let them run up and down his arms. 'You'll be glad to come back to see that Nurse Rumford, won't you? You like her.'

'Louis, really!' David protested, but the aforementioned flush shot up his neck and warmed his scalp. 'We'd better tidy up. Your Uncle Jack will be arriving soon to take you and the other boys over to the Vercoe yard to pick up scraps to make your buggies.'

'Someone else likes the nurse too,' Louis went on cheekily. 'Mr Greg's got his eye on her.'

'Sometimes, Louis –' David wagged a finger at him – 'you've got too much imagination.'

Twenty-Eight

The village was nestling down for the evening. The sun was sliding down slowly, slowly in a gentle radiance of horizontal pinks and mauves sowing tinges of the dramatic deep purples and crimson red yet to come. Mums were calling in the young children to bed. The older girls were playing hopscotch or skipping. Nearly all the boys were involved in a seriously fought game of marbles, bragging about their deeply coloured allies, or egging on the current players. Some kids were hanging about in front of their homes waiting for their working dads to appear for their hard-earned supper. An old Fordson tractor broke the relative peace as it turned off down Newton Road for Meadows Farm. Then all seemed silent, the chirping and cheeping of the birds tuned out by well-accustomed ears.

On the weedy forecourt of the Olde Ploughe a group of men were enjoying a drink underneath the wreaths of their tobacco smoke. Finn Templeton, not old enough to join in the round of beer, was supping from a bottle of Coca-Cola.

'So Elias Carey refused the invite to join us?' Ellery snorted his trivial nose at Finn. Never one to change out of his worse-for-wear work clothes until Sundays, as usual, his disreputable billycock hat, worn bald in patches, was clamped down over the remains of his coarse hair. His chin, neck, nose and ears sprouted coarse white hairs, and his steely expression showed his jealousy over Elias Carey's temporary – now ended – employment at Petherton. Ellery bitterly resented his 'elevation' to sole charge of the vast greenhouse, and Denny Vercoe taking over all his other responsibilities, although he never let on about the latter. Ellery's rheumatism and general physical weakening were getting the better of him. Pottering in the greenhouse actually suited him; he had soon regretted being talked out of retirement. He had always enjoyed a good grumble about others, and he knew that others did not really take him seriously, although there were times he had hurt people by what was in effect unkind gossip.

'Didn't except him to.' Finn shrugged his broad shoulders. He was on his feet, leaning against a porch pillar, looking cool and masculine in casual trousers and open-neck white shirt, the sleeves rolled up. 'Elias keeps himself to himself. Fine by me.'

Greg, Hector and Denny, and Johnny Westlake who was taking a break from behind the bar, nodded and murmured in accord.

Sending up a satisfied puff of blue shag smoke from his antiquated chipped pipe, Ellery cawked, 'Got something to hide, if you ask me. He worked like a navvy. A man who works up a sweat at the rate he did is likely trying to forget his past sins.'

Guy Carthewy, the long-time friend and supporter of Finn's mother, and the owner of Merrivale who was currently sponsoring Finn's studies at the art academy, was also there. Unaffectedly smart, a former officer of a tank regiment, he retorted pointedly, 'It's more likely he's trying to forget the horrors he saw and suffered in the hostilities. I know what it's like to lose some good comrades; you too, Greg. And some chaps are just naturally quiet, nothing wrong with that. Can't say I've noticed anything untoward about Elias Carey.'

'Bet his nose is right out of joint though over Mrs Howard taking on Denny full time 'n' putting him out of extra pay.' Ellery was not going to be put off his fault finding.

'I've only met him once briefly, but from what I saw he seems a fellow of simple needs. I shouldn't think he cares all that much about feathering his nest,' Greg said. 'Dorrie recommended to Verity that she take on Carey, and Dorrie's an excellent judge of character.'

'Your sister could be wrong for once!' Ellery grizzled.

'Sure it isn't you who was put out about Carey being employed at Petherton, and now because Denny has taken over your job, Ellery?' Hector bluntly challenged the other old man. There was a mutual dislike here. Ellery had complained about Hector being a 'bleddy foreigner come among us' and had made fun of his melodious Welsh accent.

Ellery retaliated by stabbing a finger at Hector. 'If you think Carey's so bleddy marvellous, then you tell me why he's always hanging round the churchyard? Eh? Eh? 'Tisn't natural.' Ellery swung his hand to point across the short distance to the raised hallowed ground.

'He goes to the services, never misses. Why shouldn't he become familiar with the church and the grounds?' Hector hurled back.

'Keep it down, eh?' Johnny told Ellery in a light-hearted manner before going back inside the pub. He would never set out to antagonise any of his regular customers, but like most villagers he found Ellery amusing and it was fun to take a poke at him.

Greg, Guy and Denny settled back to enjoy a good argument between the pair of old men. It would make their respective womenfolk laugh in the recounting of it.

Finn raised his eyes then settled them squarely on the clearly agitated Ellery. 'I can tell you exactly why Elias Carey spends time in the churchyard.' Then to annoy Ellery he clamped his wide handsome mouth shut.

Finn's victim and the other men were avid to know what Finn meant. 'Go on,' Guy prompted with urgent beckoning hand gestures.

'He likes architecture. Didn't you notice, Mr Ellery, how Elias gazed at Petherton's walls and roofs when he was taking a break? He likes the sense of history about a place. And also . . .'

'Yes, yes!' Ellery banged his thickened, work-grimed hand on the table. 'Spit it out, boy!'

'He keeps his thoughts close but he did tell me one thing,' Finn continued, enjoying making his audience agog. 'He's asked the vicar if he can have a memorial plaque put up in the churchyard.'

'Really?' Greg said. 'Who to? Parents? His wife? Children?'

Finn couldn't help grinning as he shrugged once again. 'Didn't tell me that much. Now there's something for you to speculate about, Mr Ellery.'

Ellery looked about to burst with fury. 'You cheeky young swine.'

Greg wondered if Finn really did know to whom Elias Carey wanted to dedicate a memorial plaque. If so he would reveal it when grumpy old Ellery wasn't present.

Finn gulped down the last of his drink. 'I'm off to walk Tilly back to Petherton.'

'Where's that sweet *cariad* to now then?' Hector asked.

'She's been at my place for tea,' Denny explained, as Finn left whistling a cheery tune.

'Heard any news from your other niece, Denny? Hard to think that wicked Cathy is sister to young Tilly,' Ellery remarked, with a hint of crowing.

'No, and I don't want to.' Denny narrowed his eyes at the nosey old man. 'No good will ever come from she and that's all there is to it.'

Greg went inside and ordered the next round of drinks. His whole being was energised when he spied Rebecca Rumford entering the bar. Her hair was full and bouncy on her shoulders. She was wearing just the right amount of make-up to enhance her natural country loveliness. Her dress was belted at her trim waist and her womanly curves pleasingly shaped the horizontal stripes of the bodice and vertical stripes of the full skirt. Greg took this all in and more. Then he flushed to the lips and tossed away his obvious gaze. Dr Alistair Tregonning was Rebecca's escort tonight and she was evidently very pleased about it.

Oh, well, that's that, Greg thought philosophically, *she wasn't likely to go for an old chap like me anyway.*

His musing was comfortless. He suddenly felt hollow inside. He had been loosely involved with women during his long widower years but none of them had measured up to his beloved Caroline and he had not taken things far. He was still only a year or so off sixty, plenty of life in his limbs and bones yet. His flesh desired a woman in all her femininity. It was time he did something about it.

Twenty-Nine

Sam had hid behind a hedge long enough to be sure Denny was well on the way for his evening drink. Then gulping down the rock in his throat and blinking hard, Sam started warily and hopefully with fingers crossed until they hurt, for By The Way's kitchen door. The door was ajar but there was no need to knock or call out. Tufty announced his arrival by yapping aggressively about his ankles.

'Mum! Sam Lawry's here showing his ruddy face!' bawled out young Maia, the unruly tomboy of the family. She poked her tongue out at Sam.

Sam grew heated and was vexed that it should be this girl who had popped out to see the cause of Tufty's racket. Maia put her thumb to her impertinent nose and waggled her fingers. She had grubby legs and saggy socks but her hands were clean and Sam knew, from former days as Jenna's friend, the family were soon to eat. Denny ate his supper when all the younger kids were settled down in bed.

'Shall I tell Tufty to make him skedaddle, Mum?' Maia bawled again, with malicious glee. More than once she had told Sam she hated his guts for cowardly running out on her big sister.

Adrian Vercoe was next out of the door. A tough and full-bodied fourteen-year-old he was the natural heir to Denny's protective ways for the family. 'Just because you saw Jenna home the day the Rawling hag chucked piss over her don't give you the right to think you can turn up here any time you like. Bugger off for good, or my fist will damn well do it for you.' To prove he meant it Adrian curled up his arm and showed off an impressive burgeoning bicep.

Sam glimpsed Mrs Vercoe staring out the opened window at him. She would come out and have her say but she was waiting to see his reaction to her children's style of welcome. 'L–look, I–I,' he stammered, to his horror, 'I only want a short word with Jenna, t–to ask how she is after her ordeal. To ask how Gary is,

and if she'll let me see him for a minute.' Lamely, he held out
the brown paper bag he had with him. 'I've brought something
for Gary and want to ask if it's all right if he can have it.'

'Jenna don't want nothing to do with you, *turkey-face*,' Maia
snarled tauntingly.

'Get, Sam Lawry!' Adrian thumbed in the direction of the
village. 'Or else!'

'Please!' Sam wailed, holding out the gift for his son to Jean
Vercoe as part of his plea.

Jenna appeared at Jean's side.

'Well,' Jean turned to her. 'Do you want to go out to talk to
him? Do you think he can make up for what he did? Do you
want him to?'

'I neglected Gary for a while, Mum—'

'That was different. You had postnatal depression. One good
deed on his part don't cancel out all the suffering he put you
through. He's putting his hand in his pocket now but that's no
more than it should have been from the start.'

'I know all that, Mum, but after Cathy sending those letters
to Mrs Lawry, Mrs Lawry could have gone to the cruelty people
and had Gary taken off me, but she didn't. She was really kind
about it and wished only to play a part in Gary's life. Gary deserves
to have the best and that could be letting his father see him,'
Jenna said seriously.

Having overheard Sam's plea she had quickly discussed it with
Tilly. 'I think Sam really is sorry about shunning me and Gary.
He was so good to me when old woman Rawling went for me.
It was such a comfort he was there. Without his support I don't
think I'd have the courage to go out in public again. I know he
wanted to come inside the house, but I was eager to bath Gary
and take one myself, and he didn't try to make a point of it.'

'Did he ask to see Gary again?' Tilly had asked simply. Tilly
was something of a romantic, and an innocent, but Jenna knew
her cousin was working things out in the logical, matter-of-fact
way that was also hers. Unless a crime or insult cut very deeply
Tilly was usually all for giving the culprit another chance.

Jenna nodded. 'You think I should give Sam a chance to prove
he's telling the truth, don't you?'

'I think it would be worth it for Gary's sake, otherwise he

might grow up not thanking you for keeping his father at a distance. I agree that Sam behaved like a coward. He was scared all right, of all the responsibility he should have shouldered. He sneaked off, but it seems he's thought better of it, learned a lesson, and now he's back wanting to do the right thing.'

'It must have taken him a lot of courage to come to our door today, Mum,' Jenna considered now. She felt good and she felt confident. She was in charge of this situation.

'So you want to go out and speak to him then?' Jean's frosty tone said she wouldn't be happy.

'Yes, I see no reason not to.'

Sam followed Jenna to the concrete covered well from where the Vercoes pumped up water for their pigs and garden. The younger kids tried to follow them but Jean sternly called them inside.

'Thanks, Jenna,' Sam said, almost in a whisper.

'What's in the bag?' she asked, and to Sam's ease she sounded as if she was interested.

'I bought this in Callington while out making deliveries today. The lady in the shop said it's highly suitable for a young baby. I didn't want to get anything that wasn't right yet for Gary. Can he have it, Jenna?'

Out of the bag she pulled a four-inch, soft plush fur, white Scottie dog, with embroidered eyes and snout, and a pale blue collar sewed round its neck. 'It's got a nice friendly face,' Jenna said in approval.

'The shop lady said nothing could be pulled off to risk choking.' Sam closed his eyes in relief. He had done the right thing in buying the soft toy and coming here today. Denny and Jean might never accept him but it seemed he could likely form an agreement with Jenna to have access with his baby.

'Let's get straight to the point, Sam. What exactly do you want?'

Jenna's gaze was direct and challenging, and Sam knew she would not be taken as a fool and everything depended on his answer.

'To make amends to you and Gary and I hope to be a proper father to him. What I did to you both is unforgivable, I accept that, Jenna. I want with all my heart to see Gary but only if you say where and when. I swear I'd never ever try to push you again into doing something you don't want to do. It's entirely my fault that Gary's here in the world but I don't regret it any more, please believe me. I treasure the moments when I first saw Gary. I'd love to hold him. Mum says he smiles now. I'd love to make him smile.' When Sam ended he was choked and wet-eyed.

Jenna looked at Sam and looked at the toy dog in her hands. 'Jenna?' Sam implored her.

'Well, then, you'd better come inside.'

Sam entered the huge Vercoe kitchen, where the family usually gathered. He passed through a gauntlet of unwelcoming muttering, sighing and brooding silence. He accepted it, unconcerned by it. He was going to see his son properly, and that was all that mattered. He set aside what Denny might subsequently do to him.

He reached the big double pram where Gary lay awake next to Little Jean, both tiny souls kicking their legs and making gleeful noises when their hands rattled the line of yellow ducks stretched above them and secured to the pram's sides. It was easy to tell which was Gary by his decided resemblance to Sam.

'Oh my gosh, she's just as sweet too. Funny to think she's Gary's aunt.' Sam looked at Jenna. 'Can I touch him?'

'Yes,' she nodded.

Sam was aware of Jean watching keenly as he gently reached over Little Jean and put his forefinger against Gary's tiny white palm. The tears came again as Gary made a fist around his fingertip.

'Mmm,' Jean puffed. 'Looks like he's staying for tea then.'

Finn carried on whistling as he went along By The Way lane. Hands in his pockets he dodged about sending stones to skid into the ditches. When he had moved into Merrivale last year with his depressed pregnant mother, his life had been in tatters. Thanks mostly to the support and encouragement from Mrs Resterick, whom he affectionately called Mrs R, his whole situation had changed enormously for the better, and he would never regret the hard lessons learned. His mother had finally seen her rotten criminal father for what he was, an adulterous rat, who had chosen to throw over his family, and then later his new baby Eloise, the sister Finn doted on. Finn had cared for Eloise from birth until his mother had emerged from the oppressive chains of depression.

Fiona was happy to wait for the time she could divorce Aidan Templeton-Barr and marry Guy Carthewy, the old friend who had always loved her, the man she and Finn owed so much to. Finn now had his art studies and he had Tilly. He had had previous girlfriends and full sexual experience, and had assumed he would explore new relationships for many years to come, but after the hurtful fiasco of his intense infatuation with Belle Lawry, courting Tilly in the old-fashioned way was, mysteriously, enough for him. He and Tilly were both very young, and one day he hoped to take things further with her, but for now everything was perfect.

Finn heard someone singing chirpily round the bend ahead and he stilled his lips as he tried to distinguish who was approaching. He and the other person met on the arc of the bend and Finn whipped his hands out of his pockets and balled them into fists. 'What are you doing in this lane, Sam Lawry?'

'None of your damned business, Templeton,' Sam growled. 'Still acting the arrogant swine, I see.'

'You're arrogant and a bloody fool if you think Jenna will forgive you for running out on her.'

'You can wipe that smug sneer off your mug!' Sam stormed. 'Jenna has forgiven me because she's a good person and a grown-up; she doesn't harbour grudges like you do. You've got nothing to be self-righteous about. Your father ditched his whole family. I've heard that when he comes out of clink he's going to take up with one of his tarts. Just because you stepped into your father's place doesn't make you a saint. You lusted after my mother. Blast you to hell! You would've gone with her without a thought for her being a happily married woman. You can't stand it, can you, that my mother was disgusted and furious with you. She had every right to be. You should crawl to her in shame and beg for her forgiveness and own up to your sin, as I've done to Jenna. Then you should crawl under a stone. But you're not as much of a man as mè, Templeton. You're shit beneath my shoes. Now get out of my way,' he finished coldly.

'Why, you . . . !' Finn leapt forward intending to punch Sam on the nose. He thought Sam's instinct would make him swerve out of the way but Sam remained still and Finn pulled his fist back with an instant to spare. Sam was different, not shallow and sly and creeping any more. When they had first met, Sam had been friendly and chatty, but Finn had scathed his company, only tolerating him because Finn had wanted to hear all about Belle and to have an excuse to go to The Orchards.

In the instant Finn had halted his assault he had realised that what Sam said about him was true. He had no right to act the arrogant swine. In his former upper-middle-class days, before his family's comedown, he had actually poured scorn on Jenna over her lowlier background. The truth was Jenna and Sam had had to grow up fast and after some personal trials they were doing it well.

'Strike me if you want to,' Sam said, puzzled at why Finn had resisted landing his ready punch.

'Get on your way,' Finn hissed, unwilling to let the other youth humiliate him further. 'I bet Denny doesn't know you've been to his home. He can deal with you.'

Thirty

Two deaths. Dorrie was often the first person contacted by the bereaved for comfort, and now she found herself hurrying on the way to Merrivale, leaving Greg to take Corky for his morning walk.

Waiting for her on the doorstep of the pleasantly refurbished cottage Fiona Templeton was shaken and numb, but tearless. They exchanged a hug then Dorrie held Fiona a little tighter. 'You said you've had bad news, my dear, and would tell me the rest when I got here. Tell me what's wrong.'

'Thanks for coming so promptly, Dorrie. Let's go through to the sitting room. Eloise is in there playing on the rug.'

Eloise had just started to walk and the fair-haired little girl toddled to Dorrie, her godmother, with squeaks of delight. 'Hello, sweetheart, you can sit on Aunt Dorrie's lap while Mummy talks to me.'

Fiona, with her English-rose looks, her blonde locks up in a pleat, slender in a dress with shoulder pads, met Dorrie's gentle sympathetic eyes, and took a steadying breath. 'Quite simply and horribly, Aidan is dead. The prison phoned me half an hour ago.'

'Oh, I'm so sorry, Fiona. Was he taken ill?' Poor Fiona, Dorrie thought, she was happy with her life now but she had really loved the man who had spurned her after his imprisonment and who had eventually intended to set up home with his mistress. Fiona's feelings had moved on to Guy but she had remained deeply saddened for Eloise growing up knowing her father never wanted to see her. Now Eloise would never get a chance to know Aidan. Finn had seen through his father's grasping, selfish, shady nature and he hated Aidan for it, but how would he feel now Aidan was dead?

'No, Dorrie, I'm afraid his death was neither tragic nor honourable. Rather it was true to Aidan's nature. I asked the governor to tell me all the details rather than learn about them later. I wanted to get all the shocks over and done with. The newspapers are going to be full of it. Aidan was running a protection racket in the prison. He had set himself up as top dog. Inmates were robbed of their tobacco, threatened and beaten up on his say-so. It seems someone tougher and more wicked was then gaoled and orchestrated a takeover. Aidan's henchmen turned against him, and in the early hours a sheet was thrown over his head and he was stabbed to death with a makeshift knife. The governor said that no one has been charged or is likely to be because it will be hard to prove who actually did it.'

Unshed tears glistened above Fiona's lashes, but Dorrie could see she had no particular feelings over Aidan's death. Fiona was glancing between Eloise and a photograph of Finn, sorry and concerned for her children.

'It's a dreadful thing to happen, Fiona. Have you got in touch with Guy, or would you like me to do it? And Finn? Is he doing an odd job somewhere or is he out painting?'

'Thanks, Dorrie, Guy is on his way here, and Finn is meeting up with some other students from the academy today. I'm not sure where to reach him, but I want him to learn about Aidan here at home. I'm all right really. It's just the shock. I'm sorry Aidan's dead but now it means I'm free of him. I can marry Guy and we can start our lives together. Although I shouldn't want to really I just want to laugh with joy. I owe Aidan nothing. He can never hurt me again. Does that make me a bad person?'

'No, Fiona, its perfectly understandable how you feel. What happens now – about Aidan, I mean – will you have arrangements to make? If I can help, do say.'

'I haven't thought that far yet. I'll talk it over with Finn and Guy. I can stump up the money for his funeral.' Fiona was thoughtful. 'I don't want to be hard about it. If the other woman wants to be involved, even to take over the funeral completely, then she can. I certainly don't want to see Aidan or anything like that. I'll ring the governor tomorrow and ask what's the next step. Aidan hurt me and Finn so much. He died how he lived. Now I won't have to go through the humiliation of a divorce. It even means Guy and I can be married in church. I've never felt so free in my life, Dorrie. I know it's wrong but I could almost sing and dance about it.'

These same sentiments were expressed to Dorrie the very next day. Once again her morning walk with Corky was interrupted, this time by Nancy Howard. Nancy had asked to come to Sunny Corner. Corky was left disappointed and ambled off into the garden, grumbling in his throat, for Greg had decided not to substitute his sister again and he remained at home to hear Nancy's sad news. He showed Nancy into the sitting room with exaggerated gallantry, to Dorrie's amusement, and Dorrie noticed how grateful Nancy was in return.

Greg hung on to Nancy's every word, exuding sympathy that was gilt-edged.

'I've had a telegram from Soames, from Egypt. Cassandra is dead. She had a massive heart attack. He's coming home. It was Cassandra's wish to be buried next to Eugene. Her lawyers will see to all that. I'll be damned if I'll fly out to Washington for her funeral. People can think what they like, but I'm confident she won't get a huge turn out. Cassandra's acid put-downs will see to that.' As Nancy went on a sense of bitter elation grew in her. 'I'm free of her now. I feel as if a heavy weight has fallen off my back. There were too many times when that woman made my life a misery. I know it's spiteful of me to say this, but I'm sure Soames won't be too sorrowful over her sudden end either. By now he was probably no more to her than a gofer who could never do anything right for her. I gave him a little warning, you see. I suggested he should keep on the Stores. When he gets home, I'm sure we'll all find he's well and truly over his former loneliness, glad to resume his old place, and will enjoy his autumn years to the full.'

'I'll look forward to seeing Soames again,' Dorrie said, not issuing the usual condolences. They would be just tired expressions to Nancy. 'Now, is there anything we can do for you, Nancy?'

'Yes, my dear,' Greg ploughed in, leaning forward and taking Nancy's hands. 'May I ask if Cassandra's death will affect you in any way?'

'I certainly can't imagine she'd leave me anything in her will, Greg,' Nancy replied softly, smiling a smile just for him. 'Or that she'd have Petherton taken away from me; she saw the old place as a final punishment for me marrying Eugene. If my allowance stops, it won't press me all that much. I have my own means. I accepted money off her because it was Eugene's wish that I get something. She very slyly tied up what should have been Eugene's inheritance from his father. I like Petherton, but wouldn't mind at all if I ever had to leave it.'

'Really?' Greg intoned huskily.

Dorrie slipped quietly out of the room. Nancy had no more need of her.

Thirty-One

Noise. All too often there was noise and confusion in the house. Verity hated the regularity with which Jack had his nephews and nieces over for play and meals. She had stalled his suggestion to have one or two of the children to sleep over. 'I love Louis and the little Greys, but I want to be allowed to enjoy my pregnancy and take plenty of rest.'

'Fair enough, it's important you look after yourself.' There should have been a 'darling' at the end of Jack's reply but he rationed endearments nowadays. There were times Verity bit back an addition to his words. *For the baby's sake. That's what you mean, don't you?*

Verity preferred to see the children at Olivia House or else-where. The Greys enthusiastically joined in every village event eager for the local children to understand that their disabled little ones were no different to them. Sadly, some older children referred to the Grey children, even the twins, as 'the retards'. Jack had boxed the ears of a couple of early teens after hearing their jeers. He had complained to their parents and been satisfied the culprits had received further punishment.

Verity was also protective of Louis and the Grey children, but she resented the amount of Jack's attention they and Stella stole from her. Jack could be distant with Verity, showing his resentment, she thought, over the wretched business of having Lucinda's remains removed. He approved of the new staff she had engaged; he was polite to them and showed some interest in their lives. He occasionally shared a cigarette with Elias Carey, and Verity had heard him telling Carey the origins and history of the grounds and gardens, and about the wide range of coloured heathers Jack had added in recent years. He told Carey his wishes for future work in the house and grounds, and to Verity's hurt, Jack did not discuss them with her after-wards. It seemed the blissful start to her marriage ended the day they arrived back from honeymoon. She and Jack were nurturing resentments against each other and it was pushing a wedge between them.

After a particularly stony atmosphere over dinner one night Jack had declined to join her in the drawing room for coffee. Verity had followed Jack into the library and blurted out, 'I'm sorry, Jack!'

'What on earth for?' He reached for his cigarette box.

'For wanting Lucinda to be buried elsewhere, I know you resent me over it.'

Jack had stared at her. 'Don't be ridiculous.'

'Ridiculous? That's a very unkind thing to say. I made an understandable request, but sadly, I demanded it in a totally thoughtless manner. I recognise how you doted on Lucinda and had a strong desire to protect her always. You did as I asked, and I'm sorry about the distaste it must have caused you, but please don't go on punishing me over it. Please stop cutting me out. Jack, I love you desperately. I'm sorry I made a dreadful mistake so early on. Can't we go back to the way we were? Excited and loving every minute together?'

He had frowned heavily. 'I thought we were. Why are you accusing me of failing you? It must be your hormones. You had better have a talk to Nurse Rumford. An unhappy mother makes an unhappy child. Really, Verity, you're talking such nonsense.'

'Am I indeed?' Verity had run to him, shocked at his coldness. 'Then why don't you make love to me any more?'

'What? I was being forbearing for your sake and the baby's. What the hell are you talking about? Am I a monster?'

Verity had dissolved into tears, giving Jack further ammunition to blame her hormones. Finally he used familiarity but in a way Verity found patronising. 'Darling, you really need to lie down. Up you go. I'll get Joan to bring you up some hot milk with nutmeg.' He had kissed her lightly on the forehead. 'If you want a little passion I'll see to you, don't worry.'

Verity found his last remark offensive. He made it sound like she was sexually frustrated, and he would 'see to her' as if it was some necessary and troublesome task. He had made her feel a bother to him and a little of her love dropped off her heart.

The Greys having five children and Louis under their guardian-ship meant endless picnics, seaside trips and birthday parties to attend, with the village kids joining in and the dogs scampering about. Jack insisted on going every time and Verity hated the occasions more and more. There was so much noise and jollity, entreaties to play hide and seek and sardines and board games to endure. Too much of furry pets being plonked on her lap to admire and pet. Dolls to be dressed, dressing-up games to participate in, nursery rhymes to sing and storybooks to be read, all with the smug Stella watching Verity to see if she was doing everything the right way according to *Stella Grey's vast experience in child rearing*. If Verity received one more piece of advice about the best way she should bring up her child she would scream her head off.

Her ploy to offset the irritations was to take up her wartime pastime of knitting. Verity could knit rapidly, and she had helped produce sacks of socks and mufflers for servicemen and service women. She had also knitted for the poor. She could afford to buy the best for her baby, and Dorrie had knitted a stack of baby clothes for her already, but Verity was now busy adding larger clothes to the bundle. As a treat for Pattie and Daisy she had turned out a stream of dolls' clothes, and for Libby a little stripy teddy bear.

It was immensely satisfying to knit for her baby, and she was busy forming a winter bobble hat, relaxing on the terrace sensibly wearing a tweed coat and fur hat, her legs covered with a thick blanket. In the periphery of her vision she could see the stream tinkling on its merry way. Just like a chirpy bird, Verity thought, sighing in the peace of the day. Joan brought her daily hot, spiced tonic. 'Thank you, Joan.'

'Shall I straighten your blanket, Mrs Newton?' Joan bobbed a curtsey, an etiquette Verity had told her was not necessary, but Joan liked to do it. Verity knew it made her feel entrenched in her job.

'Yes please. I haven't asked you lately how your family are. How is your sister getting on as dairy maid?'

'They're all very well thank you, madam, and Norma's taken to the job like a duck to water. Is there anything else I can do for you, madam?'

'You can fetch my shawl from the breakfast room please, Joan, in case I need it.' Extra warmth was not needed in this sheltered spot, but Verity liked to pander to Joan's delight at waiting on her.

Verity sipped the tonic and knitted on until she was casting off the last stitch at the hat's crown.

'Begging your pardon, ma'am.'

'Oh! It's you, Carey. What is it?' Verity found his combination of ice-blue eyes and carelessly curly hair and rangy physique strikingly attractive. It irritated her for some reason and she was always sharp with him. She was determined to dislike him; a person inhibited was likely to be hiding something.

'Sorry, ma'am. Mr Newton asked me to come here at this time.'

'Mr Newton is out. Why did he ask you to come here?'

'To meet him and the puppy, ma'am.' Elias Carey raised his strong brows in querulous fashion.

Verity bristled. Now what was Jack planning without discussing it with her first? Damn him, it was really too bad. He was treating her like she was superfluous to his life except as a brood mare for his heirs. Then she chided herself. Darling Jack, he was going to spring a lovely surprise on her; that was it. He knew how much she loved Corky, and before she had got so big with the baby, how she had enjoyed playing with Cosmo, Basil and Rags at Olivia House. Jack was getting her a puppy of her own in time for it to get used to its new home and mistress before the baby was born. 'Oh, of course, the puppy,' she bluffed gaily. 'I can hardly wait. Has Mr Newton asked you to help train it, Carey?'

'Yes ma'am, and to show how it's done to Master Louis.'

'Master Louis?' Verity only just managed to keep the terseness out of her question.

'Well, it's to be his dog when he stays here. Mr Newton wants Master Louis to learn how to keep it under control so it doesn't bother you. Mr Newton asked me if I'd board the dog in my quarters when Master Louis isn't staying here. Rest assured, ma'am, I'll make sure it doesn't wander into the house. I'm used to dogs.' He shuffled his boots and looked down, plainly unwilling to reveal anything more about himself.

Somehow concealing her hurt and rank disappointment, Verity marshalled her dignity. 'Tell Mr Newton I've gone up to lie down. I'm a little weary.'

'I'll do that, ma'am. Do you need a helping hand?'

His tone was gentle, and Verity felt his sympathetic respect and was not annoyed over his unexpected forwardness. To receive kindness from a man so withdrawn was comforting. Suddenly feeling heavy and lethargic, she made to trudge up to the old-fashioned day bed in the master suite.

'Ma'am, your knitting.' Carey was there beside her. 'You dropped it.'

'Oh.' She took the wool and needles from him, meeting the thoughtfulness in his lowered glance. Aunt Dorrie had been right about him; he was the right man for this job. 'Thank you, Carey, thank you very much indeed.'

A short time later there was a knock on the bedroom door and Jack came in. 'Verity . . . darling,' he whispered. 'Carey has told me you are unwell. I asked Joan if she had taken you up anything and she became anxious because you didn't mention it to anyone else. Do you need anything?'

'No,' she replied curtly, not bothering to open her eyes. She had a headache brought on by the stress of her anger with Jack. 'The last stages of pregnancy can be rather tiresome. Please go, Jack. I'll be fine soon.'

'What a shame, I've bought a puppy as a surprise for Louis, a golden Labrador.'

'I thought I heard a dog outside,' she said sternly, aiming to make him feel guilty, hating how happy he sounded about his latest trick to spoil his long-lost nephew.

'I hope it didn't disturb you. I'll instruct Carey to keep it away from this side of the house. I was hoping to tell you all about the puppy. Never mind, I'll do so later when you're up to it. I've phoned Stella to bring Louis over this afternoon. Don't worry, I'll keep things quiet.'

'What?' Verity levered herself up on the day bed to half sitting. 'You could only have been home about five minutes and you've phoned Stella about the wretched puppy before coming up to see how I am? Well! It's nice to learn where your priorities lie.'

'I beg your pardon?'

Fuming at him for taking the moral high ground, she struggled to her feet. 'You know exactly what I meant. Answer me this, why do I come so far down on your list? I'm your wife yet you concern yourself with your family before me. You're deliberately shutting me out. You should have discussed with me first about this puppy. For one thing, I might like to have it in the house, but no, as far as you see I'm not entitled to an opinion. I take it you'd previously mentioned this puppy to your sister. Am I right?'

Jack pulled an expression of impatience.

'So, yes you did.' Verity wanted to go at him blazing but she was suddenly short of breath and overcome with weariness. 'I don't count to you about anything, do I?'

'Of course you do, Verity, calm down, it's not good for you. I apologise, I've been a thoughtless bastard. I really am sorry. Sometimes I . . . I don't know.' For a moment he looked forlorn and very young. 'Look here, darling, do you think you could manage to go downstairs on my arm? We'll have a fortifying cup of tea and you must have a couple of plain biscuits. Have you taken any aspirin?'

Verity nodded, taking in the rapid change in him back to adoring bridegroom. 'Oh, Jack, I thought I'd lost you.'

He held out his arms, she went into them, and he caught her close. 'Whatever do you mean, darling? Have I been really cruel?'

Cruel? He had been cruel in a way, but she wasn't going to risk alienating him again. Her old Jack was back and she would concentrate only on that, and try to never upset and distance him again.

On the way down the stairs, he said, 'I'll phone Stella and put her off today.'

'No, don't do that, darling. Louis must already be looking forward to coming over. I wonder what he'll call the puppy.'

'We can have fun helping him to choose.'

The name given to the gorgeous playful puppy was Jakes, suggested by Stella and heartily approved of by Jack. All the names nominated by Verity were passed over by Jack and Stella and even scoffed at.

Thirty-Two

Elias Carey waited below the well-scrubbed granite doorstep of the Victorian vicarage for the Reverend Wentworth Lytton to emerge. Elias had called to inquire if a decision had been made yet by the ecclesiastical powers-that-be permitting him to have a memorial plaque placed in the churchyard.

The daily cleaner, a thick-bodied, grey-haired woman wearing a wraparound apron and her outdoor hat, fetched the vicar from his study.

'Yes? What is it you want?' Lytton demanded in his breathy voice, making watery coughs, an unpleasant habit of his. He appeared shorter than he was. The rheumatism in his shoulders made him stooped. He had a bulldog neck and a bullfrog face. His fingers were ingrained with black ink from writing his memoirs, said to be a long-winded work never near completion.

Elias had overheard Greg Barnicoat mock the vicar. 'He's probably only doodling his time away to avoid attending to his pastoral duties. Apparently, no one cared much that the vicar was lazy and insufferably rude at times, even to the pleasant middle-aged Mrs Resterick, sister to Greg Barnicoat and aunt to Mrs Newton. She attended Matins now and then. Elias always bid her 'good morning' on those occasions, after which she always went silently to pay homage at two graves.

Elias explained his presence at the doorstep in the least number of words.

'Ah, the plaque, it will take a little longer, I fear.' The cleaner dumped down a metal bucket and mop beside the heavily carved credenza in the hall. Lytton stared at her with impatience. There was obviously no mutual respect between the vicar and his cleaner. Elias was not in the least interested in the reasons why. He sought only peace for his soul on Sundays. 'I can't get on here at present, Carey. Wait there and I'll lead the way to the churchyard where we may discuss the matter further.'

Lytton did not invite Elias inside, in fact he shut the door on him, but Elias would have declined anyway. He hated how the high thick walls afforded cloying blockades. Originally from tinker folk he preferred living in a tent, a shack or loft, or as at Meadows House, in a small sparse cottage where he could leave the windows open and doors thrown wide. He had trained the puppy Jakes to run about in close proximity to him while he was working. Jakes barely left his side and was really his dog and not Master Louis's. Master Louis had been overwhelmed with the gift of the chubby healthy puppy. The boy, having in common with Elias a rough start, was happy to share Jakes with him. The boy liked getting his hands dirty and after watching Elias had asked if he could help with the planting and weeding, any painting and polishing the three cars. 'I won't be a bother to you, Mr Carey. I know you like to keep mum,' the boy had coaxed. 'Jakes would love being with both of us, see, his tail is wagging.'

'Well, as long as Mr Newton approves,' Elias replied. He wouldn't have been pleased if any of the Grey children had requested this. Master Louis just wanted to be a mate. 'It'll be good for you to learn about nature and her ways, and about engines. Quiet's the way though. Deal?'

'Deal!' Master Louis had shaken on it.

The Reverend Lytton emerged from a side door in his long flowing black cape and gaiters, as he always did when without, and a parson's hat. He motioned with a podgy hand for Elias to follow him, then turned his back and started off for the church, stepping high to the end of School Lane. He turned smartly to parade across the invariably quiet main road. He mounted the four gritty granite steps and swept in under the iron arch, its missing ornate wrought-iron gates sacrificed for the war effort.

Elias followed the vicar past the church tower and porch and through rows of older resting places, with few headstones, finally coming to a stop near the perimeter wall, on the other side of the pub. Holly bushes and yew darkened and sheltered this area of the gone and forgotten. 'You're a man of great reserve, Carey. You may have your plaque placed here where you may remember your lost ones in relative solitude.'

'That's very thoughtful of you, Mr Lytton.'

'It must be unequally hard to lose all one's family.' The vicar spoke with a compassion that would have surprised his other parishioners.

'It is. Sometimes I don't believe it happened . . . travelling on that back road . . . picked out by that German Stuka . . . One blast and they were all gone, my family. I should have been with them.'

'You were doing your duty to your king and country, where you should have been, Carey. You have an excellent position now. Will you be tempted to take to the road again any time soon?'

'I don't know, to be honest. I take one day at a time.'

'It's no more than what our Good Lord taught us to do. Now I've got lots to do. I'll inform you when a decision has been made about the plaque. There is no need to call on me again.'

Alone, Elias pictured the slate plaque he hoped to see here. People wanting to learn something about his family would be disappointed. The words etched on the plaque would be the same as others he had had placed on his travels.

In Loving Memory of my Family
The Careys

'Dor! Why do you keep shifting away from me?' Greg demanded under his breath. 'You're not jealous of me stepping out with Nancy, are you? I know for the past few years we've been content with our own company. Don't you approve of me forging a romance?' Then he was troubled. 'You don't feel I'm making a fool of myself, do you?'

They were at Petherton for lunch. Also invited were Jack and Verity and Oscar and Stella. The vicar was making a very unsatisfactory fourth man. 'I'm afraid I couldn't think of anyone else to invite,' Nancy had apologised. 'Do you mind terribly if I put the old thing next to you, Dorrie? You'll be able to tolerate him, won't you?'

'Don't worry, Nancy,' Dorrie had laughed kindly. 'The good reverend will scoff down every course offering barely a word, listening to no one at all, then hastily excuse himself to scuttle off back to his study.'

To Greg, she said while again leaning aside from him, 'Of

course I don't mind you having a romance with Nancy. You've simply overdone it on the aftershave again.'

'Damn it, Dor! Why didn't you say so before we left home?' He whipped out his pocket-handkerchief and made furtive swipes at his throat and chin.

'I tried to. You were in too much of a hurry. Instead of us walking here, you even had to drag out the old motorcar you were in such a hurry. You know, if you really want to impress Nancy you should consider getting a new car.'

'You really think so?' Greg fiddled with his tie while thrusting out his chest.

'It would give you something to do instead of nervously pacing about at home and planning your next date with Nancy,' Dorrie said wryly. 'Ask Jack about it. It will give him something else to think about too.'

Greg was too excited to glean her underlying meaning. Sherry glasses in hand Jack and Stella were standing apart, next to a window, closed off from all others. Rain was teeming down and there was a draught at that particular window but the pair did not seem aware of it. Not for the first time Dorrie noticed the brother and sister were leaving Verity and Oscar out of their eager company. Louis was much mentioned. Verity had been upset lately about being made to feel sidelined.

'Jack never considers my opinions any more, Aunt Dor,' Verity had confided, 'and I'm not just talking about choosing a name for the puppy. He never seems interested in what I've got to say unless it concerns the baby. I wish to God I'd never lost my temper about Lucinda. It might have been Cathy who played that cruel trick but Lucinda still haunts Jack and he willingly allows it. Why can't he be happy with me? I should be the one who counts. He said he loved me, he promised he would never let me down, he made sacred vows to always put me first, but Stella and Louis come first to him. I'll be even lower on his list when the baby is born. I was so happy for Jack having his sister back in his life, to learn what had happened to Tobias, but now I wish it had never happened. Well, not immediately after our honeymoon was over.'

'You believe if you and Jack had had some time to establish your marriage things would have been different?'

'Yes, Aunt Dor, I would have shown him how good a wife he'd got for himself.' Verity had banged her fists together. 'Aaargh! But Cathy would still have carried out her malicious plan. Of all the awful bloody rotten luck.'

'All that has happened and it can't be changed, darling.' Dorrie had uncurled Verity's fists and held on to her hands. 'Leave it in the past, forget all about it, you must try to for the sake of your marriage and the baby's future. Show Jack you are the wife that you'd intended to be. Jack obviously has issues from the past. He probably can't help the way he feels. Make a happy home for him, Verity, to help him forget about his hang-ups.'

Oscar did not seem to mind being forgotten. He was gallantly engaging Verity in talk about her baby. She was slumped on a high-back chair from where she could more easily rise. 'If I may say so you look radiant, Verity. It's not long now, is it?'

'Six weeks,' Verity answered tiredly.

Dorrie worried about the lack of Verity's usual verve and energy. Verity had once been so daring. Looking to take on the world.

'It seems endless. You're very kind, Oscar, but I don't look radiant, rather a cumbersome lump. It takes me a lot of time to get going in the morning.'

'I'm sure things will be better after the birth.'

Verity glanced at the husband oblivious to her. She could only manage a half smile at Oscar.

Dorrie sighed inwardly. It was awful not seeing the old Verity – confident, alert and always daring. But, Dorrie reminded herself, Verity was impatient by nature and pregnancy could be trying in the last weeks.

'Hello all.'

'Soames!' Nancy, Dorrie and Greg all cried at once.

'I told Tilly I'd announce myself. I got the taxi to drop me off here. I'm delighted to see some of my dear friends in one place.' Soames' sentiment did not include Jack, the distant cousin who had always casually ignored him. He did not know the Greys well. He and Lytton had passed few words even though Soames had been a churchwarden.

His friends' delight was tempered by them being appalled at his dramatic loss of weight. His sharply cut suit hung off him and his paunch had disappeared.

'As you can see I'm quite worn out. I've had enough adventure to last me a hundred lifetimes.'

'Thank heavens you're back safely, Soames,' Nancy exclaimed. 'You're badly in need of more than a few hearty meals. You must stay for luncheon. Cook always makes plenty.'

After the genially eaten meal of onion soup, baked mackerel and boiled apple pudding, Lytton, Jack, Verity and the Greys left.

The others congregated round the cosy hearth in the south-facing sitting room. Avid faces waited for Soames to spill all. He lounged back in a shabby well-stuffed Victorian armchair, chain-smoking expensive cigarettes.

'Phew.' He mopped his sweaty forehead with the back of a wobbly hand. 'It's the best feeling in the world to be back home in Nanviscoe, I can tell you. Can't think how I could ever have left it. Can't think how I was taken in by that bloody woman. She was the most heartless bitch on earth, begging your pardon, ladies. But Nancy knew that only too well. Thanks for your advice about keeping the shop on. I soon saw that it was a friendly warning to me.' At times his voice squeaked with tears and he was forced to clear his throat. 'Sorry. When her maid wasn't around Cassandra treated me like a slave. By the time we reached Mesopotamia it was "fetch me this, fetch me that, get me another cocktail". She even made me walk behind her. Within days she shut me out of her luxury cabins and hotels rooms, and went on to have affairs. Heaven help me, that woman was insatiable. She flaunted her liaisons and ridiculed me in front of her lovers. She left a few heartbroken wives in her wake too. If she hadn't died of that sudden heart attack I think I would now be in jail for her murder, me or one of those poor wives.'

He gave a crazed laugh. 'We were having dinner at a hotel and she was knocking back the wine as usual when she clutched her arm, clutched her chest, howled the most terrible scream and fell face down in her dessert. She dropped as dead as a doornail, and the rest of us guests, the maître d' and the serving staff could only look on, frozen to the spot. When an elderly French doctor, a chap she had sneered at for being rather short in stature, announced she was dead there was a strange hush. I half expected a round of applause. God help me, I wanted to clap and cheer that the bitch was dead. All I could think was that I was free, and desperate to return home.'

Soames let all his pent-up tears and the horror gush out of him. Dorrie laid her arm round his quaking shoulders. 'Don't stop, Soames, until it's all spent.'

Nancy poured him a large brandy.

Greg passed him a clean handkerchief. 'Let it all go, old chap.'

'Free is also how I felt, Soames, when I got your telegram,' Nancy said. 'Dare I say it was most welcome.'

'There's more good news, Nancy,' Soames said, his voice raw and husky, after he reclaimed his wits. 'Her lawyers had quite a lot of eye-openers for me. Seems the bitch didn't really have a bean of her own. The money she had splashed around was actually Eugene's and therefore by right should have been yours. I'm afraid she'd got through the bulk of it, but there's a goodly sum left, enough to keep you as you are for the rest of your days. Also, Mrs Mitchelmore made no such clauses outlined by Cassandra in the sale of this house that you must keep it as a shrine to Sedgewick Mitchelmore's family. I managed to get in touch with her and she said her time away in Switzerland had made her see the Mitchelmore history had come to a natural end. Petherton is truly yours, Nancy; your name is on the deeds and it's yours to do with as you like.'

'Phew,' Nancy whispered under her breath. 'Could anyone have been more vindictive? She was evil. She caused poor Eugene a great loss of peace. Makes me wonder if she actually loved him, or was just out to exploit him. It's quite a revelation, a lot to take in.'

'But you can now make a really fresh start,' Greg smiled at Nancy and reached for her hand.

'Well, seems I've got a lot to catch up on,' Soames said, making short of the brandy.

'You certainly have,' Dorrie smiled. 'It's good to have you back where you belong, among us, Soames.

'The rain has eased off. Will you walk with me to the shop, Dorrie?'

'I'd be delighted to.'

'One last thing I would like to know, Soames, before we put that dreadful gag out of our minds forever. What did you do with her body?' Nancy asked. 'As she had no money of her own did you arrange that she be shipped back to America to be buried next to Eugene?'

Soames smiled a wide smile. 'Cassandra had planned an elaborate funeral. As her husband it fell to me to dispose of her. I had her buried at sea, and good riddance.'

Thirty-Three

'Fetch!' Elias threw an old tennis ball and Jakes tore after it and brought it straight back to him. 'Good boy, you're a good boy, the best.'

Sprawling on his back on his own patch of lawn Elias playfully tussled with the handsome pale-coated puppy. Yapping wildly, Jakes stood on his chest and licked his arms and face and Elias laughed and laughed. He liked this place that went with his job and the old gardener's cottage. When first taken on by Mrs Newton he spent the first night in the big house in the servants' quarters, as his predecessor had done, and found it horribly claustrophobic. Next day he had explored the grounds and quickly come across the small abandoned thatched dwelling with over-hanging eaves. Against the peeling whitewashed wall was a bench of criss-cross split logs and flat planks. There was no door lock and he had gone inside. This would suit him perfectly. He did not shun dust and cobwebs but it would not take long to clean things up. It had the necessary sticks of furniture except for a bed, but he had slept on enough floors in his life – including bombed-out buildings in war-torn France – to care about that.

'You'd rather live in The Nest?' Mr Newton had asked. 'But it hasn't any running water and needs attention after all this time. There are no amenities. You'd need to cut back the surrounding trees.'

'I'm happy to draw my water from the well, sir, to cook over a primus or the hearth, to use lantern and candlelight, and the outdoor privy. To sweep the chimney and see to the other jobs.' The Nest was the perfect name for Elias's borrowed home.

Jakes' wild licking tickled his neck and Elias chuckled. 'You're a character, Jakes boy, a dog and a half.'

'He certainly is. Sorry. I'm disturbing you, Carey, during your own time. Don't get up,' Verity said, smiling down on him. 'I was taking a stroll and heard you having fun and it drew me to take a look. I hope I'm not intruding.'

'Not at all, Mrs Newton,' Elias said softly, getting up and keeping the squirming Jakes in his grasp. He was training Jakes not to greet people too enthusiastically, but he did not want to risk Jakes toppling Mrs Newton over. She had been looking emotionally fragile for too long, and she was hopelessly pale, her skin pressed hard against her cheekbones. Elias knew that pregnancy didn't agree with all women but he, and all the staff at Meadows House, knew that was not the case for Mrs Newton. They all knew who was to blame, and rumours were beginning to steal out into the village, that Jack Newton had quickly thrown off his mantle as a loving husband. It marred Elias's time here but rather than move on, as he would usually do, he felt a loyalty to the woman who had taken him on. A few nights ago she had been taken ill, a dizzy spell after some unpleasantness, apparently. To his knowledge this was the first time she had been out of the house without the nanny, Deborah Weston, at her side.

'You're as fond of Jakes as Louis is. It's easy to see he's longing to take him home.'

Verity had mentioned something similar to Jack the night after Nancy's luncheon while they were getting ready for bed. She was brushing her hair at her dressing table and Jack had just come out of his dressing room, wearing pyjamas. He had taken to wearing nightwear only recently. Verity saw it as him putting more than a physical distance between them. 'It's a shame to watch his disappointed little face, Jack. Stella says it would be all right for Louis to have Jakes at home. Why not let Jakes move there?'

'Has Louis asked you to ask me this?' Jack had said, in the way of a challenge. It was the way he often addressed Verity lately. More and more he was away from home, sometimes leaving the house without a word as to where he was going.

'No, I was thinking of Louis.'

'Don't you mean thinking of yourself?'

'I beg your pardon? What is that supposed to mean?'

'It seems to me you have no real interest in Louis and you don't like the bother of having Jakes about the place when Louis is here.'

'How dare you say such a thing? I think the world of Louis. One of my favourite times is when I play Ludo or read to him.'

She had continued with a sarcastic tone. 'I'm very sorry if I can't run about with him, but it seems to have escaped your notice that I'm heavily pregnant and need to take things carefully. You know very well that Nurse Rumford said I must go slowly as my blood pressure tends to be high. Jakes isn't allowed upstairs. It was something that we both agreed on. Otherwise Jakes has the run of the house. I've always made a fuss of him and I've always loved dogs. I want our child to have a dog of his or her own. What has got into you? Why do you continually pick on me? Have you stopped loving me?'

'Don't be childish, woman.' He had turned away from her.

Stung into a furious passion, she had jumped up and grabbed his arm, squeezing deliberately to cause him pain. 'Woman? You dare call me that in such a derogatory tone? You bastard, Jack Newton, don't you ever speak to me like that again. You're turning into your father. I've had enough of it.' Jack peeled off her clawing fingers but she continued yelling. 'I won't be treated like dirt in the same manner your father treated your mother. You've even gone as far as ignoring me in public, more than once. Aunt Dorrie and Uncle Greg have noticed, so you can't accuse me of imagining it, as you often do. I don't know what on earth I've done to make you turn against me and I'm beginning not to care. If you want our marriage to work you'd better revert to being the adoring husband I went on honeymoon with pretty damned quick, do you hear me?'

'Of course I can hear you. You're shrieking loud enough to wake the dead!' he had hurled back.

Verity had not thought she could get into more of a rage. 'Even your first insane wife?'

She had felt herself losing her legs and her balance and it seemed the look Jack gave her was of pure hatred, contorted and ugly.

The next thing she knew she was coming to, lying on her bed, and Deborah Weston was leaning over her, rubbing her wrist. 'Don't try to get up, Mrs Newton. You fainted. Mr Newton is ringing the doctor.' She was aware of Jack standing at his side of the bed speaking on the telephone, of Mrs Rabey and Joan peeping anxiously into the room.

Jack had sat on the bed and lifted up her other hand. 'It's all right, darling. I shouldn't have quarrelled with you and forgotten your delicate condition. It was very unkind of me.' He'd kissed her hand. 'It won't happen again, I promise.'

He had turned to Deborah Weston and the two other women. 'It started as a tiff over a silly thing and I let it get out of hand. I feel such a swine. I can hardly forgive myself. Now we must all club together and look after Mrs Newton.'

Verity knew Jack was insincere. He was a stranger to her. At that moment she hated him and the fact that he was the father of her baby.

Now she had ventured out alone for some fresh air and regretted it. A muddled sensation threatened to overwhelm her and she put up a hand to her head. 'Oh . . .'

'Come and sit down on the bench, Mrs Newton. I'll set Jakes to play then fetch you some water.' Elias was sure the last thing she wanted was to return to the dreary old house. He saw Meadows House differently then, as a sort of prison, a cold set of walls where despair and madness could grow. He had the strange sensation, something that had happened to him before and proved to be right, that he had ended up here for a reason.

When he returned with a tumbler of water, Verity's head had cleared. She had taken a few deep breaths and gazed around at the surroundings. Elias had made the spot pretty with pots of petunias and geraniums. An old tin kettle was bursting with delicate violas and an old frying pan served as a birdbath. To her delight a sparrow flew down and splashed in the water and preened its wings. At the edge of the grass Elias had made a border of marigolds, poppies and begonias. Jakes chased a butterfly until it flitted away. He padded up to Verity, climbed up beside her and settled down to doze with his soft head on her lap. Verity found it soothing to stroke his broad velvety head.

'Thank you, Carey, I'm fine now.' She sipped the ice-cold water. 'You've just drawn this from the well. It's delicious, refreshing. You've made it very homely here, and it's peaceful.'

'I'm very grateful to you, ma'am, to live and work here.'

He watched her circumspectly for further signs of distress.

'Do you miss the open road?'

'As long as I can come and go easily as I do here I'm quite content.'

'I understand you've lost all your family. I've heard about the memorial plaque. I'm sorry. I know it must be awful. During the war I took details from distraught people who had lost every single loved one, every single thing. One girl aged about seventeen was wrapped in blankets for she had even had her clothes blasted off. I'll never forget the uncomprehending look in her soot-streaked face, her empty eyes.' Knowing she was not outstaying her welcome here Verity felt at ease to ask him more. 'Have you travelled all over the country, Carey?'

'More or less. I've met many an interesting character on my travels. Some I'd travelled with for a while.'

'I've met a few gentlemen of the road in this parish, all seemingly honest men, quite harmless. Do you, um, ever think you'll settle down one day?'

'That's not for me, ma'am. My grandma, Polly Lock, her name was, used to say, "Always a loner, you'll be." She lived till she was ninety-nine, or so it was thought. No one knew for sure how old she was, or where she originated from, come to that. Her voice was too cracked to tell of an accent.'

'You won't be moving on again too soon, I hope.' Verity stared at him full in the eyes, needing an ally, someone to turn to situated closer than her aunt and uncle.

'There's a lot needed to be done here yet, ma'am. You can trust me.'

Verity caught his meaning and once more she felt soothed. Safer. 'I'd better go in or I shall have Miss Weston, Mrs Rabey and Joan worrying about me.' She was further comforted by the fact that she had engaged the three women. They were her staff, not Jack's. They were loyal to her. They all shared a mutual respect and trust. Verity's former fiancé had humiliated her and tried to grind her emotions into dust. She would not let Jack do that to her. He would do well to be very careful of his dealings with her in future.

Elias wandered through the woods, with Jakes darting off here and sniffing there, bounding over big sticks, chasing squirrels and sending up clumps of soggy leaves. Elias noted logs suitable for firewood, familiarising himself with areas still new to him. He had just about marked out the house's boundaries and the woods before Newton farmland took over.

'Interesting,' he said aloud to Jakes, who had tired at last and was trotting at his heels. He had reached a small setting that did not appear natural. Great hanging streams of ivy formed a high blockade. Someone was sheltering here. It might be someone he knew from his days on the road, but he picked Jakes up and held him close while gently encircling the puppy's jaw to prevent him yapping, and he crept forward cautiously. It might just as easily be someone shady, perhaps on the run from the law.

Elias slowly pulled back the curtain of foliage. He entered the small clearing beyond the greenery. There was sign of some disturbance but definitely no one was camping here. This was the former resting place of the master's first unfortunate wife. Although she had been dug up and buried elsewhere and the grave's trappings gone, Elias paid respect to the spot by refusing to let Jakes go, despite the puppy struggling against him. Elias had released Jakes's jaw and he growled deep in his throat. An icy thrill rode up Elias's backbone and the place darkened. He whirled round. A shadowy shape was in the trees.

'Who's there?' Elias snapped.

'You know me.' The shape defined into a figure of a tall man with a heavy pack on his back and he came forward. 'Hello, Elias Carey.'

Elias's frown shifted to a grin of recognition. The man was of sixty-odd years, of good bearing and had one arm. His clothes were rough from his transient life but he wore them smartly. 'Freddie Stanhope! It's good to see you again. What brings you here?'

'I always pass through Nanviscoe about this time of year and I always come into these woods. You have the look of a man in work, my friend.'

The men grasped hands. Freddie Stanhope patted Jakes' head. Suddenly tired Jakes snuggled in to sleep in Elias's arms. 'I can tell you there has been a great many changes since you were last on this land, Freddie. The house has a new mistress and I am part of a complete new staff, the gardener-handyman.'

'A good position for you. Jack Newton is a good man.'

'I thought he was at first but not now after what I've witnessed.'

'Oh? What's happened here? Lucinda Newton's grave has been desecrated.' There was a hint of anger in Freddie Stanhope's smooth voice. A former valet, he retained considerable respect for the class he had once served.

'The master had her body removed to a churchyard. It was his new wife's wishes.'

'The wife being the former Miss Verity Barnicoat, I take it? They were engaged to be married this time last year.'

'That's right. She's a fine lady, expecting to become a mother very soon.'

'And something is wrong in the marriage? I'm referring to the remark you made about Mr Newton.'

'He ignores her a good deal of the time and when she complains he's offhand and rude to her. All of us on the staff have heard it. I'd go as far as to say his behaviour verges on mental cruelty.'

'No, oh no, blood will out.' Freddie looked horrified. 'His father was an amoral brute. It's hard to think his son is just as cunning and untruthful. Look again at the grave, Elias. What strikes you?'

Elias gazed at the length of ground running down from where the headstone had obviously once stood. His expression grew grim. 'Yes, I see. The grave is undisturbed. Lucinda Newton's body still lies here down under the sod.'

Thirty-Four

Louis was hiding halfway up a cedar tree. Timmy was likewise on a lower branch. Stanley's leg irons prevented him from climbing and he had his front pressed behind the tree trunk. The boys were wearing cowboy hats and outlaw masks and had wooden toy guns. Their quarry were coming slowly up the garden path, Pattie and Daisy pushing their dolls prams crammed with dolls and stuffed animals. Rags liked to join in the fun and he was peeping out of Pattie's pram, a doll's bonnet awry on his little hairy head. Philly was with them, her pannier pockets bulging as always, nibbling on her occasional treat of a hunk of toffee, allowing the girls to take tiny bites.

'Right,' Louis whispered, 'here comes the loot. Get the toffee, Rags, and the dolls and we'll hold 'em to ransom.' Louis had suggested this game so he was in charge. He and Stanley were the most imaginative and started most of the mischief.

'Don't be rough,' Timmy said. 'They're only girls and Philly's old.'

'Don't be a sissy,' Stanley hissed. 'Philly likes a laugh and the girls aren't weak.'

'I'll count to three and we'll jump 'em, making a hell of a noise, pardners,' Louis said. 'One, two, three!'

He and Timmy jumped down from their hiding places and Stanley clanked out of his, all whooping and yelling, 'Stick 'em up, stick 'em up or you're a dead 'un,' all pointing their toy guns. Yapping loudly, Rags struggled out from under the doll's pram covers and added to the confusion by flying at legs.

Taken by surprise the girls shrieked in shock. 'Get away from us, beastly boys, you're spoiling things.' Pattie glared with her crossed eyes.

Quiet Daisy backed off but then she was peeved. 'Don't be so stupid. Hold up someone else.' She picked a stone up off the path and threw it at Louis. It struck the side of his right eye and blood gushed out.

'Owahh, you little cow.' Louis tore off his mask smearing blood through his hair, and fresh blood trickled down his temple.

'Serves you right, pig!'

'That wasn't called for.' Stanley was indignant. Timmy was pulling on his jumper trying to get his attention but Stanley pushed him off. 'I'm telling Mum and Dad and you'll be sent to bed without any tea. Philly, you tell her – Philly, Philly!'

'That's what I've been trying to tell you,' Timmy cried.

Philly was clutching her chest, her breathing was thin with strange sucking sounds and she dropped to her knees. She hit the ground and her head fell forward and rested on the end of Pattie's pram.

The girls, Stanley and Timmy started screaming and crying in fear, Rags kept yapping and leaping at everyone and there was chaos. Louis backed away. There would be trouble now.

Stella and Miss Lucas came running.

Miss Lucas put her handkerchief to Louis's deep cut and pressed it tight.

Stella went to Philly. 'Move back, children, move back.' Daisy had petrified and her screams were now silent ones. Stella lifted up her rigid little body and the nursemaid Gladys Geach was there to carry her away, taking a white-faced Pattie with her. Stella reached for Philly's shoulders and found their boniness unyielding. 'Philly, it's going to be all right. It's Stella, can you hear me?'

Oscar was wheeling himself to them. 'Stella, I saw what's happened to Philly and I've rung for the doctor. My God, Louis, your face. For goodness sake, Miss Lucas, take the boys inside.'

'Come along, boys,' Miss Lucas ordered tensely, looking over her shoulder as she walked them away.

Suddenly Philly went floppy and Stella caught her fast in her arms. 'She's had a turn of some sort. She's so limp.' Stella turned Philly over and put her ear to Philly's chest. 'No!'

In a panic Stella shook Philly, now a heavy dragging weight. 'I can't hear her heartbeat. Oscar!'

Philly's head lolled over Stella's arms.

'Her eyes!' Stella gave an almighty scream of anguish. 'They're staring; she's dead, she's dead. No, oh no, not Philly, it's not fair!'

★　　★　　★

Jack arrived at Olivia House immediately after the frantic phone call from Oscar. The whole household seemed to be weeping. A stifling sense of gloom had stooped down. The family had been dealt a tremendous blow. Oscar, Gladys and the children, except for Louis, were huddled round the kitchen table. The three dogs were shivering together in one basket.

'Where's Louis and Stella?' he demanded. It was always his first priority to learn their whereabouts and welfare.

'In our bedroom; the doctor is stitching the cut near his eye,' Oscar sniffed, choked. He had Libby on his lap and she was hiding her face in his jacket.

'What? You didn't mention this before, Oscar. I'll join him and Stella and she can explain. I'm so sorry about Philly. I can hardly believe it. I thought she was the sort to go on forever. Gladys, why don't you make some tea? Put some biscuits on the table for the children. Look, it's going to be all right, kids. I'll be back shortly. Oh, I've let Mrs Resterick and Mr Barnicoat know what's happened. They'll be here shortly so you'll have plenty of support.'

Jack went straight to the adapted downstairs bedroom. His guts twisted to hear Louis whimpering and Dr Alistair Tregonning telling him he was a very brave boy. Not wanting to startle the doctor in his treatment and perhaps inadvertently hurt Louis, he waited for silence then tapped on the door. 'Stella, it's Jack.'

'Jack! Come in.'

He went in. Louis was flat on the bed and Stella was easing him to sit up. The doctor was taking a wound dressing and a crepe bandage out of his bag. 'I heard the doctor telling you that you were very brave, Louis. Well done.'

'He's had three stitches.' Stella beckoned Jack to her and she grasped and squeezed his strong hand. 'Oh, Jack, it's been so awful.'

'I killed Philly.' Louis burst into tears. Stella held his head firmly still for the doctor.

'No you did not, Louis,' Tregonning said keenly, tucking in the end of the bandage and taking him by the shoulders. 'Listen to me now and listen well. I don't want you to feel guilty for the rest of your life about something that couldn't have been prevented. I'm pretty confident that Philly, Miss Lindley, had an underlying serious health problem. She would have died anyway, do you understand? You're not to blame. She died while playing with you children and that would have made her happy. It's unfortunate that the stone cut your head but Daisy didn't mean it to hit you. Another minute and you would all have been laughing about the game. I'm sure that is how Miss Lindley saw it.'

Louis turned his stricken face to Stella and then Jack. 'It's true, darling.' Stella hugged him to her. 'You may not have heard it but Philly passed away laughing and she's now laughing up in heaven, and one day we'll all be up in heaven with her, laughing forever.'

Jack knelt down to Louis. 'It's all right to cry and be sad, Louis.' With pain, he glanced at Stella. If their father had heard them crying as children he would beat them more. Jack would hold his breath to stop himself crying until he passed out in a panic. Stella would wet herself and had been forced to steal away to their mother to clean her, hopefully, in secret.

'Thank you for coming, Dr Tregonning,' Stella said, as he wrote up Louis's notes.

'I'll get Nurse Rumford to call in tomorrow,' he said, packing his bag. 'Please accept my condolences again for your sad loss.' He left quietly.

'Things won't be the same without her.' Stella leaned against Jack's shoulder. 'How we will we cope?'

'You will cope, Ste. You have me. Dorrie and Greg will see to the meals and anything else you need today. Where is Philly?'

'We laid her on a sofa in the sitting room. Miss Lucas is with her. We couldn't leave her alone. Jack, can you recommend an undertaker? When Philly's been settled, Oscar and I will sit with her throughout the night.'

'I'll ring the undertaker. Would you like me to ask the vicar to call too?'

'Oh, yes, Philly had many favourite hymns. She wrote out her wishes for her funeral during the war. We'll make sure she has everything she wanted. Oh, Jack, I can't believe this has happened so suddenly. Philly always said she wanted to go like a puff of smoke, bless her.'

'Her love will always be with you. Come along to the kitchen and join the others. Gladys will have made tea. I'll take a cup into Miss Lucas and pay my respects to Philly, if I may.'

'Of course. Oh, and I must get in touch with David Garth. It's quite likely he'll want to come down for the funeral. He and Philly got on like a house on fire. Everyone who knew Philly quickly took to her. Let's go.'

Treading the passage to the kitchen, with Louis clinging to her waist, Stella asked, 'Jack, does Verity know what's happened?'

'Yes, don't worry, I've left her in the capable hands of Deborah Weston.'

'Good, I don't want her to be upset so near her time. Verity hasn't been well for a while now. She needs a lot of support, Jack.'

'She's got it,' he said sharply.

Stella gazed at him as he strode at her side. He was facing ahead and seemed grim. 'Support from you too, Jack.'

'What does that mean, Ste?'

'Don't get defensive,' she whispered above Louis's head. 'I've noticed things aren't right between the two of you. What's happened?'

'I can hardly tell you now,' he replied gruffly.

'Oh, Jack, are you unhappy?'

'Sort of, don't worry. I'll sort everything out. Verity's just a bit moody, that's all. Nurse Rumford's says some mothers-to-be are like that.'

'But she's got everything to look forward to. Oscar and I would so love to have our own children to add to our brood but it's never happened for us. I suppose Verity as someone very independent is finding it hard to be somewhat restrained. I owe her a bit of an apology actually.'

'What on earth for?' Jack said crossly.

'Well, I have been a bit patronising, passing on my ideas of how a child should be reared; it's one of my faults. And I have rather monopolized you, Jack.'

'You're my sister, for goodness' sake. I haven't seen or heard from you in years. We've got a lot of catching up to do.'

'Maybe so, but Verity is your wife. She returned home from her honeymoon and got a whole bunch of new relatives. It takes a while for a woman to get used to her new home, and poor Verity had all that unpleasantness with Cathy to face too. It spoiled her homecoming. Then your staff deserted you. I've never bothered to congratulate her on her excellent choice of new staff. Verity's a wonderful person. You've got a great wife in her, Jack. You must look after her. She needs you.'

They reached the kitchen and Stella halted and waited for Jack to reply. 'Jack, have you nothing to say?'

'Not for now,' he answered with a sigh. 'You've given me food for thought.'

Stella opened the kitchen door. Before she and Jack had the chance to usher Louis into the room, Stanley bellowed through his sobs, 'Don't bring that boy in here, Mummy! It's his fault Philly's dead. It was his stupid game jumping out on her that made her die of fright! I wish he'd never came here.'

Thirty-Five

Freddie Stanhope ambled into the back yard of the pub. 'Good morning to you, Johnny.'

Johnny was whistling raucously while brushing down the rough court with careless abandon. 'Eh? Oh, 'tis you, Freddie, back this way again and as polite as ever. How's life been treating you then?'

'Pretty good, if I'm honest, and yourself and Mrs Westlake?' Nanviscoe was one of Freddie's favourite places to stop on his yearly travels that started in spring at St Ives and took him round the north coast to Padstow, and then back down through countryside to St Ives once more.

'Oh, we're right as rain here. Got a little granddaughter now, the apple of our eye, I can tell 'ee. She's the prettiest little maid that ever was. The wife is always clicking away with the knitting needles making clothes and toys for her. Florence Mary Rose, she's called. Come on in, Freddie, and I'll show 'ee a photo of our little beauty.'

'I'll be delighted to do that, Johnny. Have you got some jobs for me as per usual?'

'I have that; the old stable loft is waiting for you to give it its annual birthday, and there's plenty of tidying up in the back garden – a hearty bonfire to be made like you always do. You'll be joining us for meals right through the day, and the wife's been keeping a few bits and pieces you might like to have. Margaret's slipped over to see the baby. She'll be back when she can tear herself away. This year seems to be flashing by, don't seem long since you were round this time last year. A heck of a lot's happened since you were last in these parts.'

'So I've heard. I saw the new chap at Meadows House yesterday. We travelled the road together for a while after he was demobbed. He told me about the changes there. I couldn't believe how wickedly Cathy Vercoe behaved. I didn't go to the house. I know Miss Verity, the new Mrs Newton, would have given me a welcome but I didn't like to intrude now she's in a delicate condition. I bedded down in the woods last night then first thing I called on Mrs Resterick and Mr Barnicoat, but they were hurrying out to some sort of crisis at Sawle House, well it's Olivia House now, so they said, and with new people called Grey. From what I gathered it seems someone there has suddenly died.'

'Oh my Lord, can't think who that can be, although young Mr Grey is crippled and in a wheelchair, and the youngest little maid they adopted can't grow no more with some sort of condition. All the children there are adopted, except for young Louis Newton, of course.'

'Louis Newton?' Freddie said, using his one arm to pull his canvas bag and bed roll off his back and putting them carefully out of the way on the kitchen flagstone floor. 'Who's he? Someone connected to Soames Newton?'

'Elias Carey didn't tell you about him? He's the son of Mr Tobias, now the late Mr Tobias. He drank himself into the grave. First Jack tracked down his sister Stella, Mrs Grey she is now, then—'

'Miss Stella?' Freddie gasped. 'Is she Mrs Grey?'

'She is,' Johnny confirmed as if he had achieved a triumph. He reached up to the high mantelpiece above the range and took down a wooden framed photograph of a baby lying on a shawl in its christening gown. 'Here's our little sweetheart, Florence. Gorgeous, isn't she?'

'She most certainly is, bless her. You're a lucky man, Johnny. She's like her mum, and your Florrie always was a lovely girl. Anyway, you were saying about Miss Stella.'

Kissing the image of his granddaughter, Johnny replaced the photo. 'Just a mo, first a drink, tea and a drop of run?'

'If you please, Johnny.'

'Take the weight off your feet then. You're welcome to jump in the bath later on. There's a bed indoors for 'ee but if you prefer the old stable, we've a mattress that can be carried out.

'The stables will do me well. Perhaps one day soon I'll accept your kind offer of a bed inside, when my bones complain a little more.' Freddie waited at the table for the laced tea. He appeared as always, patient and unhurried, but his guts were flipping over and over. He had watched the girl Stella Newton growing up and it had tugged at his heart all too often to witness her sweet face frightened and bewildered. Tobias had often clung to her, his witless eyes displaying pain after a brutal beating. Jack had hovered over them protectively, but as for himself he was like a slammed book. Their mother, such a dear pearl of a woman had had her peace and beauty leached out of her by her brutal husband. It had hurt Freddie to see her suffer. It still hurt him. As a valet to one of Randall Newton's acquaintances, Freddie had loved the exquisite bride Marina Newton from afar. Newton had furiously noticed and saw to it that Freddie was dismissed without references. Losing his arm at the Somme during the Great War, Freddie had then gone on the road. He had secretly spent more time about Nanviscoe to catch glimpses of Marina. Eventually, she had fallen in love with him, but she had been too afraid to leave the odious Randall. Freddie was rapt at the thought he would be able to see his daughter Stella again. And he was deeply concerned about Jack Newton's lies about having his first wife's remains removed from the grounds.

'She turned up at the house while Jack and Miss Verity were away on their honeymoon. She moved her family down here quick as you can say knife, and there was a happy reunion the very day the Newtons returned home from their honeymoon.'

'I would call there to see if Miss Stella, Mrs Grey, remembers me, but,' Freddie added with heartfelt regret, 'I can't do that while she is mourning.' A terrible thought made him pale under his weathered skin. 'Oh God, I hope it wasn't her who died.'

Verity was resting in the sitting room. Deborah Weston, her constant companion nowadays, had lifted her feet up on the sofa. Deborah was in a nearby armchair, filling in *The Times* crossword.

Verity pointed at the swollen mass pushing up her breasts and seeming to spread down to her knees. 'It's grotesque, isn't it, Deborah?'

'No, Mrs Newton.' She smiled to placate. 'But I know what you mean.'

'It's what I like so much about you. You're always aware of my feelings.' Verity admired the other woman's pinned-back, sweeping waves of her light brown hair. She was a good needle-woman and wore pretty collars that turned her plain dresses into something special and individual. Together, she and Verity had cut and stitched pram and cot bedding from soft white cotton. Verity had helped with the crossword answers until her brain fogged up. Sometimes this unnerved her, but Deborah soothed her without a fuss. 'You're my friend.'

'Well, I'm very grateful to you for giving me such a delightful position. You have my total respect and loyalty. I'm honoured you think of me as your friend.'

'You've proved that you are over and over. I trust you and like you very much, Deborah.'

'Mr Newton wouldn't trust me if he knew about my past. He'd throw me out,' Deborah whispered, after making sure she was not overheard. Her moon face darkened with shame.

'He'll never know. Nothing is written down. You've wisely changed your name.' A short while ago, when Jack had stayed away overnight, Deborah, in her nightwear, had come to Verity in tears, wringing her hands hard enough to strip off her flesh. As often in the case of someone feeling depressed and low, Verity found strength and a lighter heart after listening to someone in deeper distress. 'You've been so good to me and you deserve to know the truth. I love it here and I'm so looking forward to looking after the baby, but of course I'll pack up and leave this instant if it's what you want, Mrs Newton,' she had ended, sobbing in great watery gulps.

Verity had got out of bed and after a minute of listening to Deborah draped an arm round her. 'You're not the one who should have gone to prison, Deborah. Every decent-minded person would agree. I would have done the very same thing to a man who was trying to rape me. I read about the case, and my friends and I took your side throughout. It's wicked and it's not justice how things were turned against you, because the man was a politician. My father is a retired high court judge, and I can assure you he always thought that particular judge was too hard on women; a bloody misogynist. He's a total bastard like that rotten politician. You gave him a well-deserved crack on the head. I wasn't at all sorry to learn he'd been killed in the Blitz.

'Now, Deborah, dry your tears and take heart. You can start a new life here with the baby and me. Your secret will go with me to the grave.'

On the sofa, wriggling her toes, which she could not see over her huge belly, Verity said, 'Call me Verity from now on. Friends don't stand on ceremony with each other. Look at the movement inside me.' She was always fascinated when the baby was lively inside, and she was relieved to know it was going strong. 'I've been willing my labour to start. I think I'll take some castor oil tonight to see if that will get things going. It's supposed to work for some women.'

'Gosh,' Deborah laughed. 'You might explode, if you know what I mean.' She looked out of the window. 'It's Mr Newton's car back from Olivia House.'

'Poor things,' Verity shuddered. 'Can't think what they must be going through. Philly was such a dear and they all adored her. Help me to sit up properly, will you, Deborah.'

The women heard the sounds of two doors of the car being slammed. Verity made a face. 'He's brought someone with him.'

A minute later Jack joined them and holding his hand was a nervous Louis, trailing him. Verity's heart went out to the mournful boy with his bandaged head. His chin wobbled and he was on the verge of tears. 'Oh, darling, I'm so sorry about what happened to Philly. Your poor head, are you badly hurt? Come to me.' Verity flinched when she saw Jack's hand tighten round the boy's.

'I hope it won't be too much of an imposition. I've brought Louis to stay here for a while.' He raised his dark head as if he had been challenged. 'It's necessary. He can have the room next to ours. I'll keep an eye on him and otherwise he can trot about with Jakes and Carey.'

How dare Jack behave as if she was making Louis unwelcome, Verity thought bitterly. 'Of course Louis must stay for as long as he likes. I'll ask Joan to fetch Jakes inside now. I'm sure you'd like to curl up with him, eh, Louis? Miss Weston will be glad to fetch a blanket and you can cuddle up here on the sofa.'

'Thanks, Aunty Verity,' Louis mumbled. He tugged away from Jack and Jack had to let him go, and Louis ran to Verity. 'They're saying it's my fault Philly's dead! I don't ever want to go back to that place again. Can I live here? Can I have my mice here, ple—ease say I can.'

Verity pulled Louis in to her as much as her bump allowed. She gazed harshly above his head at Jack. He said nothing. She said nothing. She just wished he would turn round and go to his precious sister.

Thirty-Six

Dorrie was too worried to sleep. She was sitting up in bed, the book she had tried to read fallen shut in her hands. There was no point in switching off the lamp and lying down in the dark, the total darkness the countryside afforded when there was no moonlight. Slipping out of bed, she put on her dressing gown and went down to the kitchen to make some hot milk.

'Dor, come and join me.'

Greg was in the sitting room, where she had left him over three hours ago. He had not been up to bed. 'Can't drop off, old thing?'

'I'm too worried about Verity, Greg.' Rain pattered hard against the windowpanes as if it was trying to get inside and soak them. Dorrie shivered although she wasn't cold. There was an ominous shadow over her that she could not shake off, a growing instinct that Verity was desperately unhappy and in need of help and comfort.

'Me too, we both know things aren't right between Verity and Jack, and that Jack is mainly responsible for it. I should have had a word with him long before now, but of course I didn't want to interfere, and until lately Verity was always a fighter. But our dear girl is too low for that now. I can hardly tackle Jack about his cool attitude with Verity now this tragedy has happened. Do you think things will be different now Louis is staying there?'

'No, I don't, Greg. You heard how the children blamed Louis for shocking Philly to her death. Apparently Louis had turned their games more into pranks and had made them quite rough. In the children's minds everything was well until Louis showed up. Daisy told me she and the other children are put out because Jack favours Louis over them. Verity's baby is due in ten days' time. Louis was very upset when Jack took him away from Olivia House. He might prove to be difficult and that is the last thing Verity needs. It might be too much for her. Thank goodness she's got Deborah Weston to call on. I'd suggest I should stay at the house until Verity has had the baby but I'm afraid Jack would resent it.'

Greg hung his head in guilt. 'I should have remembered that although Jack has many fine qualities, he always had a certain coldness about him. Deep down I'd thought he had an unhealthy fixation for the peculiar Lucinda before and after her death.' He looked up with pleading eyes. 'My God, Dor, what has Verity married into?'

Dorrie was nibbling toast at the kitchen table. Greg had gone out into the steady rainfall to fetch some women's magazines to take to Verity later in the morning and check how she was coping. Corky was in his basket, warm near the range, alert for any crumbs Dorrie dropped, and waiting eagerly for the square of toast she would leave him.

There was a loud knocking on the back kitchen door and Dorrie's heart lurched and she darted to her feet worried someone was bringing bad news about Verity. 'Yes, who is it?' She wrenched the door open. 'Oh, Elias Carey, has Mrs Newton's labour started? Why didn't someone ring?'

'It's not that, Mrs Resterick.' The young man was dripping wet in his Army greatcoat and a cap. 'But I'd like to talk to you and Mr Barnicoat about Mrs Newton, if you don't mind. I have worries about her. I hope I'm not speaking out of turn.'

'Not at all, Carey, come in, come in. My brother has slipped out to the village but he'll not dally there.'

She told Elias to hang his wet things on the hooks behind the door. He pulled off his heavy boots and followed Dorrie into the cosiness of the kitchen, leaning forward to pat Corky. Corky thoroughly sniffed him then returned to his basket, grumbling in his throat that his titbit of toast had been delayed. Dorrie cut off Corky's rightful treat and gave it to him.

'Sit down, Carey. I can squeeze another cup out of the teapot, and then I'd be grateful if you'd get straight to the point. Mr Barnicoat and I are very concerned about our niece too. Has something happened? Are there problems with young Louis?'

'Thanks for the tea, ma'am,' Elias said, sitting at a respectful distance from Dorrie. 'Master Louis seems to be fairly settled. He's happy that Mrs Newton has said he can have Jakes inside with him all the time, even to sleep in his basket in his room. I'm here about something I discovered, with Freddie Stanhope, just yesterday.'

'Something about Mr Newton?' Dorrie raised her neat ginger eyebrows. Alarm grew in her.

'Yes, ma'am, we were in the woods, at the site where the first Mrs Newton was buried, and we realised that the grave had never been dug up. Mr Newton lied about having the lady buried elsewhere.' Dorrie could see he was feeling uncomfortable about bringing this information to her. 'I thought you and Mr Barnicoat should know. Mrs Newton should be told, shouldn't she? But it isn't my place to go to her, and right now, well, if I may say so, all is not easy . . .'

'I'm very glad you've told me.' Dorrie chewed her lip. 'And you are right about the present situation being fragile. I'll discuss this with Mr Barnicoat when he returns and we'll decide what's the best thing to do. We are planning to call on Mrs Newton this morning. If I think Mrs Newton is not . . . safe, I will not leave her side.'

Thirty-Seven

Verity woke confused for a second, believing she was still living her old uncomplicated, comfortable life at Sunny Corner with her doting aunt and uncle.

'Sit up sleepyhead, I've brought your breakfast.' She thought she must be mistaken about the owner of the voice but when she fully opened her drowsy eyes she saw it really was Jack, with her laden breakfast tray. And he was smiling. Warmly. Handsomely.

He put the tray down on the foot of the bed, gently hooked his arms under Verity's armpits, sat her forward, placed the pillows to support her and then eased her back comfortably. He caressed her hair away from her tense forehead and kissed her there with tender pecks. Verity was too surprised to respond, except with caution. Her trust in Jack had gone, and right now his kisses or any other sign of affection from him were unwelcome. She would not allow him to play mind games with her. She wasn't a disturbed, unworldly child like Lucinda had been. A noxious thought stabbed her. Had Lucinda been as mad as she had ended up when Jack had first brought her here?

'Thank you, Jack,' she said blandly. 'Is Louis up yet? I was going to sit in with him last night until he fell asleep, but I heard you talking to him and knew you had everything in hand.'

'He slept in fits and starts, darling. I sat up in a chair in his room. I took him down for breakfast at seven-thirty. He's had a bath and he's now out in the garden with Jakes and Carey. The weather has cheered up, thankfully. He'll fare much better with us where he can get plenty of one-to-one attention. He thinks the world of you, darling. He loves you reading to him.'

'I think the world of Louis. He's got some rough edges but they're a part of who he is. He could go far.'

'Darling, that's what I think too. Eat your scrambled egg. I'll pour you some tea.'

She picked up the butter knife and spread a triangle of toast. 'This is all I can manage. I'm not very hungry.'

He dashed milk in the tea. 'You ought to try to eat your egg, Verity darling. You need to be strong for the time ahead.'

Verity took a tiny bite of toast, thinking, *It's too late to show me care and concern now.*

Deborah appeared, and met Verity's gaze with meaning. 'Can I get you anything, Mrs Newton?'

'I'm here for Mrs Newton, Weston,' Jack said in a dismissive manner.

'You can run me a bath in half an hour please, Deborah,' Verity answered her brightly. 'And could you look out the book *Peter Pan* − it's Master Louis's favourite − and some other books suitable for boys. When Master Louis comes in we will all sit cosily in the sitting room and I'll read a chapter. My aunt and uncle are going to pop in. Nurse Rumford is due here at eleven o'clock to give me a check-up and you can keep Master Louis occupied.' *Get this, Jack, you're not included in these arrangements.*

'Certainly, Mrs Newton.'

When Deborah had gone, Jack continued as if she had never been there. 'I'm pleased you think that Louis could go far. We could do a lot for him. I think he should live here, it's only right he lives where his father grew up. I'm going to keep him here. He doesn't seem to fit in with Stella's tribe. We'll be so happy, me and you, Louis and the baby. It will be perfect.' He stared at Verity, the hateful challenge she was beginning to know so well back in his penetrating gaze.

Verity did not have to think about it. She truly cared about Louis, and because he would spend time with Carey she would get plenty of quiet. But she felt a stir of unease for Louis. Jack's phrase, 'only right he lives where his father grew up', was not a fine sentiment. How could Jack have forgotten how his tragic brother had suffered terrible violence under this roof and ran away as soon as he was able to? What quickly followed was unease for her baby. What kind of father was Jack going to be? Would she then be more or less superfluous to him?

'I think it would be wonderful. Louis can really be himself here, but won't Stella object? When will you tell her?'

'I'll tell her today. She can't really object. I was the one who looked for her and Tobias. David Garth first came here to see me. It will be more comfortable for David to stay here when he comes down to Cornwall. He's going to ask for time off to attend Philly's funeral, by the way. I'll get in touch and let him know to come here.'

Verity finished her breakfast. 'I wonder how they're all bearing up at Olivia House, poor things.' Her thoughts for the Greys were sincere, but she hoped Jack would take the bait and go over to the grieving house and see for himself.

She was not disappointed. 'I'll go there soon but I'll be back in time for lunch.' He took her tray away. 'Will you be all right, darling? Perhaps I should be here for when the nurse comes.'

'It's not really necessary, Jack. It's really a women's thing. Right now Stella and the children need you.'

He kissed her on the lips before he left. Verity rubbed her mouth with the sheet. The kiss had not been at all like Jack's warm passionate kisses of old. *I don't know who you are any more.* She massaged her taut brow. 'How the hell did I get myself into this horrible marriage?' Her baby moved above her navel and she gently pressed her hand there. 'But at least you're worth it, darling.'

Verity had her bath with Deborah in attendance to help her in and out safely. Verity dressed in a tweed skirt, a midnight-blue pleated smock and a warm cable knit cardigan. Deborah knelt to put Verity's slippers on over her woollen stockings. Then Jakes suddenly bowled into the room, muddy all over, and jumped up on to the bed.

'Oh no!' Verity shrieked.

Louis rushed in after the puppy in his grey socks. 'Sorry, Aunty Verity, I was too late to stop him. We had such a lovely time running about the garden and Jakes got all excited. Jakes, here boy.' Fortunately Jakes obeyed immediately.

'We'll let it go this time, Louis,' Verity said, with a sense of fun. It was funny and she would laugh later this morning about it with Dorrie and Greg. 'Please be careful that he never ever goes into the nursery.'

'I'll try very hard. I'll keep hold of him when we come in.' Louis was excited himself. 'Uncle Jack said I can wander in all the rooms, that all this will be mine one day if you have a girl and not a boy.'

Deborah gasped loudly, her mouth gaping open. 'Oh, Verity . . .'

Shaken to the roots of her soul, Verity fought to control her voice. 'You run along now, Louis. Ask Joan to help you clean the mud off Jakes. I'm sure Mrs Rabey will make you some hot milk and find you something tasty to eat. Wait in the kitchen until I come and fetch you.'

Verity was consumed by a blazing fury and it came off her in waves. 'The bastard!' She choked. 'How could he? How could he say such a thing to a child? How could he ignore my feelings in the matter and to cast our baby aside if it's a girl? How dare he treat the baby and me this way?'

A monumental thought tore through her, shocking her in such a manner it should have shattered her, yet somehow through her horror she acknowledged something she should have known for some time. How could she not have seen it before? Jack was only able to love his sister and he loved Louis because he was a part of Tobias. He was generous to others, but his traumatic upbringing had robbed him of all other important emotions. It explained his fits of depression and moroseness. When he had fallen in love with Verity, or thought he had loved her, he had lived a lie. The moment he was reunited with Stella it was all he really wanted, his family, and now he had Louis. He had probably planned to get Louis to live under his roof all the time.

She aimed her heartbreak at Jack's image. You must wish you'd never set eyes on me. You don't love me, you never really did. I was probably just another distraction for you, like your fast cars, acts of charity and all the women you'd bedded. Even if our baby turns out to be a boy, are you capable of really loving him? If she had not agreed to take Louis under her care she would have got Deborah to drive her straight to Sunny Corner, to stay there with her, and she would never return to Meadows House.

Thirty-Eight

'Aunty Verity isn't happy,' Louis said. 'Is she worried about the baby?'

'Oh, she's just a bit tired, that's all, Louis,' Dorrie replied. She was looking out of the sitting-room window, watching the last stubborn leaves up on the high branches lose their grip to the determined breezes and cast down on the lawn. 'Nurse Rumford is upstairs now giving her a check-up. She'll make sure Verity keeps well. Look, it's Jakes running about, with Carey. Do you want to go outside and join them?'

'Not yet, Mrs R. I'm worried about Aunty Verity.' Dorrie felt Louis's head resting against her arm and she put a comforting arm round him. 'I'm afraid she might die like my mum did. Having babies is dangerous.'

'It's very rare for a mum to have really bad problems, Louis. Verity will be fine, you'll see.' Dorrie took a deep breath. Verity could make her eventual labour an added trial for herself if she did not calm down. She had been a ghastly hot colour and shaking to her toes on taking Dorrie and Greg aside. 'That disgusting creature I married has had the effrontery to tell Louis that if the baby is a girl, if we never have a son, then Louis will inherit this house – what a thing to say to a child! If I have a daughter she won't be good enough for Jack. He's made it clear in a hundred ways that I'm certainly not what he wants. I hate him! I'd leave him this moment but I don't know what to do about Louis. I can't send him back to a bunch of kids who blame him for Philly's death, and I dare not leave him with Jack. Goodness knows what he'd say to him next.'

'That settles it,' Dorrie had said. 'I will stay here until after the baby is born and you are back on your feet.'

'Where is Jack now?' Greg asked tightly.

'He's gone to Olivia House to talk to Stella about his plan for us to raise Louis. He said he won't be terribly long.'

'Right.' Greg had gone purposefully to the door. 'I'll wait for

him at the gates. I shall have a lot to say to Jack Newton. He's
not going to continue to treat you with such blatant disrespect,
Verity. Take heart, darling, if things don't get better immediately
your aunt and I will be taking you away to Sunny Corner. I
understand David Garth is coming down for the funeral. He'll
help, I'm sure, to sort things out about Louis.'

Greg strode off down the long drive. Rebecca Rumford, a
friend to Verity, had arrived early, took one look at her patient,
and exclaimed, 'I'll bet your blood pressure is sky high. It's bed
rest for you, Verity.'

Louis pointed outside. 'Do you think that's the tree the lady
jumped off to break her neck?'

'What?' Dorrie was appalled that Louis had something so
morbid on his mind. She pictured him staring up at every tree
in the grounds wondering, perhaps almost seeing, if this tree or
that tree was the one Lucinda Newton had used to kill herself.
'The tragedy happened nowhere near the house, Louis. I don't
know exactly where it happened, hardly anyone does. It was all
a long time ago, and it's nothing for you to worry about. How
did you come to hear about it?'

'I overheard Aunty Stella and Uncle Oscar talking about all
sorts of stuff that's gone on here. One day Timmy and I walked
down to the village for our sweet ration and we got collared by
this old man. Said his name was Mr Ellery and he had an important
job at Petherton. Then he prattled on 'bout Merrivale being
haunted – don't know how, Nanny Lucas took us to play in the
small woods there and the cottage looked, as Nanny Lucas said,
"a charming place". Then the old man said the place is cursed
and that my grandfather Randall was a devil, and that he cursed
my dad to drink himself to death. And how the lady Uncle Jack
first married went crazy and hung herself and a maid called Cathy
went crazy and did bad things. That Uncle Jack is sex mad and
peculiar. He said to watch I don't get cursed too. I told Aunty
Stella and she said Ellery's a nasty-tongued gossip and to take no
notice of him. She gave the old man merry hell.

'There's nothing cursed or evil here is there, Mrs R? In
Merrivale or in this village? Philly moved here and soon died.
And now Aunty Verity isn't well. She won't die, will she?'

Chills ran up Dorrie's neck at the thought of Verity being in danger. Jack was behaving as if touched by some madness. One thing Greg would tackle Jack about was why he had lied about having Lucinda's body reinterred. She eased Louis away from the window. 'I promise you that Verity will be absolutely fine and that there is absolutely nothing evil or bad about this house, any other house or in the village. Life is pretty ordinary here as it is everywhere. Would you like to play draughts?'

'Are you sure the house is safe?'

'Cross my heart.'

'OK.' The boy grinned. Dorrie had at last convinced him. 'I'm brilliant at draughts. You won't beat me. I always win against Aunty Verity.'

'We'll see about that, young man.'

While they were in the throes of the first seriously contested round, Rebecca Rumford peeked round the door. 'All is well with mum and baby. I've ordered Verity to stay in bed all day and to eat as many nourishing meals as she can. I'll call in again tomorrow. My instinct tells me she could start labour at any time, so I might see you even sooner.'

'I'll see she eats, and Deborah or I will be with her every minute,' Dorrie said. 'I'll be staying here until after the baby is born. I've got a bag packed. Greg will fetch it later.'

'Wizard.' Louis pounced on his next successful move on the draughts board.

Stella stared at Jack in disbelief that he could make such a demand at this time. 'It's a good idea for Louis to stay with you for a while, Jack, but I don't agree you should take him over for good,' she said with conviction. 'You're soon to become a new father. You and Verity need to concentrate on the joy and upheaval a new baby will inevitably bring into your lives.'

Jack had approached Stella outside in the garden while she was taking a quiet minute at the spot where Philly had died. She was dressed all in black, hat, scarf and gloves, her hands clenched over her heart. He lit a cigarette and offered Stella a puff. Stella had never taken up smoking but when Jack had filched a cigarette as a boy, she had always asked for a puff. They blew out the smoke adding to the plumes of their warm breath in the chilly air. 'We won't find the baby a struggle. We've got staff in the house including an experienced nursemaid, and I'm in the fortunate position of not needing to work for hours away from home. Verity is good with Louis and in fact Louis is good for her. I want to take Bod and Bim, his mice, and his things. To have Louis settled in as soon as possible. I'll pack his stuff myself so it doesn't take any of you here away from the children. How are they?'

'How do you think?' Stella replied tartly. 'Libby doesn't understand, of course, but the others are inconsolable, as is to be expected. Louis needs to be reassured that it wasn't his fault Philly passed away, and *I* am the best one to do it. She had a heart condition and it was worse than we'd thought. She could have gone at any second. It's such a dreadful thing she died in front of the children. Oscar and I will get them through it. On the practical side we need a new cook. Know of anyone?'

'Not really. You could ask the oracle, Dorrie Resterick.'

'Jack! You said that with resentment. What's got into you? Dorrie and Greg were wonderful with the children yesterday. Oscar and I have great respect for them both. Has Dorrie done something to upset you?'

'She's an interfering old cow where her niece is concerned.'

'Verity is like a daughter to Dorrie. The Dorrie I knew from old, and now, wouldn't dream of interfering with anyone.'

'She'll tell me what to do!' Jack's sudden scream of rage made Stella start in fright and her hands flew to her face. Jack came straight at her, shoulders raised, head forward in the same way their father had used to when about to deal out a punishment, and she backed away. 'Everybody tells me what to do!'

'Stop it, Jack, you're scaring me.'

'Damn you! You're all the same, even you.' Still he advanced on her but his arms were crossed in front of his face as if expecting a blow.

'Who tells you what to do? I don't understand. Jack, what are you talking about?'

'Father!'

'Father? What's he got to do with here and now? Get a grip on yourself. You're not the Jack I knew. You always cared so much about others.'

'You don't know anything about me after you left, what I went through every minute of every day when that evil bastard was at home,' he yelled, thumping the air with his fists one moment, the next smacking the heels of his hands against his head. 'Boy, make yourself good enough to be called my son. Do this. Don't do that. Don't slouch, boy! Mind your manners, Jack! Do it again until you get right, you little bastard! Keep your head up, boy, or I'll knock it off your shoulders! Do better at your lessons or I'll whip you again.' Now it was Jack who backed away, trying to get away from his lifelong pain, the agonising memories plaguing him.

'And Verity started telling me what to do. Verity who swore she loved me for who I am and would support me in all I do. She demanded I dig Lucinda up, that poor sweet girl who couldn't help being what she was. Meadows House was her home, she was safe under its ground. Safe . . . safe from . . .'

Stella went after him. 'Stop it, Jack, for your own good. You'll make yourself ill. Come inside with me and let me help you.' She was recalling the terrible times when after their father's savage, unjust attacks Jack would find it hard to breathe and get into panics and near hysteria, and only Stella or their mother could calm him back to normality.

He did not hear her pleas, or the love and caring in her tone. 'When I brought Lucinda home she . . . she . . .' He cocked his head peculiarly to the side and brought it up in tiny jerks as if his mind was really a machine and it was malfunctioning.

'What did Lucinda do, Jack?' Stella said firmly, but softly. 'She was just a rather strange child, wasn't she? You protected her, you gave her a good life for as long as you could.'

'She . . . she . . .' His face warped and it wasn't his normal voice but a chilling, seething hiss. 'Don't touch my dolls. I want a doll in a red flounced dress. Get it for me, Jack. Get me some paints, lots and lots of paints, and red paint. Get me clothes fit for a princess. I want to dress like a princess. Don't go near Polly or I'll tell her to bite you. Go away! You can't share our tea party. The dolls don't like you. I'll tell them to bite you, to eat you. To kill you.'

Then Jack's own voice, anguished, full of disgust. 'I wish I'd never come across you. How can you treat me like this? You're mad. You're evil. It's no wonder your guardian signed you over to me in all haste. He hated you. I was a fool. I didn't see what you were. I wish you were dead. Do you hear me, dead!'

Lucinda's jeering had come alive inside Jack's head. 'Then I'll do it and it'll be your fault, then see how you feel!' And then came a crazed laugh that made Stella scream in horror. Jack had backed all the way until he struck the tree Louis and Timmy had jumped down from and Stanley had hid behind. It brought him to his senses, but not his true senses. He blinked, blinked hard again, not believing what he was seeing. 'St-Stella? Is that you? Wh-where are we?'

'It's all right, Jack. You're not well. Come inside with me.' She reached for him.

'No! Don't come near me.' He flailed his arms to keep her away. He ran off to his car, the closer he got to it the more his legs buckled under his weight.

'Jack! Come back, you're not fit to drive.'

Stella raced after him but he fell into the car and after fumbling for a few seconds he roared off. 'Jack!' Stella made a grab for the car but it left her hands like a blazing bullet.

Jack didn't see the drive ahead but somehow he reached the end and swerved out into the lane, the wheels scattering out stones and dust. The car bounced off the rounded hedge and Stella could hear its engine protesting as Jack crashed the gears and ploughed on in the direction of home.

She turned frantically towards the house and saw Oscar wheeling himself towards her. 'Darling, what's going on? What was all the shouting about?'

'Oscar!' she screamed. 'Jack's having some sort of mental breakdown. I tried to stop him. He's going to kill himself!'

Thirty-Nine

'Stop right there, Jack Newton, I want a serious word with you right now. I want an explanation over your behaviour towards Verity, and we're not moving from this spot until I get it. What's got into you since you returned from your honeymoon? What's this about only a son of yours or Louis inheriting your property? How do you think that makes Verity feel when you say something of that nature to Louis and not to her?'

Greg was rehearsing the confrontation he was determined to have with Jack when he heard the roaring engine and screeching of tyres out in the lane. 'So you're on your way home, driving like a madman, of all the foolhardy things to do,' Greg said aloud and indignantly.

There was an almighty deafening crash before the hedge close to Greg shuddered and the nearby bushes shook. Hordes of birds took flight from trees and hedges and set up a terrific ruckus.

'Jack! Oh my God!' Greg felt his guts lurch.

It took a second for Greg to gather his wits, and then he was running as fast as he could, dreading what he was going to find when he left the driveway.

Jack's Triumph 2000 Roadster was a twisted mass of metal embedded by its bonnet in the ditch. Jack had been thrown clear and was lying flat on his face, one arm hanging at an odd angle with a bone sticking out. He had rolled over and over and there were blood and deep cuts all over him. He raised his head and gazed about from senseless eyes.

Greg cried, 'Thank God!' He wasn't dead, not yet anyway. 'Keep still, Jack, don't move.'

Before Greg reached Jack, Freddie Stanhope appeared on top of the opposite hedge, then jumped down and knelt down to Jack. 'How he wasn't killed, sir, we'll never know.'

'He's not out of danger yet. Freddie, run to the house and tell them to ring for an ambulance. I'll stay with him.'

Greg pulled off his jacket and laid it over Jack, tucking a folded sleeve under the side of his face. An ugly gash furrowed through his scalp. Jack's mouth was opening and closing. Greg bent his head to listen if he was trying to say something.

'Didn't mean it . . . love Verity . . . sorry.' He mumbled the same words over and over, and Greg kept talking to him, telling him not to worry, that all would be sorted out, knowing it was important not to let Jack slip into unconsciousness.

Greg heard a car coming along the lane and he got up to flag it down for safety's sake. It was Stella. An instant later she was down on her knees beside Jack. 'It's all right, Jay, darling, it's Ste. Greg is here too. An ambulance is on the way. We'll soon have you better.'

'Verity. Ve—ri—ty . . .'

'Verity will understand, she loves you very much, Jay.' Stella tenderly stroked his battered face. 'Verity will understand that you were ill, that it all got too much for you. Just fight to stay alive, darling Jay. We all need you so much.'

Forty

'I should be with Jack,' Verity insisted, gritting her teeth through the pain.

'You can't go to the hospital in the middle of labour,' Dorrie said patiently, padding a cool damp flannel along Verity's sweating brow.

Verity pushed the flannel away. She breathed out grumpily like a gust of wind. 'But he might finally come round today and I want to be there to comfort him, to tell him how much I love him. How I do understand everything after Stella told me what happened. It's just not fair, damn it. Not fair that everything went so wrong for Jack and me the moment we stepped back inside this house. Not fair that he had a breakdown and it's not bloody fair he had that dreadful accident. I want to see him. Don't make me stay in this bed!'

'The old feisty Verity is back, I'm glad to hear.' Greg popped his head round the door. 'Welcome back, darling.'

'Out with you, Mr Barnicoat, this is no place for a man.' Rebecca Rumford waved him away and shut the door in his face.

'You've done your bit for Jack by being at his side for the last three days at the hospital,' Greg called through the door. 'Now be a good girl and give him a healthy, happy baby to come home to.'

'Ring the hospital, Uncle Greg, and ask them if Jack is awake yet!' Verity bawled.

'Righto.' Greg made for the downstairs telephone.

'Try not to make an unnecessary fuss, darling,' Dorrie said. 'The doctors say Jack has a long road to travel. After he fully regains consciousness he has a long recuperation to get through to recover from his physical injuries and his emotional issues.'

'I know, Aunt Dor. I just hate the thought of not being able to see him even for a day. Jack and I have a lot of making up to do. I should have had more faith in him. I should have realised there was an awful reason behind his cold behaviour.'

'You mustn't dwell on any of that, Verity. Jack wouldn't want you to. Just look forward to the future. Your baby will be born quite soon. Jack has showed signs that he understands what is said to him. I'm sure news of the baby will be a tremendous breakthrough for him.'

Three hours passed and Deborah brought in a light lunch. She was about to go downstairs and fetch afternoon tea when Verity cried out, 'I want to push! Can I push?'

Rebecca made a quick physical check. 'You're fully dilated. You can bear down on the next contraction. Dorrie, you're quite an old hand to all this now. Miss Weston, you go round the other side of the bed. All being well, Verity will soon be drinking her first cup of tea as a mother.'

'Alice Newton,' Greg said, holding his twenty-minute-old great-niece. 'Aren't you a stunner? Beautiful just like her mother.' From the side of the bed, he beamed at the proud new mum. 'You've done a brilliant job, precious girl.'

'Alice Jacqueline Newton, her second name close to Jack's. I couldn't be more happy,' Verity replied, taking her daughter back, wanting her in her arms every second. 'I wish I could have been there when the Sister on Jack's ward told him he has a daughter. I hope Jack understood.'

'I'm sure he did, darling,' Dorrie said softly, smiling in wonder at the new little life and Verity's joy.

Louis stared at the baby from where he was leaning on elbows on the bed. 'She's so tiny. My baby sister who went to heaven must have been that tiny. It'll be ages before she's big enough to play with.'

'In just a little while she will like to be amused and at six weeks old she'll smile at you,' Dorrie said.

'She's perfect,' Deborah said, so pleased and happy she looked as if she wanted to dance around the room.

'Not too much excitement for mother and baby now,' Rebecca warned gently. She was packing her bags, satisfied at another successful straightforward birth. 'I must say Alice is one of the loveliest babies I've seen.'

The visitors were ushered out. Verity gave her baby its first feed then she was left to rest in a darkened room with Alice snuggled down in the cradle close beside her.

Later Stella looked in on her. 'Is it all right to come in?'

'Of course,' Verity said. She had been too excited to sleep and had only dozed. 'Come in and say hello to your niece.'

'Thank you, Verity. I wasn't sure if you'd really want to see me. We didn't get the chance to talk at the hospital. Before Jack's accident, I'd come to realise I was patronizing towards you, Verity. I admit that although I was thrilled Jack had fallen in love and married the perfect woman for him, I didn't really want to share Jack with anyone. I got in your way, didn't I?'

'Whatever happened, it's all in the past, Stella. Let's be friends as well as sisters-in-law.'

'I'd like that.' Stella gazed down in the cradle. 'Oh, Verity, she's gorgeous. You deserve your little girl. I've also come to tell you that I rang the hospital and Jack is awake, he knows about Alice and can't wait to see you both. He's very weak still but he's quite his old self again.'

'Will it be all right if Louis stays here until Jack gets home, Stella? He'll be good for Jack. He's good for me; we get along famously.'

'Jack's head was muddled but he was right about Louis living here. I can see how much he enjoys being with Jakes, and with Elias Carey, and you, Verity. He talks very fondly of you. Louis needs the space he's got here to become his own person.' Stella looked all round as if seeing the room and the whole house completely differently to how it was when she had lived here. 'The ghosts are all gone from this place at last.'

Forty-One

Greg drove Verity to the hospital to bring Jack home. Jack would need help to master the hospital steps. He had the odd occasion when his mind switched off and he got a little confused. The doctors were confident if Jack underwent a sensible convalescence – and they thought at home would be better than a nursing home in his case – he would make a complete recovery.

In the drawing room of Meadows House, a roasting fire warmed the air. Dorrie was holding three-week-old Alice up to her shoulder and patting her back. Alice was wearing a new dress, and a matinee jacket and matching bootees Verity had knitted, and she had the hiccoughs. Dorrie laughed with delight. 'You look just like your mummy when you do that, but you have your daddy's dark hair.'

The day after Alice's birth, ignoring Rebecca's frown, Verity had taken the baby to Jack in the hospital. 'He was sleeping, Aunt Dor. I whispered to him that Alice and I were there and his eyes opened and I literally saw the life flood back into him. He was my Jack again, the man I fell in love with and who loved me back. There's just one little problem to see to now.'

That 'little problem' had been seen to. In a rare moment of sympathetic pastoral duty, the Reverend Lytton had arranged with a fellow clergyman a special dispensation to have Lucinda Newton re-interred in an anonymous spot in the fellow clergyman's church-yard. Only the two vicars knew where the grave was. Tragic deranged Lucinda would haunt no one again.

Stella arrived to welcome her brother home. Only she had come today to allow Jack to settle in without being overwhelmed. 'Hello, Dorrie, hello, darling Alice.' She paused, and Dorrie could see she was using all her senses.

'What is it, Stella?'

'I can't help marvelling, Dorrie, how the old house has taken on a new serenity since the day I returned and startled you. There's peace, peace at last, and a sense of freshness. All will be well for Jack and Verity and little Alice. Even the photos on the piano seem happier now everything has changed.'

Smiling, Dorrie took a good long look at the familiar photos. She opened her eyes wide. 'Mmmm.'

Stella's household too was returning to normal. Philly had been laid to rest in Nanviscoe's churchyard. Freddie had introduced himself to the Greys the day after the funeral. He could work well with his one arm and he had been hired to clear an oval-shaped piece of ground and plant it with evergreen shrubs and winter and spring bulbs. Bedding plants would be put in for the summer. Stella, Oscar and the children had all helped Freddie prepare the memorial garden to Philly.

Stella noticed movement outside through the window. 'I see Freddie is still here, out there with Carey and Louis. I remember it's unusual for him to stay for so long. He must have waited to give Jack his best wishes. I've told Freddie how grateful we all were for him coming to Jack's aid that day. He's a good man. Oscar likes him and so do the children. We've got a great new cook but it's not the same as having Philly. Do you know, I actually believe Freddie would fill in some of the emptiness left by Philly. She would have approved, bless her. I've always liked Freddie. I'd ask him to stay around, the summerhouse could always be adapted for his use, but I'm sure he'd rather move on; gentlemen of the road like to keep to their adopted lifestyle. He used to be a valet but I think he's quite a gentleman himself. I think he must have been rather good-looking as a young man.'

Dorrie was still gazing at the photographs of Stella throughout her young life and snatching glances of Freddie at each angle as he moved about. 'I agree with all you've said, but do you know, Stella, I believe Freddie would very much like you to ask him to stay.'

'Do you really think so? Why are you so interested in . . . Oh . . .' Stella followed Dorrie's eyes. Slowly, then picking up speed, she went to the window and stared at the man in question. He seemed content to be where he was. 'While Freddie worked in the garden he spoke highly of my mother, and then apologised for speaking out of turn. I thought he was rather emotional at the time. I told him I didn't mind him mentioning Mother. They . . . they must have known each other very well, don't you think, Dorrie?'

Swaying gently with the baby in her arms, Dorrie said, 'I most certainly do, Stella. As a valet he would have seen your mother on many social occasions before and after she married Randall Newton.'

Stella's eyes shone with emotion. 'He actually told me he hadn't had the heart to go on in service or to do anything else after someone special in his life died. That someone must have been my mother. Freddie must be my father. You saw my resemblance to him in the photos just now, and now so I do. It's why I felt I could trust him the instant he came to Olivia House, why I thought he could fill Philly's shoes. Philly was a grandmother to the children. Freddie is not related to the children but as my father he is their grandfather. It's wonderful to know the man who meant so much to my poor mother, to know the one who gave some happiness to her miserable existence. Dorrie, do you think if I went out there he'd . . .'

'Stella, from the way I've seen Freddie look at you I'm certain he'd love to take his place as your father. He's a humble man and he wouldn't make the truth known to you. He would fear he'd upset you. But there he is, there's no need to wait. He will be overjoyed. I'm thrilled for you, my dear.'

Freddie watched Jakes chasing the ball Elias threw for him, but Freddie was thinking about his packed belongings, joined by the generous offerings of the locals. Nanviscoe would always be his favourite place to come to. The place where he felt close to the only woman he had ever loved. In the past he would be itching to move on after a while but now his heart was heavy. Now he must tread the road again and leave his beautiful, successful daughter behind until this time next year.

But Stella was hurrying towards him and she had a lovely smile, a special smile for him and he knew what it meant. The hollowness fled from his heart. At last he could stay put and know what real freedom was. He glimpsed someone spying from the window and she was beaming like the sun. He knew whom he had to thank for this wonderful moment that would last for the rest of his life.

'Well, Alice.' Dorrie bobbed lightly on her feet. 'As well as your daddy coming home another wonderful thing has happened today. Your Aunt Stella is meeting her real father, the love of your grandmother's life, and it will make the new peace of your home complete.'